Becoming Kate

jc konitz

Becoming Kate
Copyright © 2020 by Judith Konitzer
ISBN: 978-1-970153-19-4
Library of Congress Control Number: 2020914427

La Maison Publishing, Inc.
Vero Beach, Florida
The Hibiscus City
www.lamaisonpublishing.com

"Life is a tragedy for those who feel, but
a comedy to those who think."
Horace Walpole

Acknowledgment

My thanks to the members of the Vero Beach Writers Pane
for their suggestions and encouragement.

CHAPTER -1-

"Star Light, Star Bright, first star…" Betty Parker whispered as she lifted eyes shimmering with unshed tears to the night sky. *Why? Why me?* She looked back through the sliding doors at Ralph Parker's profile illuminated in the soft glow of the television. He lay back in his recliner engrossed in some silly program. His silhouette only emphasized her loneliness.

Betty slumped into a faded lawn chair. *Only children and fools wish on a star. Next thing you know, Betty old girl, you'll believe in love and happily ever after. Accept it,* she chided. *This is as good as it gets — all there is for you.* Still, she hesitated. If there was the slightest chance… She whispered one last desperate plea. "Help me. Help me find true love."

A tear leaked from her eye as her fingers stroked the yellow Lab at her side. Both the woman and the dog had left their youth behind them.

*****

Angel Second Chance slipped into the majestic hall. He glided across the snowy marble floor. Browsing, he paused now and again to scan the tablets that adorned the walls.

Ah, at last. He contemplated his entry in the Celestial Directory for a breath or two, tracing it with a slim finger — *Angel Second Chance, Project Angel, known as Zvie (Zěv'ē).* Occasionally he needed this reminder of who and what he was. Satisfied, he searched the room. Then left as he had entered.

Zvie had recently returned home and completed his debriefing which signaled the end of a successful mission. Most mortals were unaware all angels didn't float on clouds and play harps. *No offense to the cherubim.* He had provided comfort and guidance to survivors and victims of earthquakes, hurricanes, and war in the Middle East. It had been a busy year, and a leap second had further extended it.

Weary, he looked forward to visiting with his peers, sharing experiences and stories on the terrace. It was heavenly to be home again.

*****

Colin O'Brien closed the glass door of the high-rise apartment. Cynicism marred the handsome actor's face as he leaned against the railing of the terrace and gazed at stars dimmed by the city lights. The hum of conversation, the clink of glasses, and an occasional shriek of laughter he had left behind disturbed his brooding. Away from it all, he didn't have to hide his unhappiness.

He tensed as the door opened, and his agent's voice boomed. "What's the matter with you? You can't score out here. Come on. You gotta meet the broad with the humongous..." Sam wagged his eyebrows and gestured, his hands extended from his chest.

"Give me a minute, Sam. I need…to escape," he muttered under his breath and waved him away. He rolled his shoulders to ease his irritation with his agent, the party—a rubber stamp of so many others—and his life.

"If anyone is out there, if you can hear me, prove to me that love is real," Colin challenged, then added in a barely audible voice. "I have to know if love is real or an illusion, a scam perpetrated by the entertainment media. If it exists, help me find it or give me the good sense to remain alone. Don't let me play the fool again."

CHAPTER -2-

Zvie hid his dismay when his phone vibrated. "Angel Second Chance. How may I be of service?"

"The Archangel wishes to see you," a voice replied. "Please come now."

"Michael?" he asked.

"No, Archangel Rafael."

Zvie gazed wistfully at the open bottle of wine on the countertop, but left his quarters. Loose white robes billowed around his tall frame as he made his way to Administration.

He paused before the carved silver door to take a deep breath and then pushed the door open to enter a spacious white room. A wall of windows overlooked a garden, its colorful blooms and flowerbeds tended by workers in pale green robes. Darker green–clad figures manicured the perfect lawn. He strode across the snowy marble floor to a grand desk near the windows. In the distance a pale blue haze cloaked a globe, an indeterminate mosaic of muted colors.

The ruffled, silver fringe of hair circling the Archangel Rafael's bald pate was a certain sign that he wrestled with a weighty problem. His smooth, unlined face bore a frown as he bent over a desk strewn with bits of paper, folders, photographs, and other detritus of his office. He looked up, raised bushy white brows, and directed a preoccupied look at his visitor.

"You summoned me, Chief?"

His superior gazed at Zvie for a moment before he remembered why he'd summoned him.

"Yes, I did. And, please remember to knock and wait for permission to enter. I could have been in conference."

"Sorry, Sir, but your secretary implied there was some urgency."

"I have an assignment for you." The Archangel rummaged around his cluttered desk and picked up a memorandum. "Two disillusioned mortals question that love is real—romantic love, that is. One believes she experiences travail for our entertainment, although she does not specifically name us. Angels," he hastened to clarify. "She believes her problems are a source of amusement to us. We, however, know that is not true, don't we, Angel Second Chance?"

"Of course," he agreed, although there was a touch of irony in his voice as his thoughts strayed to the refreshments waiting for him.

Rafael arched an eyebrow and gave him a penetrating look before he continued.

"These mortals share the same desire. The Celestial Appeals Committee believes the two of them may be complementary, considering their petitions are similar. Matching them is most unusual."

Zvie thought he saw the Archangel shudder.

"This project will require delicacy." The Archangel frowned and weighed his next words. "I have strong reservations about the wisdom of intervention, but the Committee voted contrary to my views, and I must bow to its will. These mortals are so dissimilar they would never meet without our aid. It is regrettable that their life choices have been such poor ones."

"I've never worked a dual project. Will I be working alone? And," he began, but the Archangel had definite ideas of when and what he would discuss.

"Patience, Angel Second Chance. You will receive all the information you require, but you must have a preapproved plan of action before you begin this project. You must keep me in the loop at all times. If you encounter any difficulties, you must come to me. Do you understand?"

Zvie nodded, swallowing the urge to remind the Archangel that he was not a neophyte project angel.

"This is a complicated project. Betty's second chance will affect not only her, but people close to her. That is why I must approve your campaign."

"I understand," Zvie said, shelving his former plan.

"I hope so. Let us look at Colin O'Brien first, a less-complicated individual. We will discuss him when the presentation ends. Please make yourself comfortable." The Archangel waved his hand to indicate the choices.

Zvie considered his options and sprawled on a padded settee.

"Files, please," the Archangel prompted. A slight figure in soft gray robes swept in, left several devices and scurried away. The Archangel's hand hovered and dropped. He leaned back in his desk chair and snapped his fingers; images scrolled before them.

A small, dark-haired boy kneeled on a window seat in a stark room he would share with three eight-year-old boys.

This would be his home while he attended boarding school. His lower lip quivered, and a lone tear trickled down his cheek as he watched his parents get into a black sedan and drive away. Alone, he stared after the car long after it vanished in the distance.

The boy grew into a slender youth, and candid shots showed him on the edge of groups of people. From the physical resemblances, Zvie guessed they might be family. A pattern emerged as Colin stood aloof in other social settings.

Colin matured into a tall, broad-shouldered man. He wore his tousled, dark hair short to disguise its tendency to curl. Aviator sunglasses hid his blue eyes, and his sensuous mouth slanted up, lending him an air of amusement. His straight nose was a little on the large side. Taken as a whole, however, Colin was a handsome man. Even as a youth, his clothes distinguished him from his peers, preferring sport coats, khakis, and loafers rather than the leather and ragged jeans popularized by rap stars.

Colin discovered an aptitude for acting in college. He found it easy to pretend and enjoyed recognition and acceptance through acting.

Sam Lewin, a talent agent, saw Colin in a college play, approached him, and arranged an audition. Colin got the part in a TV series called *Lovers and Liars,* received excellent reviews, and became a television celebrity. He was often in the company of people who flattered him and talked at him but did not listen *to* him.

Two failed marriages followed, but Colin didn't appear heartbroken by either woman's departure. Finally, Zvie watched Colin slip onto a terrace alone and issue his challenge. "I have to know if love is real. If it exists, help me find it." The image faded, but Colin's words lingered.

"And, you are here because his challenge touched a member of the Celestial Appeals Committee." The Archangel pushed a heavy volume toward the edge of his desk. "This was a cursory presentation, but you may review the entire file at your leisure. Your impressions?"

"Handsome man, magnetic. He may have realized his youth is slipping away, and his lonely childhood may have stunted his emotions. His career depends upon his looks, or so he believes. He's drawn to beautiful but shallow women. Might I suggest he is following the dictates of his second brain?"

"And might I suggest, Angel Second Chance, this is not the time for levity."

Zvie considered his superior stuffy and lacking a sense of humor, but he readily apologized.

"Sorry. I'm not surprised his relationships failed based on his selection criterion and their brief acquaintance. He is lonely, frustrated, and approaching the juncture where he may not be salvageable."

"Very astute. However, he has undeveloped depths. We believe the second subject may help him turn his life around. If she can overcome his cynicism and if he experiences love, he will achieve the emotional growth important to his future happiness and professional success. Currently, he sees no further than the dissatisfaction that colors his life."

"Why does the Committee think the woman is complementary?"

"She is caring and creative by nature. She had a bright future and displayed wit and intelligence before her unfortunate life choices. Her marriages forced her to be practical. She yearns for a relationship with a man she can lean on, one who will cherish her, although she has yet to find one."

Zvie formed a question, but the Archangel held up his hand for silence.

"Just… watch."

*****

A young girl crouched in a corner, her eyes scrunched shut. Her hands covered her ears to block out the angry shouts and gestures of a man and a woman. When the scene changed, Zvie watched her eat and dress with an eye on the clock before boarding a school bus. She returned home on the same bus and let herself into an empty house with her key.

"A latchkey kid," Zvie murmured.

"We prefer the term *child*," Rafael corrected.

Zvie rolled his eyes.

Betty called out, "Is anyone here?" and looked relieved when no one answered. She exchanged her school clothes for jeans and T-shirt and read the list of chores left for her. She drew a line through each one as she completed it. Similar scenes repeated as she grew older. Homework, babysitting, assorted domestic chores: her life was one of responsibility.

She went to work after high school graduation and six months later married a shallow, immature young man. His brash, outgoing personality had attracted her, so opposite from her own. Early on he was unfaithful and belittled her at every opportunity. Reluctantly, she divorced him.

"Reluctantly? I should think she'd be relieved," Zvie ventured.

"Reluctantly," the Archangel repeated. "The sexual revolution of the late 1960s was slow to gain acceptance in Betty's middle-class community. Divorce was uncommon and not viewed with favor in her family and rightly so. She married to escape the hostile atmosphere of her parents' house, and young marriages were the norm for girls of that time. She wanted to call off the wedding the night before but lacked the courage to face the public scandal and family censure."

"Pity," Angel Second Chance observed. "What changed her mind about divorce?"

"She discovered her acquaintances either felt sorry for her or labeled her a fool. Once one loses respect, the relationship is over."

At thirty, she listened to her biological clock and, succumbing to Ralph Parker's swagger and charm, they married. Before long, however, she confided to a friend she had mistaken lust for love.

"Have you grasped the delicacy of this assignment, Zvie?" Archangel Rafael consulted his notes. "We cannot simply pluck Betty away from her husband."

"Her husband is alive?" Zvie interrupted.

"Yes, yes he is," the Archangel verified "Now do you see why we cannot simply arrange an introduction, let matters run their course, or perform a small miracle?"

"But we try to save marriages; we do not break them up," Zvie protested.

"Her marriage failed years ago despite our efforts to save it. She and her husband share nothing."

The presentation continued. Betty struggled to cope with their move to Florida and the demands of an infant daughter without the emotional support of family and friends.

"She is not only married but has a child!" Zvie straightened, all trace of complacency gone as he struggled with this new piece of information.

"Yes. Yes," the Archangel replied with a touch of asperity. "If you would refrain from interrupting, we might get to the end of this presentation."

Later scenes showed Betty fulfilling roles of treasurer, housekeeper, cook, nanny, chauffeur, occasional nurse, and caretaker for family pets besides full-time employment. Zvie watched her grow increasingly weary, and her marriage become silent and cold. She and her husband rarely discussed anything personal outside of Ralph's health. When he discovered the internet, he developed cyberchondria.

"They are strangers who live in the same house." Archangel Rafael sighed.

The last image showed Betty's husband announcing his retirement plans. "I'm going to buy a boat and learn to sail." He was unaware of the effect of his words although he knew Betty suffered with seasickness.

Though she hadn't told anyone, Betty had hoped her marriage might improve when Ralph retired. Zvie watched the play of emotions cross Betty's face as her last fantasy died.

"Well, Angel Second Chance?"

"Her second husband is an older version of the first with the same disappointing results. Betty and her daughter seem close."

"Yes, but her daughter's recent engagement forced Betty to examine her life. She is now in the autumn of her years, and her time for fulfillment is running out. If she refuses her second chance, you will return for reassignment. It is possible Betty and Colin will not strike sparks off each other. However, we can exert some influence to sway them." The Archangel allowed himself a slight smile. "If they can overcome their pasts, and if… if… if…" The Archangel ticked off the obstacles.

"A handsome television actor and a faded, over-the-hill housewife?" Zvie questioned the Committee's judgment.

"I *told* you this will require planning and delicacy." The Archangel moved several volumes toward Zvie. "And, I do not envision Betty as an aging housewife when the project gets underway."

"How did Betty come to the Committee's attention?"

"Something in her plea struck a chord in that same member of the Appeals Committee," the Archangel said, "although we have been aware of her unhappiness for some time. She believes love has passed her by, that it exists only in the pages of novels, that it is a foolish fantasy. She believes romantic love is mistaken for lust and cannot last."

"Ouch," Zvie replied.

"Betty's youth and her looks have flown along with her dreams. She would not attract Colin in her present form. When you meet her, you will agree she'll need time at the Spa. She will require emotional adjustment and a physical makeover. She can be attractive again, or so I have been told. You will guide her through her transformation. My advisers recommend the complete course at the Second Chance Academy. Shall we say one month?"

"The works? None of my prior projects have needed the complete course!" He frowned at the implications.

"You do not have unlimited time for this project, but it will not begin until Betty completes the Academy program." The Archangel paused, lost in thought. Then, he stressed. "This is important, Angel Second Chance. The program begins only if Betty *accepts* her second chance." He added with a pointed look to Zvie. "You might benefit from some time at the Academy too."

The loose white robes Zvie wore had not disguised his expanding waistline, and he nodded his acknowledgment.

"What happens if they don't strike sparks off each other?"

"Please do not consider failure before you begin. But since you asked, Colin O'Brien will remain much the same, although he will become more jaded and bemoan his choices and missed opportunities. Betty's life, however, intersects with others. Consequently, failure for her will be serious. She cannot pick up her former life, nor would she want to read or hear about Colin if their relationship flourishes and then fails. That leaves only one alternative."

"Welcome to my world?" Zvie asked.

"Crudely put, but succinct. We are reminded of the adage: *Be careful what you wish for.*"

Zvie nodded his appreciation of the platitude.

"Chloe is an important factor. Do not discount Betty's loving relationship with her daughter. Chloe is frustrated by her mother's reluctance to change. Betty's role in her daughter's life will be greatly reduced after Chloe's wedding to James and the independent future they have planned. Although she grew up in the shadow of her parents' unhappy marriage, I think Chloe will manage without Betty."

The Archangel consulted his file once again. "Ralph Parker, the husband, will follow his desires without the occasional twinges of guilt his wife inspires. No doubt he will move on after the initial shock." He contemplated the steeple formed with his fingertips. The tick of the Great Clock broke the silence in the room before he straightened in his chair.

"Take the files with you and draft a plan. Make a follow-up appointment with my secretary on your way out." The Archangel turned back to his desk.

"Yes, sir. This case will be a challenge. I'll..." Zvie stopped his search for the right words. His superior had shifted to other matters and waved him on his way.

*****

Back in his quarters, Zvie poured a golden liquid into a crystal goblet, closed his eyes and enjoyed the wine's bouquet.

He reclined in an easy chair, sipped his wine, and let his thoughts wander to his mortal life. His father had steered him into the clergy. Although not his choice, he had been comfortable in his robes and accepted the convoluted path of his life. His wife, the eldest of three siblings, was not his choice either. Her family had feared she would not only suffer the stigma of spinsterhood, but they were not wealthy enough to arrange her continued support outside of marriage. Consequently, their marriage had been an arranged one according to the custom of the time. Zvie had been content with his small country parish, but his wife had worn her dissatisfaction openly and often expressed it. When she contracted a fever and died, he mourned her, but privately he gave thanks that his life had become easier. Zvie resisted his parishioners' matchmaking attempts, encouraging their belief that he had loved his wife and could not accept anyone in her place. He empathized with Betty Parker. He, too, had suffered a joyless marriage.

Zvie considered Betty the primary challenge and considered at length how she might be changed to attract Colin. He would have to trust the experts at the Second Chance Academy to work their wonders with her.

A connoisseur of good food and wine, Zvie's thoughts turned to Colin. A television actor, he mused. Colin no doubt enjoyed elegant dining, interesting companions, stimulating conversation, and entertainment.

He refilled his goblet and raised it. "To you, Colin, and to you, Betty." He hummed and drummed his fingers on the arm of his chair: "All You Need Is Love." Dum de dum de dum… She Needs Love… Dum de dum de dum… Love is what she needs.

CHAPTER -3-

Betty Parker leaned toward the mirror and studied the woman who looked back at her. The demands of raising her daughter, keeping house, and full-time employment had made the passing years insignificant except for dates on letters, her checkbook register, and the calendar of activities. Now, those years were making themselves known. Creases and crow's feet once were laugh lines. Drooping eyelids partially obscured warm golden-brown eyes. Furrows ran from her ordinary nose to the corners of her stern and unsmiling mouth. She struggled to reconcile the image in the mirror with the woman who didn't feel that old, most of the time. When had she become her mother?

"Tomorrow I'll schedule a facial," she murmured, but knew even as she spoke the words, she would not make the effort. She needed a hair appointment too. That was another decision she would put on hold. She pulled on her uniform—drawstring pants and an oversized T-shirt—and slipped her feet into rubber clogs. Then, she bent over the bathroom sink and splashed lukewarm water on her face.

She could remember when she had spent precious time on makeup and her hair. She had enjoyed shopping for fashionable clothes and had even felt attractive and desirable. That was another lifetime, one before she realized her dreams would not come true. She left the bathroom, looking away from the mirrored closet doors.

She heard her dog whine and called out as she made her way to the kitchen. "I'm coming, Maggie; I'm coming." She hurried to open the screen door. While her dog inspected the backyard, she spooned coffee into the coffeemaker, pressed the switch and listened to the first gurgle of water through the filter. She switched on the radio. This morning she needed distracting—another voice, reassurance she wasn't alone on the planet.

Ralph never brings me flowers. They didn't talk anymore just like in the lyrics of the song on the radio. Oh, Ralph delivered lectures on things he had discovered on the Internet, his new best friend, or in the newspaper while he expounded on what was wrong with the country. He talked on his cell phone to Walt, the man he had worked with on his last out-of-town assignment. When he came back home, Betty had been puzzled, then amused at the animation in Ralph's voice when he spoke with him. Chloe had dubbed the man Dad's girlfriend because their conversations were so frequent and lengthy. When Betty let that slip, Ralph had been indignant. Now, however, the label and the friendship annoyed her.

She walked to the screen door at Maggie's I-want-in-now bark and let her inside. It was approaching 8 a.m. and the temperature was climbing, although it had little to do with the dog's demand. When Betty brought Maggie home, the dog had recognized a friend and determined that she would not live outside ever again. Ralph believed dogs belonged outside and this was just one more entry on their lengthy list of conflicting views.

She poured coffee into a mug and promised to feed her dog as soon as she drank her first cup. Maggie thumped her tail, assuring Betty she understood. The Neil Diamond/Barbra Streisand duet continued.

Ralph might have learned how to lie, but he hadn't learned how to love, and, she hadn't either. And how many times had she imagined telling him goodbye? *You Don't Bring Me Flowers* might have been written for her. She brushed at the tears that trickled down her cheeks. *Stop it, Betty.* The medication the doctor prescribed and that she took each evening was not easing the suffocating sadness, her constant companion. Tears were always near the surface. Sad, mad, and glad were basic emotions, but her equation eliminated glad.

Before her forced unemployment, Betty had handled anger and resentment easier when she could vent with fellow workers. but the law firm had downsized and terminated her. After all the years of struggling to find enough time to fulfill her responsibilities and perform her chores, Betty now had the leisure to brood on her unhappiness.

She fed the patient old dog and poured herself a second cup of coffee. Zapping the lukewarm brew with the microwave, she considered how to fill her day, but her favorite wicker chair beckoned to her from the patio. She did her deepest thinking there.

Maggie finished eating and joined her. The dog plopped down and brushed her feet.

"You big old fur ball," Betty said and nudged Maggie with her toes. She grew misty eyed again when she considered the dog's white muzzle and slow steps.

She should call her sister but put off doing that too.

'Betty, hindsight is a wonderful gift but a waste of time. Make the best of each day.' Mary's voice rang in her ears without the benefit of electronics. Her sister would add before they hung up, 'God loves you and so do I.'

Betty envied her sister's sunny nature. Was it the result of a fortunate marriage, or was her happy marriage the result of her sunny disposition? She loved her sister, but her pious remarks grated on her last nerve. As far as Betty could tell, God wasn't interested in her or her marriage. He hadn't been interested in her first marriage either. She had offended Mary when she'd insisted she was a character in a heavenly sitcom and God and his minions enjoyed watching her sorry attempts to climb out of the tangle of her life's problems.

It had taken weeks to mend their relationship after that conversation.

Ralph was coming home this afternoon after several days on his boat. Betty felt heartburn's onset. Her gut cramped. She knew it wasn't from the cup of coffee. He had called yesterday from the middle of the Bay to describe the sights, the colors, and the other boats. Amused and proud, he wanted to boast that his boat had stopped traffic when the tender raised the bridge so he could pass through. She'd been cleaning the oven, her hands greasy and her head reeling from the chemical cleaner when she took his call. This wasn't the first time he had called while sailing. He had done so while she had been churning out documents in the word processing department of that sealed office building, breathing recirculated air, with not even a window to relieve her workstation.

The phone rang, and she toyed with ignoring it, but dragged herself to her feet. That would be Chloe. She hoped her daughter wouldn't request another monetary or emotional withdrawal from the Bank of Mom.

"Hello?"

"It's me. Anything going on?" She recognized Ralph's voice.

"The usual, thanks for asking." Betty felt a measure of guilt at her sarcasm. She waited for the coming zinger.

"Uh, Walt and I are taking his boat to the Bahamas for a couple of days. It's perfect sailing weather."

"I thought you were coming home today, Ralph." *Walt again, always Walt!* She clamped her lips before she said something she might regret.

"Well, that was the plan, but Walt and I agreed we won't have many more opportunities to go out with summer coming. The heat, humidity, and the mosquitoes and flies from hell will be real bothersome soon. And, there's the hurricane season." He paused, waiting for her response, but she gave none.

"Well, just wanted you to know. Nothing you can't handle, is there?"

"No, I'll manage," *as usual,* she added silently, resentful that she would deal with the responsibilities once again while he played. The grass was ankle high; she would have to mow it if she could start the old lawnmower. She'd have to call a plumber to fix the leak under the kitchen sink.

"Right. See you in a couple of days."

Betty laid the phone in its cradle to keep from slamming it down as she wanted to do. *It would be a cold day...* The phone rang again before she could complete the thought.

"Hello."

"Hi Mom. How's your day going? Heard from Dad?"

"He and Walt are sailing to the Bahamas for a couple of days. Last chance before… You know the drill. Maggie and I are on our own for a few more days."

"O-kay." She drew the word out. "You don't really care, do you?" and rushed on, already knowing the answer. "Come out with me tonight. Don't sit around by yourself. It's yoga on the beach night, a beginner's class, and a chance for you to get back into it. We're a fun group, and it will be beautiful by the water. You'll meet new people, and we'll go out for a bite to eat after."

"Oh, honey. I can't wear yoga clothes anymore, and it's hot. Maggie—"

"Mom, the dog will be fine," Chloe interrupted. "I worry about you being alone all the time. You have to make an effort."

After a moment's hesitation, she gave up her plans to spend the evening with a glass or two of wine and the DVD movie she had picked up at the library. "All right. I'll meet you at your place, and we'll go together. See you about six o'clock?"

"Perfect. And, Mom, turn your cell phone on and leave it on, so I can reach you. See you later."

"Love you," she said and dropped the receiver in its cradle.

Betty groaned and thought of excuses she could give later, but her refusal would hurt Chloe's feelings once again. If she didn't show, her daughter would call her every couple of hours to see if she was all right. Making a face, she headed to the bathroom, stripped, and stepped into the shower. She needed groceries, and she could stop for a latté. She dressed indifferently in black drawstring pants, a white-and-black patterned knit shirt, and flip-flops.

Betty parked her car and started for the Best Ever Coffee Shoppe. She passed her bank, then for reasons she couldn't explain, made a U-turn and walked into the lobby. She stood for a moment while she removed her sunglasses and dug in her purse for her savings book before she approached the teller. A half hour later, she tucked the signature card for her new account into her purse, completed her shopping, then sat in the coffee shop puzzling over her actions. *Betty Parker, where did this bit of nonsense come from?* She didn't have a clue, but signed the signature card as Kate Dunning, the fictitious joint owner, before returning it to the bank officer.

Back at home, she considered the contents of her closet. It was nice to have plans even if it was with a group of lithe youthful women who would make her feel frumpy and ancient. She found dark blue jersey pants that Chloe wanted her to donate to Goodwill and hoped the seams would hold. She added a navy sports bra and a long white T-shirt to cover her expanded derriere. Years of sitting at a desk hadn't helped her figure. Neither had the bags of Peanut M&Ms she snacked on every afternoon when the hands of the clock slowed to a crawl. Betty added lip gloss. Additional makeup would slide right off her face in the afternoon heat and the sweat generated with yoga asanas.

Betty took Maggie out one last time, promising her a walk when she returned. She adjusted the volume of the radio and avoided the dog's sad eyes. Shouldering her bag, she locked the door and climbed into her car. She slid a Diana Krall disk into the CD drive, cranked the volume, and opened the sunroof. Backing out of the driveway, she felt upbeat.

Her neighbor, Mrs. Watson, sat by her front door monitoring the neighborhood activities, and Betty waved. She avoided the kids playing ball in the street and admired the new landscaping in front of the house at the end of the block. She and Ralph should do something to their house. It was looking shabby. They still used the same furniture they'd had when Chloe was in elementary school. She lacked the motivation to shop alone. They didn't like the same TV programs and watched in separate rooms because they couldn't or wouldn't compromise. Often, he escaped to his boat or the computer, and she sat with Maggie.

Their middle-class neighborhood had been different when they moved there, and she and Ralph were nicer to each other. Chloe had been the only child on the block. And, they had a dog; Betty always had a dog, had always needed one. They had installed a privacy fence so the dog would not upset the neighbors. They reasoned they were being good neighbors. After the last section of fence was in place, the next-door neighbor had marched over to tell them it obstructed her breeze. Since that incident that house had changed hands as had many of the others. Most of the houses now had privacy fences. Neighbors didn't know each other except to nod or wave as they passed from their air-conditioned cars to their air-conditioned houses, and the fences enabled them to keep it that way.

Betty left the neighborhood, joined the east-west artery to the toll road, and merged with the commuters. The vehicular gods were in a good mood, and the congested five o'clock traffic moved at a slow but steady pace. She arrived at Chloe's apartment after a forty-five-minute drive and two phone calls from her daughter pinpointing her location. *Kids are so dependent on those damn cell phones.* Sometimes she wondered if Chloe thought she was losing her grip. Their roles were reversing.

Her daughter had expected her arrival and waved before she locked the door to her apartment while Betty chose a parking space. Chloe planned for her to drive to the class.

"Hi, Mom. I'm glad you came. I expected you would cancel on me." Chloe's smile accompanying her playful jab didn't reach her eyes. She inspected her mother. "Isn't it hot?" She tossed her bag in the back seat.

"Yes, it is, but you look cool. Is that new?" Her daughter wore an ankle-length gauzy skirt in turquoise with a skinny white knit shirt and turquoise sandals with varied colored beads on the straps. A clip tamed her shoulder-length, tawny hair and a fresh, light scent Betty didn't recognize accompanied her daughter into the car. Chloe looked fresh from the shower.

"I picked the skirt up on the sale table at Merlin's, and I already had the knit top. Aren't these shoes the cutest? I couldn't pass them up."

"How many pairs does that make?"

"Oh, Mom. You know you can never have too many pairs of shoes." Chloe laughed. "You had a closet full of wild and crazy shoes, and I remember playing with them when I was little."

Betty followed Chloe's directions and listened to an account of her day. The temperature had dropped a few degrees, but it still would be hot on the sand although it was early evening. The sunbathers and swimmers were leaving. They looked sweaty, frazzled, and in need of a shower, their skin reddened from exposure to the sun. Mothers struggled under enormous beach bags, towing tired, cranky kids as they made their way to their cars. Betty waited while an SUV backed out, then took the vacant parking space. She looked at the near-naked bodies and the trim figures in body-hugging knit shorts and tank tops that jogged or power walked past. She made a mental resolution to hide in the back row, but Chloe had another plan.

"Let's spread our towels over here. Oh, there's a new guy here tonight. He looks friendly and close to your age. Now, Mom, I want you to smile and make nice."

"I'm not interested, Chloe. Never, never again."

"Mom!" she wailed. "Coffee and conversation. I'm not suggesting you sleep with him."

"Chloe!" Betty wanted to lecture but didn't want to make a bigger scene than her daughter already had. She rolled her eyes heavenward and hoped no one had overheard. Chloe dropped her skirt exposing the knit knee-length shorts she wore underneath it and removed her shoes. The instructor took her place, and the class began.

Profusely sweating after an hour of deep breathing, stretches, and postures, Betty congratulated herself for completing the class. She felt good. Her hands and face tingled. She had renewed acquaintance with muscles she hadn't met in a while and would remember them tomorrow. She stooped to pick up her shoes and car keys, shook the sand from her towel, and walked to the shoreline, welcoming the faint breeze. The sun was settling on the horizon and she waited while Chloe visited with her friends.

Betty felt someone near and whirled in that direction. The unfamiliar man stood beside her. She met his blue eyes and couldn't look away. Something about him drew her interest. Chloe was right; he and Betty were the oldest in the class. Blonde hair sprinkled with silver, receding hairline, he dressed in white from drawstring pants and T-shirt to his tennis shoes. He was pale for someone who lived in Florida.

"I didn't mean to startle you. I'm Zvie." His grin charmed her.

"Betty Parker. I didn't hear you coming."

"I'm sorry. You must have been deep in thought. This is the first time I've been here. Do you come often?" Zvie laughed at Betty's raised eyebrow. "That isn't a pickup line."

"It's my first time too." Betty had the oddest feeling she had met this man somewhere before. They exchanged small talk until Chloe joined them.

"This is my daughter. Chloe, meet Zvie."

"We're going to The Snack Shack for a bite to eat," Chloe said. "Would you like to join us, Zvie?"

"Thank you. I'd like to, but I don't have a car."

"We'll give you a ride. Right, Mom?"

Chloe! We must talk. What can I do but agree... this time? Betty nodded and, following Chloe's directions, drove to a small beachfront restaurant. The interior's painted block walls boasted autographed pictures of celebrities, the restaurant's only concession to décor. Four women from the beach yoga class had claimed a long, lacquered table near the front window. They waved to Chloe.

"We saved places for you." They moved chairs and borrowed two more from nearby tables to accommodate their party. Betty wedged in between Zvie and Chloe. They were a lively group, friends who attended the yoga class each week, and conversation turned to the latest reality shows and television series.

"Anybody watch *The Biggest Loser* yet?"

"I caught it last week. What could those people have been thinking?" An anorexic-looking young woman at the end of the table made a face for emphasis.

"I'm rooting for them. I wouldn't have the courage to weigh in on television!" A slim young woman defended.

Betty wanted to warn them. They might find out how it was possible. Trying to cope with a crying baby in the middle of the night made cookies look and taste delicious, but their calories lurked and hovered, until one day they took up permanent residence on a once slim pair of hips.

"Anybody see the intern on that new medical show? Is he hot or is he hot?"

"I did. My boyfriend thinks it's lame. He doesn't understand I watch the show to drool over the actor," another responded.

They argued good-naturedly over the sexiest male on television. Betty guessed that medical and reality themes were in vogue this season. She did not recognize the celebrities they talked about, and the celebrities whose names she could recall wouldn't mean anything to them. She made a mental note to watch some of the programs they were discussing, the one with the so-called hottie to see if he's as good looking as Colin O'Brien, an actor they might not know. They talked about the characters as though they knew them.

Despite the age differences, Zvie took part in their discussions. She marveled at the ease with which he conversed with them. When the party broke up, she and Chloe dropped him at a small apartment hotel on the beach. He seemed like an old friend. From time to time he had turned to her with a casual comment making her feel part of the discussions swirling around her although she had ventured no opinions.

"Join us again next week?" Chloe called to him.

"I'll try. Thanks for the ride. I enjoyed the class and the conversation."

Betty felt he was talking to her, but that couldn't be. She had been a spectator.

"Did you enjoy yourself? How do you feel?" Chloe asked.

"My body will protest tomorrow morning, Chloe, but I had fun."

"We'll do it again next week, okay? Whether or not Dad's home. Zvie seems very nice. Maybe he'll come again."

"Chloe, don't…"

"Mom, you need a friend, just like Dad has a friend. What difference does it make if he's a man? Relax and go with the flow."

They arrived at Chloe's apartment, and Betty got out of the car and hugged her daughter. She held on for a moment longer than usual. She loved the woman Chloe had become, but there were times she missed the child.

"Call me when you get home, Mom. That's what you always asked me to do."

She agreed and waved. Betty sang along with the radio and even the careless South Florida drivers didn't ruin her mood on the way home.

"Maggie, I'm home," she called as she turned her key in the lock. Her dog met her when she opened the door, and they made a slow circuit around the block. The phone was ringing when they got back: Chloe checking on her. After assuring Chloe she had arrived, and that Maggie was fine, she showered and changed into pajamas. Tuning her radio to the oldies FM station, she poured a glass of wine and replayed the evening. Zvie intrigued her. *How could he survive in South Florida without a car?* She tried to remember where she could have met him, but she had worked in many places and couldn't place him. After a while she lay back and drifted while the music played. Her thoughts turned to her favorite fantasy—what-if. What-if there was a handsome man somewhere who would adore her? Betty sighed and poured another glass of wine.

CHAPTER -4-

Betty had planned her life to the minute for so long that free time forced her to review to-do lists and her calendar for a forgotten appointment or task. Now, after a month into unemployment, she was learning to relax. Her housekeeping chores and laundry were lighter with Ralph on his boat. Reclaiming her bicycle after years in the storage shed, Betty wobbled when she first climbed on. Soon she rode around the neighborhood. She attempted an aerobics DVD Chloe had left behind, something she wouldn't do if Ralph were home to discourage her. Betty was more relaxed than she had been for weeks. When Chloe called to remind her of yoga, she was looking forward to it.

Dressed in new exercise clothes, she picked up her tote. Car keys in hand, she was reaching for the doorknob when Maggie barked. Betty heard the beep that signaled locking a vehicle's doors. *Who could that be?*

Ralph opened the door, surprising her. "What's for supper?"

"Hello to you too. I didn't know you were coming home today, Ralph. I'm meeting Chloe."

"Give me a few minutes to get my gear from the car. I'll grab a shower and come with you. Where are you going?"

"To a yoga class on the beach."

"You? Yoga? Pull the other one!" He smirked and wiggled his eyebrows. "Be careful you don't get fleas rolling around in the sand." He reached over to lift the hem of her shirt, then shook his head. "Stretch pants? Oh, babe."

Betty turned away. He had some nerve, with his belly hanging over his belt, although Ralph was still a good-looking man. His suntan flattered his gray hair and intensified his blue eyes. His legs were tan and smooth, smoother than hers, and she wondered if he shaved them.

"Unless you plan to take part in the class, don't bother coming with me."

"Take part? Hell no! I'm not twisting myself into knots."

"I don't know when I'll be home, so don't wait up."

Betty was still on edge when she and Chloe arrived at the beach and spread their towels. A gentle breeze blew in from the ocean. Waves slapped the shore and receded, taking grains of sand each time. *Like Ralph does to me.*

Her daughter wandered away to chat. Zvie arrived late and claimed a spot in the back as the class began. Betty had wondered if he was a beginner. Now she wouldn't be able to watch him.

After class, most of the group had plans and didn't linger as they had the previous week. Zvie, however, was available, and the three of them—Chloe, Zvie and Betty—decided on a sports bar nearby. As they approached their destination, Chloe let out a whoop after her phone chimed. "James texted me. He's been out of town and got back earlier than expected. Would you mind if I pass?"

Chloe! That's just too darn convenient! Zvie was already in the car. How could she take him home without looking silly?

"I know you haven't eaten. You and Zvie should go without me," Chloe urged. "Then neither of you will have to eat alone."

"I'm harmless," Zvie said, coaxing her with his soothing voice. "And I would enjoy your company."

Betty looked at him in the rearview mirror. She sensed he knew what she was thinking. Did the twinkle in his eyes mean her hesitation amused him?

"That's settled, then." Chloe gave her mother a sly grin. "We're close to my place, so it's not out of your way. I'll call you tomorrow, Mom." She turned to Zvie. "I'm sorry. I didn't expect James tonight."

Betty noticed the lights in Chloe's apartment and the car in Chloe's second parking space.

"Looks like James is here," Betty observed.

"Have a nice evening," Chloe said over her shoulder as she hurried away.

Betty waited while Zvie moved into the passenger seat.

"There's a little restaurant off the lobby of my hotel. Let's go there. You won't have to make a second trip."

Again, Betty questioned his motives before she replied. "I planned on a place like the one we went to last week," and gestured at her workout clothes.

"You're perfect the way you are."

Betty suppressed a shiver. She gave him a sharp look to see if there was a hidden meaning, but his expression was bland, almost innocent.

The hotel, on a street that branched off the beachfront, was in a row of small family-owned and run hotels. The landscaping and exterior appeared a tad more luxurious than the ones on either side. Betty surrendered her car to a valet before accompanying Zvie into the restaurant. A few diners seated about the compact room evidenced their day at the beach. Their sunburned faces labeled them as tourists.

Assorted Florida beach scenes and posters of native birds adorned two walls of the establishment. A third windowed wall overlooked a pool. Underwater lights turned the water to a clear aqua blue, and a light breeze rippled its surface. The hostess showed them to a table, and a waiter brought menus listing the specials and the typical sandwich and salad fare.

"Would you care for a glass of wine, Betty?" Zvie asked. "They don't have an extensive list, but the house wine is decent."

"Thank you, no. I have to drive home."

They ordered, and any awkward feelings she'd had soon disappeared. He was easy to talk with, and Betty confided in him as if he were an old friend. "I don't believe in love, except in movies and the pages of romance novels," she said.

"You don't know anyone with a loving relationship?"

"Not really. At the office where I used to work, divorced or separated women and men made up half of the firm. Oh, we had the occasional newlywed with stars in her eyes."

"I know many happy couples," he said, and he related some happy-ever-after stories. Then he startled her with his next question. "What if you could have a do-over? Would you risk it? Are you brave enough to change your life?"

Betty stared at Zvie. *Where did that come from?* "I've thought about it, but where would I go and what would I do? At my age, a do-over is so much dreaming."

After coffee, he waited with her until a valet brought her car and held the door while she slid in.

"Will I see you next week at the class?" He asked.

"I plan to be there."

"Until next week. Good night, Betty."

The population of this South Florida area was in a growth spurt, and coastal cities had grown until they shared boundaries. She drove home through the adjoining cities rather than on the expressway. She pulled into the driveway and didn't get out of her car right away.

Betty thought of her conversation with Zvie and how it had turned to her. *What was I thinking, confiding in him as I did?* She was embarrassed as she remembered they had discussed not only her marriage, but her previous marriage and the brief liaison she'd had between marriages. *How had that happened?* She had never even mentioned his name to anyone.

She had told Zvie she believed love only existed in the pages of romance novels. He had tried to reassure her she was wrong, and they'd debated at length. Zvie had described the couples he knew. He couldn't make all that up, could he? *Was he a marriage counselor?* He had almost convinced her of his argument… until she arrived home.

With a deep breath, she got out of the car and let herself into the house. Maggie padded down the hall to greet her. Her husband was not in his recliner in front of the TV, and he had dimmed the lights. Finding his door shut, she sagged with relief.

Betty and Maggie sat on the patio, and she reconsidered the question of the night: the *what if*. What if she could have a do-over, would she risk it? She thought about her daughter. Any changes would have to wait until after Chloe's wedding. She could end up alone, but she was alone most of the time anyway, wasn't she?

She had spent endless hours regretting and wishing but had never planned an alternative life or thought about the consequences of failure if she tried. Zvie had opened a whole new menu of thought. Was she brave enough? Or was she like that man she dated in between marriages, always talking about what he would do and doing none of it?

Did she only want to tell anyone who would listen about "poor me"? Could she face a second failed marriage? She had often entertained her co-workers with her sarcastic anecdotes of Ralph and his sailing buddy, referring to them as the Skipper and Gilligan. They thought she had exaggerated for their entertainment when she had added with a smirk, "except there's no Ginger sailing with those two." *But was there?* She knew very little about Walt.

Would Zvie play a part? She didn't detect sexual tension between them, but conceded she hadn't known him long. She didn't think he was interested in her beyond friendship but couldn't explain what it was about him, or why she thought so. He just didn't seem to be a sexual man. It occurred to her at that moment that for all their lengthy conversation she knew next to nothing about him.

CHAPTER -5-

Over the next several days, Betty obsessed over what-ifs. She filled her every waking moment with questions and the myriad arrangements that would be necessary should she pursue a do-over. When she wasn't trying to reach a decision, she was daydreaming of a changed life or expecting a calamity. Her mother had always told her, 'Better the devil you know than the devil you don't know.' Betty's depression and gloom circled to anxiety and apprehension. She was neither happy nor sad. She supposed her medications were taking effect.

Dark shadows under Betty's eyes testified to her sleeplessness. She was tired and preoccupied, fearing her decision would come down to an impulse or an insignificant incident leading to the ultimate irritation. It must not come to that. She needed to feel comfort in her decision.

Did she want to go through another divorce? A divorce would be evidence of yet another failure. Perhaps she and Ralph should separate. What good would that do if she met her soul mate? Maybe soul mates didn't marry in the current social climate. Could she *live* with someone? That would mortify her sister even more than Betty's divorce. That led to another round of puzzles and considerations.

During their next yoga session, Chloe remarked on the changes in her. Betty tried to pass it off as fatigue, but Chloe didn't buy it. "Mom, please schedule a doctor's appointment. Maybe you should talk to a psychologist. Something is troubling you."

She spent hours on the patio in her favorite wicker chair with Maggie at her feet. She imagined standing on the fulcrum of a seesaw. Selecting one side of an issue over the other tilted it, upsetting her balance.

Neglected projects needed her attention, whatever her personal move. First thing tomorrow, she would buy archive boxes at the office supply store. She would sort through her books and photos and clean closets. It was time to reduce the clutter in her life. She would get organized.

Betty felt better after that decision. She could postpone the big personal issues in the smaller act of downsizing. She would take small steps until she knew when and where to leap.

She threw herself into sorting belongings over the next several days, making several trips to the Good Will store with donations. That trimmed her closet to less than half the size it had been.

Next, she threw out the duplicate, faded, and out-of-focus photographs and prepared packets for mailing the pictures of nephews, nieces, and friends' children to their parents. Betty wrote an accompanying note telling them she happened across the photo and the change in little Jackie, Janie, or whoever had amazed her. She just knew they would enjoy seeing their children at that cute stage. She bought a scanner and preserved her very favorite pictures from the past.

Betty walked through the house noting any furniture she would like to take, as though she were moving out and furnishing an apartment, and took pictures of the contents with her digital camera. Even if she didn't end up leaving, she had intended to compile an inventory for insurance.

She had remained luncheon friends with Nancy, an attorney she had worked with and who had agreed to guide Chloe and Ralph through the probate process when she died. She would take her friend to lunch and refresh her memory.

Sorting through their important papers, she made a detailed list of everything that might hold any value and its location. She made notes where she kept the title to her car, the deed and homeowner's policy to the house, updated a previous document on her laptop, and included passwords for any website or account she had ever had.

The third bedroom was a catchall. Betty's mother's books and family mementos were still there years after her death. Betty pulled the sealed boxes to the middle of the floor and tore off the tape. Immediately, childhood memories inundated her.

She had been an imaginative child, afraid to be alone in the basement of her childhood home. A coal-burning furnace heated the house and made scary, unexpected noises. Betty had thought it a monster with a belly full of flames. The smell of fermenting grapes drifted from the crocks in a dark corner. They contained wine her father made from the grapes he cultivated.

Betty's family attended church services on Sunday, the only day they relaxed. On special occasions the family went to a restaurant afterward, but it was more usual for her mother to cook the big family dinner. Automobile drives through the country had been a treat, and visits to her mother's sister's family and the farm came alive in the old photographs.

She stretched her back and leaned against the bed. Her mother and father had been hardworking people who had held labor-intensive jobs. They had instilled a sound work ethic and a sense of responsibility in their daughters. Her parents had survived The Great Depression, had experienced a great world war, rationing, and an explosion of technology. Life must have confused them with their limited education. At last she understood that her mother and father had been too busy earning a living to have time for romance or coddling a sensitive little girl. With this new insight, she felt guilty at the resentment she had carried for so long.

She selected several snapshots and put them aside. Next, she sorted boxes of books and kept those by her favorite authors, and some of her mother's favorites. Then she packed and resealed the boxes. She drove to the postal substation and shipped them to her sister. Mary loved old stuff if it related to their family. The boxes would delight her when she received them. Until Betty reached a decision, the family mementos would be safer with Mary. Perhaps that was the answer to her dilemma. She would visit her sister. Away from her home, she might arrive at a calm and reasoned decision about what to do with the rest of her life.

Betty felt so much better she called Chloe. She'd become self-centered, and she should have shown more interest in her daughter's wedding plans. "Chloe, it's Mom. I thought you and I could spend an afternoon shopping. Perhaps we could get manicures and pedicures."

A brief silence ensued before Chloe answered. "Mom? I left voicemail messages, and you haven't returned my calls. Are you feeling better?"

"Yes, I am. That's another reason I'm calling. Are you free Saturday? We'll go to lunch, my treat, and have a fun day. How about it?"

"I'd like that. I should register at the department stores, too."

"Have you and James made any more plans? Honey, I'm sorry I haven't been more involved. You know you have only to ask, and I'll do whatever I can to help with the arrangements."

Chloe and Betty discussed the pros and cons of a big wedding versus a small, more intimate one.

"Perhaps you should have a small wedding with a big party later. Your father and I will give you money. You could put it toward a party, your honeymoon, or anything else you want. Talk it over with James. Personally, I think big splashy weddings are a frivolous way to spend money, but it's your decision. I want you to be happy."

Chloe agreed to come on the weekend to sort through the belongings she left behind when she moved out of her parents' house. Betty didn't understand her compulsion to spend time with Chloe, but her feelings were too strong to ignore. After Chloe and James married, Betty's role in their life would be a minor one. Her baby had become a woman, and she felt more alone and lonelier than ever.

*****

"Wow, you've been busy!" Chloe said when she saw the gaping spaces in the closets, the empty book shelves and absent bric-à-brac. "Still have this old thing though, don't you?" She bent to give Maggie a hug.

"I can't get along without her. She's my best friend," she answered. "Chloe, I want to visit Aunt Mary for a few days.

Will you take care of Maggie? Your dad will leave her outside, or ask the neighbor to feed her if he goes on his boat. I need to know she'll be with someone who will be kind to her."

"Of course, I will. I won't let anything happen to Maggie. When are you going?"

"I'm looking into flights. I'll let you know when I have definite plans." They walked together to Chloe's old room.

"These boxes with the big *C* on them are yours—dolls, sticker books, crafts you used to do, and so on. Do you want to put them in your car and look at them later, or go through them now? If you do it now, I'll take whatever you don't want to the Good Will or put it in the trash collection."

Chloe stirred through the contents of the boxes. "I can't believe you still have the rag doll Aunt Mary made." She pulled the string on a stuffed lion and listened to the electronic roar. Chloe chuckled as she leafed through her school yearbooks. "Look at me, gawky and braces." She set them aside. "Remember when I did the macramé bracelets? I spent hours selecting just the right colors."

"And I remember waiting in the store wishing you'd decide."

Chloe agreed to take her yearbooks and the box of accumulated yarn and thread. "Give away the party dresses; they're too yesterday for me. Trash the rest. I'm running out of room in my storage locker, and James and I won't be buying a house soon unless we win the lottery." She paused. "Have you talked to Zvie?"

"Not since the last time I was at yoga. Why?"

"No reason. I thought he would call you." Chloe looked disappointed.

"I think you should get any ideas about Zvie out of your head. He knows I'm married, and he doesn't strike me as a man to get in the middle of a triangle."

"Maybe," but she sounded unconvinced. "Are you coming to yoga Tuesday?"

"Planning on it. We'll talk before then."

Betty walked Chloe to her car, waved, and watched her drive away. Why was her daughter so interested in Zvie?

Chloe called on Tuesday to remind her of the yoga class, and Betty agreed to pick her up. When they arrived, she experienced a stab of disappointment. Zvie wasn't there.

"I'll skip eating out, Chloe. Do you want a ride home?"

"No, I'll hitch a ride with somebody at the restaurant, or I'll call James."

They embraced. "I'll talk to you tomorrow," Betty said.

All the way home, Betty speculated about Zvie's whereabouts and reasons he hadn't been at the class. *Had our what-if discussion been a come-on, and I was too naïve to know it?*

The next morning Betty packed for her trip. She also packed mementos she wanted to keep if she worked up the courage to leave. She filed her divorce decree, copies of her marriage certificates, photocopies of her credit cards, and other identification documents in a metal box and placed it on her closet shelf. She couldn't leave her favorite dog behind. Ralph thought she was nuts to keep Sassy's ashes. He would dump them the first chance he got. She would find a place to store her treasures. Betty felt foolish. *All packed with nowhere to go.*

"Hello?" she answered her cell phone.

"Hello, Betty. It's Zvie."

"We missed you at the yoga class last night."

"I was out of town. I got back too late for the class. Would you like to have lunch with me today? Do you have any plans?"

"Uh, no, but do you think it's wise?"

"Betty, it's lunch," he chided. "I won't pick you up at your house if you would rather I didn't. Tell your neighbors that I'm an insurance salesman, or you can meet me at The Chateau."

Betty bristled at his note of laughter and heard herself answer. "What time should I be ready? Do you need directions?"

At one o'clock Zvie pulled into her driveway in a sporty convertible. He looked dashing behind the wheel, his cap angled just so. When they left, Betty waved at her neighbor. Her spine tingled, knew she watched them until they turned the corner.

After they ordered, Zvie eyed Betty. "Time for the moment of truth," he mumbled under his breath.

"I'm sorry, Zvie, I didn't hear what you said."

"Did you think over our last conversation?"

There was no point in pretending she didn't know what he was asking. "I've done nothing *but* think of it until I think I'll go crazy. One foot says go, and the other says stay. I've sorted, thrown out, and packed. I suppose I've symbolically said goodbye to my life in the house, except for Maggie. That's my dog," she explained at his raised eyebrow. "This is harder than ending my first marriage."

Zvie nodded. "Do you know how unique you are? Few people have an opportunity at a second chance or come to a time in their life when the circumstances are ripe for it. Make no mistake, however, once you decide on a do-over, going back is not an option."

"Everything is negotiable while you're still breathing.

What do you mean going back isn't an option?"

"Trust me. I've had a lot of experience."

The waitress brought their lunch, and Zvie shook out his napkin. "The food looks delicious; let's enjoy it. We'll talk later."

Just like turning off a light! What if I don't want his help? What's it to him? His nonchalance annoyed her. How could he switch from the serious conversation they had been having to the prosaic one they were having now? He told her about his trip to New York—the people, restaurants, and the apartment he rented.

"I can't wait to experience the theaters, museums, and five-star restaurants." His travelogue enticed her. He made it sound like a grand adventure.

Over coffee, Zvie resumed their earlier discussion. "Be honest, Betty. You find living for yourself, walking away from responsibility for the first time in your life overwhelming. You're worried about impacting Chloe's wedding plans and whether you'll find a pet-friendly place to live with Maggie."

She nodded, not surprised at his perception.

"This is the time to accept your life, make the best of it, or change it." Zvie gave her a penetrating look. "Is that what you want? More of the same for another thirty years?" He waited until she shook her head.

"I've been unhappy for a long time, but I want to wait until after Chloe's wedding. Her happiness is important to me. And, being on my own frightens me," she admitted.

"You can't please all the people all the time. That's restating the Abraham Lincoln quote, but it still is true. Shillyshallying over a decision and its effects is more damaging to you than acting. As far as being on your own—housing and finances—those things will fall into place."

"I suppose. But Chloe and Maggie..."

"Chloe has James. And Maggie will have you or Chloe."

*****

"Why don't I store your boxes?" Zvie offered. "It's a spacious apartment; I have plenty of room."

"You're moving. I don't know how long it will be before I have a place or where it will be. You might move again before I'm ready for them. We could lose contact. It's kind of you to offer, but the logistics don't work."

If she left her possessions with a friend or her sister, she would have to fabricate an explanation. If she didn't follow through, she didn't want to tell anyone what she had planned. She didn't want her sister or Chloe to question her. And she didn't want anyone combing through her keepsakes.

"I can handle it. When you decide your destination, I'll get them to you. Here's my new address, and here's my cell phone number. You'll be able to reach me here for the next several months. If you haven't settled by then, I'll return them."

Betty wavered. *Why would he offer? Did he think she had something valuable that he could sell?* He couldn't know what she'd packed in them.

"Betty, I will keep your possessions safe. I don't intend to visit the pawnshop and convert them to cash. You can trust me."

She flushed. How had he known what she'd been thinking? His blue eyes were intent, engaging hers, until she nodded.

"Do you need a ride to the airport?"

"Thank you. I'm not sure when I'll be ready, and I have to take Maggie to Chloe. And…" She stopped as she realized she was babbling. "It would be better if I take a taxi."

He stowed her boxes in the trunk of his rental car, and Betty tucked his phone number in her pocket. Again, she questioned his intent. *Why had he offered? Not for financial gain!* Her things had little intrinsic value — books, CDs, pictures, personal mementos. She'd included crafts Chloe made in grade school, sentimental items only a mother would treasure. She stifled the urge to run after him and demand he turn around and leave her things. Instead, she forced herself to watch him drive away. *Well, Betty, you've done it.* She chewed her lip. If she'd been foolish, she'd have the rest of her life to regret it.

*****

"Chloe? I'd like to bring Maggie to you tomorrow morning. Will you be home?"

"Sure Mom. Don't forget her dog bed."

She called the airline, confirmed her reservations, and printed a boarding pass. Then she called Ralph at the marina where he kept his boat.

"I'm going to visit Mary. I'll probably leave before you get back."

"When did you decide this?" Ralph asked.

"While you were sailing with Walt. Chloe is taking Maggie so you don't have to change your plans." She waited through his silence.

"How long?"

"Until I wear out my welcome. Is there a reason I need to be here?"

"I suppose not."

"Okay. I'll see you when I see you."

Betty walked through the house. She was anxious and excited to take control of her life. That night she sat on the patio with Maggie until late. For the first time in several years, she didn't think about her unhappiness or her regrets. Sometimes a poor decision is better than no decision at all, she reasoned.

She couldn't know how her life would change.

CHAPTER -6-

The morning her life changed, Betty alternated between excitement and dread. Dressing in an old pair of sweats and tennis shoes, she would have time to change clothes before going to the airport. She fed her dog and drank a cup of coffee. After rinsing her cup, Betty tidied the kitchen, then carried her bags to the front door. Maggie sniffed her luggage, and Betty could read the question in her eyes—*What's happening?*

Betty gathered meds, food, dishes, toys, and Maggie's dog bed. *Just like the old days of packing a diaper bag.* She ran through her mental checklist to see if she had forgotten anything that Chloe would need for the old dog's comfort and experienced a sharp pang of sadness. The house would be empty and sterile without her. She walked Maggie around the block, helped her into the car, and drove off. By the time she arrived at Chloe's apartment, she had logged miles on her guilt trip.

"Chloe, this is a mistake," she blurted as she got out of the car. "You have so much going on right now. What was I thinking?" She shuddered. "I'm going to turn around and take Maggie home. I've never left her before. I can't leave her."

"Don't be silly, Mom. I have my wedding plans in hand and I'll take good care of her. She'll be fine with me."

"Maggie, I'm so sorry," she apologized and stroked the yellow lab pressing against her legs. "I promise I won't stay."

"Stop carrying on. You're upsetting her. Tell Aunt Mary hi for me. Now give us a hug and get going. Have a drink at the airport!"

Betty knew her daughter thought her silly and emotional, but she couldn't help herself. Tears burned her eyes and streaked her face. Why had she listened to Zvie? She struggled to breathe past the sob that threatened to choke her, swiped at her cheeks, and turned for one last look at Chloe and Maggie. Her canine best friend sat beside her daughter. Drawing a deep breath, she waved and forced herself into her car.

*****

Betty tensed as she merged onto the southbound access ramp of I-95. No matter the time of day, the interstate was congested with cars exceeding the speed limit. This stretch of I-95 was under construction. Signs warned of trucks entering the highway. As she focused on driving, she tried to block out the regrets that gnawed at her peace of mind.

"Are you ready to begin your new adventure, Betty?" A voice startled her from the passenger seat.

"Zvie!" She took her eyes from the road to look at him. "Where did you come from? How did you get here?"

"Trust me, Betty. I'll explain later." He smiled to reassure her.

Betty turned back to the road as a tanker truck edged into her lane. She blasted the horn, but the driver didn't react. Sandwiched by cars behind and adjacent to her, she had no place to go.

Her heart raced. "No!" she cried. Panic squeezed her chest and she stomped on the brake pedal. Tires screeched; brakes locked. Betty's car fishtailed. The SUV behind her rammed the back of her car pushing it forward.

Zvie reached to cover her hand on the steering wheel. "Everything will be all right. I promise you. Take my hand. Don't let go,"

The truck's huge tires squealed against her door. Her car shot off the expressway. The molded plastic body crackled and crunched as it gave way and the seat belt cut into her chest. Air bags deployed, pressing her into the seat. The frame buckled as her car rolled. Scorching heat stole her breath and smoke filled her nose. She screamed at the approaching ball of fire

Who is screaming? She looked around before she realized the fearful sound came from her. Then, abruptly, mercifully, silence.

Where am I? She saw her car enveloped in flames. *How did I get out? Why don't I feel pain?* Zvie still held her hand. Out of the smoke and confusion a shadowy, grim-faced figure took shape. He opened his thin mouth to speak, but Zvie interrupted.

"No, NamKrad. The Archangel Rafael and I have plans for her. She will not be yours today."

NamKrad's heavy gray brows drew together in a line. He looked from Zvie to Betty. He reached out and brushed her cheek with a cold, skeletal hand. She shivered and moved closer to Zvie. She sensed conflict, but no struggle occurred.

No words were spoken between them. Finally, NamKrad retreated and vanished.

Zvie continued to hold her hand. She was conscious of movement. A gentle breeze cooled her face. She was gliding, flying, weightless. Soon they arrived at a gleaming white building. Zvie waved, and the door slid open.

They entered a high-ceilinged room where water splashed into a central fountain. Beyond it, several pink-robed figures stood behind a desk. Plush sofas with fat cushions in a muted shade of vanilla, gaily patterned club chairs, and side tables were artfully stationed around the room. Green trailing vines and bouquets of blooms added more color. Huge windows provided light and overlooked a well-tended garden where footpaths circled flowerbeds, plants, and trees. One path led to a shady alcove sheltering a secluded bench while another ended at a brightly striped umbrella table and chairs.

"Where are we? Who are you?" Betty whispered.

"We're at the Second Chance Academy. I made a reservation for you weeks ago. The staff is expecting you. In a moment your guide will show you to your room and begin your orientation, but first we need to talk."

Zvie led her to a corner table between two chairs, picked up a telephone and ordered refreshments. She stared at him when he gestured to one of the chairs.

"Please. Please sit down. I know you have questions and I'll try to answer them."

Betty hesitated before she lowered herself into a chair with the movements of an arthritic old woman. Numb, she was too stunned to do anything but obey.

"The Celestial Appeals Committee heard your plea. Your unhappiness was so great you could no longer be overlooked.

We will work to change your mind and your heart while you are in the Academy."

"As to who I am, the Celestial Directory lists me as Angel Second Chance. I have been assigned to help you. As you move through the Academy, I'll tell you more about your opportunity."

Betty stared at him in open-mouthed amazement. *An angel? Either I'm hallucinating or he's crazy.* She looked around. Everyone she saw wore flowing robes. An air of silence filled the room. *How big a fool does he think I am? Maybe this is an institution. That rat bastard Ralph has had me declared incompetent!*

"No, Betty, you are not crazy, and you are not in an institution or rehab clinic, as you know it."

She realized she hadn't spoken. "How do you do that? How do you know what I'm thinking? This isn't the first time you've read my thoughts."

"I told you. I am an angel. More particularly, I am a project angel."

She had known from their first meeting there was something out of the ordinary about him.

"If you will remember what just happened, it will not be such a stretch of the imagination to accept what I told you. Your life is changing. You must trust me if I am to help you."

"What just happened?" she echoed. "How did I get out of my car? There was a terrible accident, but I'm not injured. I'm not hurting anywhere." Her hands traveled over her body to confirm her words. "Am I in the hospital? Is this an out-of-body experience?" Then a more somber thought occurred to her, and she slowly phrased her next question. "Am I dead?"

"No, you are not dead. You are transitioning. You are not in a hospital. Yes, there was an accident. As I said, we are at the Second Chance Academy, a special place, where you'll receive treatment and instruction in a variety of areas. Completion of the course will prepare you for a new life."

Zvie reached across and took her hand in his.

"Now, Betty, listen carefully. This is very important. For a while you will retain memories of your former life. I can't tell you how long they will last or how vivid they will be. It differs with each individual. But, eventually, the memories will fade and may even disappear. I know you are concerned for Chloe and Maggie."

"But..." Betty began.

Zvie raised his hand to ward off her questions. "You *must* trust me. You can no longer have any contact with Chloe."

"No contact with Chloe! Not be a part of her life? See her? Talk to her?"

Zvie's eyes held hers.

"You can't do that. She needs my help with her wedding. I want to be there when she marries James. I *can't* leave Chloe." Tears coursed down her cheeks. She hiccoughed a sob. "Maggie will die without me. You have no right to do this. Take me back!"

The sweep of his hand silenced her. "It's too late. I cautioned you that after you made the choice, you could not change your mind."

"What choice? You didn't tell me I'd have to give up my daughter and..." Her voice broke.

"I know you didn't want to leave Chloe and Maggie, but it had to be this way. I can't explain everything over a cup of tea. As you progress in your training, I'll provide you with more details."

Zvie paused, helped himself to a meringue cookie and topped off her cup of chamomile tea.

"Chloe is a sensitive, as once you were before you became a cynic. Where love is strong between individuals, an extrasensory connection remains. How long it will exist or the strength of the connection, I can't state with certainty. Chloe needs time to adjust, just as you do, but knowing your connection may not be completely severed should ease your parting. Now, I must report to the Archangel."

"How dare you! You take my life away, drop me in some... some alien place then leave. Did you all need drama in the celestial comedy?" She turned away from Zvie. Her shoulders shook. She drew a shuddering breath. In a quavering voice she asked, "Will you come back? What about that creature you sent away?"

"He will not be back," Zvie stated with conviction. "You will find time isn't measured the same way in the Second Chance Academy. You wouldn't have known I had gone if I hadn't told you. Betty," he soothed, "you have a lot to think about. Please go with Jana." He indicated the pink-robed figure who had joined them. "She will show you to your room and begin your program. You will be very busy preparing for your new life, but I believe you will enjoy your stay here."

He turned to the aide. "She has to recover from the trauma she experienced and deal with her grief. Begin level one. I'll rejoin you soon."

Jana nodded. She led Betty to a room with a bed and a plush overstuffed chair. Drapes drawn across the lone window dimmed the light.

Betty's shoulders drooped, her head bowed. Tears dripped onto her clasped hands. She neither questioned nor resisted when Jana helped her into a loose robe before she collapsed onto the bed.

"Shh," Jana soothed as she covered Betty with a light blanket. After placing a cool mask over Betty's eyes, the mask began to glow, and Betty's thoughts scrolled in the air above her. Soft light bathed the bed where she lay.

Was I heard when I asked for love? Did I agree to a second chance? This has to be the worst nightmare ever. I will wake up, won't I? Betty sobbed until she slipped into sleep.

CHAPTER -7-

Zvie squared his shoulders and approached the Archangel Rafael's desk. "Sir, the initial phase of our project has begun. Betty is at the Second Chance Academy."

"Good." He nodded his approval. "How did she receive your revelation?"

"She was stunned and…devastated." Zvie braced for his superior's reaction.

"Devastated?" The Archangel straightened in his chair.

"Her reaction when I told her she could not have any further contact with Chloe." Zvie hastened to explain. "Her opportunity commenced with an automobile accident between her car and a tanker truck. The authorities and her family will presume Betty died. She cannot go back to her drab existence."

Archangel Rafael's blue eyes like lightning flashes turned on the project angel.

"She was not aware of the conditions attached to her second chance opportunity?"

Zvie squirmed at the Archangel's question. "I may have omitted some salient details. A slight error in judgment, Archangel."

"Slight?" The Archangel ran slim fingers through his fringe of hair and looked to the ceiling. "Choices, Zvie."

Although his voice was mild, Zvie felt the sting of the Archangel's words.

"She was to exercise her free will—choose or refuse the opportunity—if you will remember our initial discussion."

"She was so desperately unhappy. She confessed she did not want another day of her present life let alone another thirty years. You and I agreed that divorce was not the answer, that Betty Parker would never meet nor attract Colin," Zvie said in his defense.

"We did, but I envisioned her consent to our plan." The Archangel slumped in his chair and closed his eyes while the Great Clock ticked the seconds. "Well, it is too late now. She cannot go back. Let us hope the attitude alteration succeeds or she may be unhappier than she was before her second chance."

"Yes, sir. The Dark Angel frightened Betty. She became agitated when I told her I had to report. I should return. She draws a small measure of comfort from my presence."

"Hmm. In the future, Zvie, you will stay within the framework of our strategy. Understood?" His ice-blue eyes watched for Zvie's nod. "We must *not* force our will on our charges."

*****

Zvie gazed out the window at the Second Chance Academy while he waited for lunch. He was strangely subdued as he reflected on his meeting with the Archangel and the complexities of this assignment. That the Committee would consider breaking up a family unit still gnawed at him, and he, Zvie, had effected that separation, arrogantly taking Betty's choice from her. He had acted rashly in a situation that required delicacy. Waves of remorse washed over him as he recalled the Archangel's words. The Archangel was vexed with him and justifiably so.

Before his assignment to the project angel section, Zvie had been a celestial bodyguard, commonly known as a guardian angel. Exhausting work, he remembered. During infancy he guarded against the actions of ignorant caretakers and immature parents. During the oral gratification stage, he shielded the child from the dangers of safety pins, small objects, and household chemicals. And later, he'd had to contend with childhood diseases, vehicular accidents, sports injuries, sexual predators, and unsafe Internet sites. In his view, too much leisure time and too little supervision had made his job harder. A multitude of dangers, he mused. He would have to be cautious going forward. He must make this assignment a success. This section is a much more desirable place to work.

CHAPTER -8-

Zvie nodded to the doorman as he entered the New York high-rise. Nattily dressed in tailored slacks, open-neck shirt, and silk herringbone jacket, soft Italian leather loafers cushioned his feet as he crossed the marble floor. A placard on an easel announced Mogul Productions in the penthouse. He pressed the call button for the elevator, selecting the penthouse icon. When the glass elevator reached the top floor, the doors slid open. He tracked the hum of conversation, clink of glasses, and the tinkle of a piano to the Top Hat Room. A mechanical mannequin might have drawn more attention than the pianist tucked into the corner.

He lifted a glass off the tray of a passing waiter and surveyed the event room. Vast glass windows offered a vista of the city. A man in a white jacket attended the buffet table. He whisked crumbs off the white tablecloth and called for replenishment of the serving dishes as needed.

Typical reception food, Zvie observed. He helped himself to assorted crackers and cubes of cheese, added shrimps and a dollop of cocktail sauce before he chose a secluded table where he could observe the occupants of the room while he waited.

There were more women than men present, many of whom wore an air of desperation, unaware that men avoided women with that look. Most of them wore the dark day-to-evening dresses that Zvie thought of as their uniform.

An extraordinary couple approaching the buffet table drew his attention. The woman's straight, dark hair hung to her shoulders. She wore bangs in long fringes and brushed at them with a rhythmic sweep of her hand. A loose, silver tunic that appeared made of aluminum foil with footless black tights and four-inch stiletto heels called attention to her board-thin body.

Zvie heard the snatches of conversation that followed her. "So weird… Where does she shop?"

Her companion wore faded blue jeans, a black crew neck T-shirt, and sneakers. Light from the chandeliers bounced off the satin lapels of his knee-length dinner jacket and the sequined baseball cap pulled low over his eyes.

A small group of men and women stood to one side, balancing plates and glasses with ease. The women's dresses varied only in the number of sequins or jet beads that sparkled as they moved. Men revealed more latitude in their apparel: from evening attire, which indicated they'd be heading out that night, charcoal-gray worsted business suits, white shirts and ties to jeans, tees, and jackets. Now and then, a spate of laughter split the conversation in the room.

A slight man sporting tinted glasses and a goatee sat alone at a corner table. He wore authority as comfortably as he did his charcoal gray sweater and slacks. Individuals approached at regular intervals to exchange a few words with him. He appeared to accept their obvious homage as his due.

"Darlings, so good of you to come." The man with the goatee stood to greet recent arrivals whose style could have graced a magazine cover, a contrast to the previous couple.

A dark-haired, good-looking man separated from the corner group. Zvie watched him as he canvassed the room, nodding as he recognized someone.

"Come join us," an attractive blonde called. Although alone, he declined.

"Hello, handsome," a woman in a pink spandex pantsuit stepped toward him, but she met with no more success than the blonde.

He turned to the buffet table, picked up a plate, and deliberated over the selections. He spoke to a cocktail waiter then chose a vacant window table.

When Zvie was certain the man had settled, he rose to his feet. He helped himself to a second glass from a passing waiter and approached.

"Mind if I join you?" Zvie asked.

He waved Zvie into the other chair without comment.

"I'm Zvie." He extended his hand.

"Colin O'Brien," the man replied, wiping his hand on his napkin. He touched Zvie's fingers. The waiter brought Colin's glass, earning his thanks and a tip.

"Who's the man holding court?" Zvie gestured to the man with the goatee.

"He's an executive with Mogul Productions. He's rumored to be looking for a location for their new project."

"That explains it," Zvie murmured. "Are you interested? In the new project, I mean."

"In this business, I'm always interested."

"What's your gig? Actor? Scriptwriter? Director?"

"Actor." Colin faced Zvie. "I don't think I've ever seen you at any of these affairs. Are you new to the business?" Colin leaned back, waiting for Zvie's answer.

"Oh, no. I've been around for several years. I prefer to work in the background. This is my first trip to the city on business. I'm not based here." Zvie propped his elbows on the table and rested his chin on his hand.

"Agent then?" Colin pursued.

"No," Zvie replied with a smile. "It's difficult to apply a label. I suppose you could consider me a troubleshooter. If a project is in trouble, I try to find a solution. Sometimes I'm called upon to inject energy into a tired career."

"How does that work?" Colin sat up and gave Zvie his full attention.

"Sometimes all it takes is a fresh perspective and a little imagination. I've found very little effort is required if the subject is receptive."

They were quiet for a few minutes while Colin toyed with the food on his plate. Each newcomer increased the noise level in the room. Zvie watched the shifting scene with interest.

"Would you care to join me for dinner? This finger food isn't doing it for me, and I don't like to eat alone. We could talk shop." Zvie asked, breaking their silence.

Colin's blue eyes iced over before he replied. "I'm not attracted to men, if that's what you have in mind."

Zvie chuckled with genuine amusement. "I don't lean that way either, Colin. Look at me. Does it strike you I'm looking for action? Apart from that, I wouldn't think guys would come on to you. You don't project the right aura for that. I have nothing more than dinner, drinks, and conversation in mind." When Colin did not answer, Zvie pressed his invitation. "Have pity on a stranger to the city. Otherwise, I'll eat at a bar with ESPN for company." He shuddered for effect.

Colin pushed his plate away. "There's a little Italian place near here. It's quiet, not too pricey, and I like the food. It's quiet. You like Italian?"

"I like good food. Ready to go?" Zvie smiled to himself. *Agent? Entertainment business?* He supposed his mission could be described as entertainment if it is successful. The Archangel might consider him an agent, although not in the sense that Colin supposed.

Zvie guessed Colin would not be as malleable as Betty Parker. Still, he had to begin somewhere. If his mission were to succeed, Colin would become the dominant partner in the relationship, which was surprising, considering their histories. He might have to level with him. Zvie tried to imagine Colin's reaction if he came right out and identified himself.

Hi, I'm Angel Second Chance. Remember the night you were on the balcony? The powers-that-be heard the challenge you flung out to the universe. They sent me to help you in the love department. It might come to that, but he would rather it be later rather than sooner.

They walked to a small restaurant with intimate lighting. Red and white–checked tablecloths covered the small tables for four. Zvie savored the smell of herbs and spices that permeated the room. Colin had chosen well if the food lived up to the aromas. A waiter approached, greeted Colin by name, and showed them to a corner table. Zvie maneuvered his companion toward a chair so the light from the bar would illuminate Colin's face. The waiter handed out menus, and he described the specials. They chose the house wine.

Zvie took a sip of wine and leaned back in his chair. He scanned the mural that covered the opposite wall, a town in Italy. His thoughts wandered to Betty Parker and her treatments at the Second Chance Academy. He couldn't stay away too long if his mission were to stay on schedule.

"So, Colin O'Brien, tell me about yourself. What is it like living and working in this metropolis?"

Zvie watched a variety of expressions play across Colin's face as he talked about his current role in a television series. He'd played the part for three years, and in this, his fourth, he was finding it difficult to sustain his enthusiasm. His character had become clichéd, and he didn't think he could do much more with it.

"How many scantily clad women can I take to bed or lay with on a rug in front of the fireplace before the public has had enough of the meat market? How many love affairs can fail before the viewers label me a chronic loser? Sure, the names change, but the women are similar except for the color of their hair and the size of their breasts. The pay's good, but…" he trailed off.

"You're ready for something new."

"I've been ready, but good roles are hard to get, according to Sam — that's my agent, Sam Lewin. He claims the old-line Hollywood boys have first choice at the challenging movie roles. Most producers and directors won't chance an unfamiliar face that might not catch on at the box office unless the old guard is too pricey."

"Fancy yourself a dramatic actor, or do you want to try comedy?"

"I'd welcome anything that would free me from this sex object image. And there comes a time in an actor's career if you take your clothes off too often, you're open to ridicule. I don't want to become a John, Clint, or whoever where the audience isn't convinced the eighteen-year-old sex pot wants a romance with the old fart. Not unless it's clear that she's angling for all of his assets for her services."

"I'd say you're a few years away from that," Zvie reassured him. Colin moussed his crisp dark brown hair in a casual, messy style. Random strands of silver wisdom hair glistened.

"What about family? How do you and your wife survive your screen lovemaking?"

"We didn't." Colin laughed without humor. "I met my first wife in college. We jumped into marriage before we knew what we both wanted. The demands of the entertainment business—the frequent travel, extended absences, and the gossip columns—were more than she could handle. She wanted the country club and a so-called normal life. I was trying to establish myself, and I had to go wherever there was work. If I got labeled as too choosy, word gets around and opportunities disappear. We lasted little more than a year."

"You couldn't reach a compromise?" Zvie said.

"That about sums it up. If our relationship had been strong, we might have made it, but I don't think so. I still see her from time to time. I regret we tried and failed, but I don't miss her in my life."

"My mistake number two needed a boost to her career, and I was it. She was clever; I was easy. You ever been married, Zvie?"

"A *long* time ago." He didn't elaborate, and Colin continued.

"Number two is a model, and I couldn't live with the demands of her career. How's that for irony?" Colin sneered. "I run into her once in a while, but we're not friendly."

"So, where do you go from here, Colin O'Brien?"

"I want a role with substance, one that features more than skin. I wouldn't mind an honest relationship either, but not if it will end in the tabloids. That kind of publicity I don't want." Colin paused, appeared puzzled. "You're a good listener, you know? I don't talk about my life."

Zvie laughed. "Your secrets are safe with me."

"I thought I found love twice, and it was fake. How do you know a relationship is real or if it will last? I don't believe in love between a man and a woman."

"Don't for a moment doubt it's real, Colin. And when it happens to you, the sun will shine brighter. Your senses will be sharper. You'll feel more alive than you ever have before."

Colin looked unconvinced, and Zvie went on. "You'll miss her if you're not together, and I don't mean just for sex, although that will be better too. You'll accept your differences and her weaknesses and foibles because they make her who she is. Together, you'll be complete."

Zvie sat back and measured Colin's interest.

"Maybe, but that sounds like BS to me. I thought I had love twice, and I was wrong."

"You could be the greatest actor in the world and win every conceivable award, but unless you can share your success with someone who cares, your accomplishments will be empty ones. You'll know when it's real, Colin. There's not another feeling in the world to compare with loving and being loved." Zvie smiled without embarrassment. "I'll get off my soapbox now. I suppose you could tell I'm passionate about the subject?"

Colin nodded but said nothing.

"I have a previous commitment out of town," Zvie said, "but when I return, I will entertain. Give me your contact information, and I'll call you. You'll enjoy my friends, Colin. They may give you a fresh perspective." He paused and his blue eyes locked with Colin's. "Remember my name."

CHAPTER -9-

Betty tossed, turned, and moaned. Her memories flashed across the monitor, colored by the emotions they revealed. Her guide switched to neutral or pastoral scenes—landscapes, art works, baby animals—until Betty grew calm.

"Isn't that nice?" Her father's sarcasm sent a young Betty crying from the dinner table. "Clumsy, stupid," he sneered as she spilled her milk. Often, she went to bed hungry, too humiliated and timid to return to the table.

Her fingers twisted the bedclothes at recollections of laundry day. The old wringer washing machine and rinse tubs were in the basement, a dark, dank, scary place. During winter, her mother pinned the wash on lines stretched from wall to wall and it took days to dry. Towels and underwear were stiff and scratchy to the touch. Outer garments required ironing. During summer, they carried heavy baskets of wet laundry up the steep basement steps and pegged it on lines strung between posts in the backyard. The clothes dried in the sunlight, then were dampened again for ironing. She was so young and short that she'd had to stand on a box to iron the flat pieces.

A quiet Voice urged her: *Let it go.*

Her embarrassing school years followed. A teenaged Betty agonized over dates, popularity, cliques, and acne that further eroded her self-confidence.

Let it go.

Her first husband emerged from the dusty archives of her memories. She had been too young, and he was too. Had she given a thought to marriage and its duties, or had it been a fantasy like all the marriages portrayed on television during that era? She couldn't or didn't want to remember. She'd had little experience with boys or men other than her father and blushed as she looked back at her naiveté. Sex had been a taboo topic with her mother, and her initiation had been both a shock and a disappointment. Her marriage and subsequent divorce were, in her view, a public admission of failure.

Let it go.

Betty watched the man she had dated between marriages suck up to a waitress or a store clerk, always trying to get something free. A smoker, she heard his hearty liquid laugh, the same one that punctuated every conversation. When she stopped dating him, she had believed he would utter that same laugh if she had told him he was terminal. How had she ever thought him attractive?

Let it go.

As her memories continued to wash over her, a dashing, young, and handsome Ralph Parker appeared as he was when she first met him. She'd found his swagger and confidence sexy and appealing. The darling of his family, he failed to convince them to accept her. They had never told her in so many words, but she suspected they considered her tainted by her previous marriage. Perhaps that's when Ralph and Betty began their downward spiral. When they moved away from their families and friends, Betty blamed Ralph for her loneliness and subsequent unhappiness. Resentment flared anew at his conspicuous absence at Chloe's school functions. Many of Chloe's teachers assumed she was a single parent.

Let it go.

She burned over the loss of her job. She had been efficient, a conscientious employee, even calling attention to grammatical errors and inconsistencies. When the firm let her go, she had accepted that the company had to cut back, but a younger, prettier, inexperienced woman had kept her job. Betty reasoned her aging face and body were the chief reasons they terminated her. That event made her realize that more of her life was behind her than likely lay ahead, and she had fallen into depression.

Let it go.

Her unhappiness ebbed as she recalled the parade of pets she'd welcomed into her home: cats that appeared on her doorstep, dogs from Animal Control and the Humane Society. Jack the Cat had learned how to open a door. He hung from the doorknob, bracing his hind feet on the frame, until he turned the knob. When the door opened, he'd saunter to the patio, tail in the air oblivious to the dog in the house. His claw marks on the door frame attested to his time with them. Her mind's eye traveled throughout the house. Grooves, scratches, and scuffs reminded her of puppies that lost puppy teeth or cut adult ones, and where kittens had climbed.

Tears trickled to her pillow at Sassy's memory and of other pets that had died of sickness or old age. Maggie had been a furry armful when she brought her home, a far different dog than the one she had left with Chloe. She was the last in the varied collection of unwanted and neglected animals that Betty had adopted and loved.

Betty relaxed to the swishing palm fronds in a gentle breeze. She had often mistaken the sound for rain when they first moved to South Florida. The lacey leaves of the royal poinciana waved, and she marveled that the resident squirrel didn't electrocute himself traveling back and forth on the power lines. She listened to the wild green parrots early morning raucous chatter, pictured them in the trees and at the bird feeder. The sights and sounds of her backyard had entertained and soothed her.

Her memory reel ran to the day she met Zvie at the beach yoga class. And now, because of that meeting, she felt lost, confused, and unhappy.

CHAPTER -10-

Following her arrival at the Second Chance Academy, Betty held onto the hope that Zvie would restore her to her former life. She took part in the programs with reluctance, including counseling sessions that reviewed her previous life choices and would prepare her for a successful relationship. She learned about erogenous zones and pleasuring. Soon she knew more about sex than thirty years of marriage had taught her. Lectures and group discussions of current events in the political and entertainment scenes. exposure to the latest trends in fashion, food, and interior decorating made her realize how dull and out-of-date she had been. She met interesting people and practiced the art of conversation. Betty soaked up information like a sponge, and Zvie watched her blossom.

Toward the end of her first week at the Academy, Betty recalled her puzzling experience at the bank. After discussing it with Zvie, they agreed she would become Kate Dunning.

Her physical appearance was the focus of her second week, and Zvie monitored the process. The image consultants took measurements, and studied her until she felt her body had become community property. She empathized with the specimens she had seen pinned to display boards at the Smithsonian and Butterfly World.

Zvie reminded the consultants that Colin was over six feet tall and his agent had schooled him in the importance of image.

The expert opinions swirled around her as they debated.

"Change the color of her hair and eyes…"

"Must lose twenty pounds…"

"Ridiculous. Should be taller…"

After trying another unsuccessful, trendy diet in the past, a disillusioned Betty had decided she didn't need to lose pounds; she needed to gain inches. At last she met someone who agreed with her.

"The consultants are agreed," Zvie informed her over morning coffee. "They will perform your transformation today. Are you excited, Betty?"

"I… I'm a little scared. I've seen women in bandages, with black eyes and swollen faces after they had plastic surgery. It looks painful."

"Our experts don't use such antiquated methods. Trust me."

She rolled her eyes.

Betty disrobed in a mirrored alcove. Although self-conscious to expose her sixty-four-year-old body, refusing had not occurred to her.

The experts consulted their checklist, and Betty watched her body change. Numbers on the mirror increased by one-inch increments, stopping at 5'7." To her amazement, another set of numbers showed a twenty-five-pound weight loss. Every cell in her body submitted to their will. Chronological years rolled back and the furrows, lines, and wrinkles in her face and neck that had revealed Betty's age smoothed and disappeared. Cellulite and dimpled skin firmed. Her sagging breasts and derriere lifted, her stomach tightened.

A celestial assistant applied drops in Betty's eyes to lighten them although her natural brown eyebrows remained unchanged. She gained hollows in her cheeks, erasing her chipmunk pouches. Her hair grew to shoulder length. However, the transformation stalled as the experts failed to agree over her hair color.

"Blonde…"

"No, sleek brunette…"

"You're mad. She's a redhead."

"Sun-kissed, streaky shades of gold…"

Each time an expert voiced his opinion, Betty's hair color changed. She feared her hair would fall out if they didn't agree soon.

At that point Zvie ventured an opinion, but the experts rejected his suggestion.

As her alteration progressed, brown-haired, brown-eyed, dowdy Betty Parker of the past decades receded. Thirty-year-old Kate Dunning of the stunning figure, Irish setter red hair with sun-streaked gold highlights, and amber eyes reminiscent of a cat emerged. Betty/Kate reached out in awe to touch her image. She turned to study her silhouette and quivered with excitement. *Is this real? Is this me? Will I wake up tomorrow to the same Betty Parker I've seen in the mirror the past twenty years?*

At the end of the second week, Betty-Kate accepted her new identity: Kate Dunning. The stranger in her mirror still surprised, but no longer startled her. After lessons on skin care, hair styling, and cosmetics, a fashionista taught her how to select clothing that flattered, as opposed to following the dictates of fads.

During the third week, Kate-Betty continued to develop. The curriculum stressed personal care and socialization. She enjoyed the dance lessons. Her sense of rhythm, new body, and developing joyous spirit combined to make her an exceptional student. The cooking, party planning, and entertaining skills came next. She gained an overview of wine selection and the preferred brands of liquor and the know-how to prepare standard cocktails and several trendy ones. Kate-Betty questioned which had come first, the geisha or a Second Chance Academy graduate?

Kate's Second Chance Academy experience drew to a close. Her instructors reviewed and tweaked anything she had not absorbed. Together with her instructors she chose her wardrobe, which appeared one evening in her closet.

*****

Zvie and Kate strolled through the garden, and he shared a general idea of the life she would lead upon leaving the Academy.

"The Celestial Appeals Committee linked another second chance to yours, Kate. He also scoffs at love. Convincing you and him it exists is a vital part of my mission."

"Who is he? Do I know him?"

"If I told you, I might influence you. The Archangel Rafael stressed that you and he must exercise your free will. With your rediscovered sensitivities, I believe you'll recognize him when you meet. I'm not as confident he'll know you. There is another consideration. This project must succeed within a specified time span. The Great Clock will mark time the day we leave the Academy."

"Time limit? How long and what happens if it expires?"

"Let's see what happens before we worry about the ticking of the clock."

Kate wondered how long they had—a month, a year? She shrugged and continued to question Zvie.

"I've learned a lot here. What are my do's and don'ts when I leave? Can I experiment with the sexual knowledge I've gained, or am I to remain chaste?"

"We don't want you to become a call girl," Zvie teased.

"That's reassuring," she replied. "You read my thoughts before I came to the Academy. Will that continue 24/7? If I want to do a little blanket dancing with a guy, do I get privacy? Or will you send me the *not tonight dear* message? What if I'm attracted to someone other than *this guy* I'm linked with? What then?"

"Whew! You have a lot of questions. Let's decide these things when we're faced with them. I think you'll feel something for *this guy* on sight," and his fingers curved to suggest quotation marks. "He is even more cynical than you were. He may require some extraordinary measures," Zvie mused. "About your thoughts? They will become private as you embrace your new identity."

Kate nodded.

Zvie added, looking thoughtful, "I'll be working with you, Kate. I will not abandon you. There will be time to discuss your future if we know the mission has failed, but I have confidence in you. I'm *not* a novice project angel."

"Congratulations." His solemn demeanor evaporated. "Do you realize you completed two years of finishing school in the four weeks you have been in the Academy? You have presence, poise, and a delightful veneer. You are ready to begin your new life. How do you feel? Exciting, isn't it?"

"I'm more than amazed. Will I ever be able to talk about my experiences?" She rushed on before he could respond. "I suppose not. Anyone would doubt my sanity and accuse me of making it up or taking mind-altering drugs. I barely remember myself before I came here."

"That's the purpose of the Academy. You had to leave the old you behind before you could become Kate Dunning. Memories of your time here will dim after we leave, but I expect you will keep flashes of your past life. Your transformation was more complicated than the average, but you have succeeded beyond my expectations. I must compliment your instructors. You are a beautiful, sexy woman. Hold that thought. If I were not an angel, you would tempt me, Kate."

She laughed and squeezed his arm.

"I always knew you weren't interested in me that way, Zvie, but what *is* our relationship when we leave here? Are you my sugar daddy, uncle, employer, what?"

"I think you will be my assistant. We might claim a distant kinship. Let's see what transpires before we chisel it in stone. You'll develop your talents into a career while we're together." Zvie waited, expected her nod. "We can fit in a last treatment. The massages are pleasant, aren't they? Afterward, we'll leave for our new home."

Although Kate had emerged at the Second Chance Academy, all of Betty Parker had not disappeared. Kate put her hand on Zvie's arm beside the entrance. "Zvie, please. Is Chloe okay? Could I see her one more time?"

He took Kate's hands and drew her to him. His eyes reflected his compassion, and he hesitated while he framed his words.

"Chloe is...coping. You would be proud of her. I spoke with her after the accident. I told her you have a life in a different dimension, that you had loved her very much and continue to love her. And I suggested that anytime she needs you she should whisper your name, and she'll feel your presence. Her memories will comfort her."

"Does she know who you are?" Kate asked in a low voice. Tears glistened and overflowed. In that moment she was Betty Parker, Chloe's mother, not Kate Dunning.

"You must know I can't tell her. James has come through like a champion. This" he waved his hand as though to encompass the Academy, her past and present, "has strengthened their relationship. I feel sure it will be a pleasant one."

"I don't want to forget her."

"Most memories fade, Kate. I wish I could reassure you, but I don't know. Powerful memories may stay with you, buried in your subconscious. One day a melody, a voice, or an aroma could tease you, and through the maze in your mind a memory will find a path and tumble out. Aye, that's the way of it, lass."

Kate stared. He had never spoken with an accent before nor was he ever pensive. "Are you okay, Zvie?"

"Yes." He turned away, but after a minute, he cautioned. "You must not allow Chloe to interfere with your second chance. This *mission* is unusual, and the Celestial Appeals Committee will not look with kindness on failure. Oh yes, one more thing. Maggie is well and content with Chloe."

Kate's shoulders drooped as she asked, "Where are we going?"

"Do you remember when I told you about my trip—the restaurants, the museums, and the theater? A friend has offered his apartment to us while he's out of the country. We'll begin your new life there." He raised her chin so her eyes met his. "Now, what about that massage?

CHAPTER -11-

Zvie ushered Kate through the door of the unpretentious multistory building. The houseman stood and offered his hand.

"Welcome to the neighborhood. I'm Harry." He chatted while he confirmed their identification and presented each of them with a key card for the entrance and keys to the apartment.

"Max, Josef and I rotate shifts. One of us will be here from 8 a.m. to 10 p.m. We answer the door and call you to approve visitors. After 10 p.m., you must come down to admit your guests. If you're having a party, one of us can stay, but we get paid extra for that. We accept deliveries too. If it's a delivery guy that's been here before, we might send him up in the service elevator, but we'll call you so you know he's on his way. Let me know if you need a taxi or anything else." His tone and friendly expression showed a willingness to help with all and sundry tasks they would require. "You must be eager to get settled," Harry said at last.

Zvie nodded while Kate stood by, bemused by Harry's monologue and the wealth of information he had volunteered.

"Mr. Zvie? We took care of the stuff you wanted us to do. Let me know if something's not right. The furniture's here too."

"Thank you, Harry. I'm sure everything is just fine."

Harry handed them a map of the area. On it he had marked restaurants and shops. "Central Park is across the street." He added a brochure. "This tells you about the building. The fitness center and laundry are in the basement, but housekeeping service is available. You should read the rules in there. I guess that's all for now." He frowned at his clipboard. Although he circled the stairs and elevators, he walked with them, and pressed the call button for their floor.

The carved door to the apartment showed Kate this was not economy lodging. A small anteroom led to a large multipurpose room. Ceiling to floor windows and French doors created an airy atmosphere. Kate saw posh cushioned sofas and chairs arranged around area rugs, and a rectangular table and side chairs dominated the end of the room. A mixture of impressionist and modern art provided relief to the neutral almond color scheme. Potted plants added a lived-in look. Doors at the far end of the room opened into a modern kitchen and a hallway that led to the bedrooms. The decorator zoned the apartment for relaxation and social functions.

Sage and coral accessories relieved the neutrality of Kate's bedroom. She toed off her shoes and pressed her feet into the deep pile of the ivory area rug before she collapsed on the queen-size bed. She lay staring at the revolving blades of the ceiling fan, recalling their trip from the Academy to the apartment. The seamless travel boggled her mind—no waiting, no lost luggage, and no wasted time. She rose to her feet, crossed to the windows and opened the drapes to let in the late afternoon sun. She surveyed the Manhattan cityscape before she unpacked her cases. The spacious walk-in closet swallowed her wardrobe.

Kate noticed boxes at the back of the closet, but she had other things to think about. She would ask Zvie about them, but they could wait. She didn't want to deal with them now.

Her bathroom displayed the same neutral shades. *Was Zvie the decorator?* She looked forward with pleasure to the Jacuzzi bathtub. There was a separate shower. Fluffy sage bath sheets hung from the heated towel bar. A mirror spanned the wall above the twin basins. Kate unpacked her cosmetic bag and stowed her personal care products in the drawers. She brushed her hair and spritzed perfume in the air. "There," she told the image in the mirror, leaving her imprint on the room.

She made her way to the kitchen. A door by the small table opened onto the terrace. She resolved to enjoy the view. The cabinets held colorful dinnerware, cookware, and several small appliances but were otherwise bare. Kate could manage toast and instant coffee, but food shopping was a priority.

"It's too late to shop and prepare dinner tonight. Let's talk to our garrulous houseman and explore the neighborhood. Do you have a preference, Kate?"

"Casual and close. I'm starving. I don't want to take the time to change."

After a recommendation and directions from Harry, and a short stroll, they arrived at a deli. The menu offered salads, sandwiches, and a limited selection of specials. They ordered and chose a table by the window to watch the street scene.

"What do you think of our new home, Kate?"

"Impressive. The kitchen looks like we could feed an army. I love the terrace. Who is the decorator?"

"Our friends at the Academy. I think they did a splendid job for us. We'll be entertaining in my role as troubleshooter and adviser."

"Troubleshooter and adviser to whom, Zvie? What is it you do? I know what you've done for me, but I can't imagine the Archangel will let you service a legion of people who will pay you for makeovers. Or will he?"

"Bless you, no." Chuckling, he hesitated before continuing. "I told someone on a previous visit that I could revive stale careers and suggest solutions to troubled projects. I think you'll find my clientele interesting. Most of them will come from the arts and entertainment fields. I want us to host a party this weekend."

"This weekend? You know people here?"

"Let's say I've done my research. I met a few people when I was here before. I have many resources."

"Are your resources people you have helped in the past?"

"Some of them, yes, but not all. Don't try identifying the people I've helped, Kate. That could compromise our project. As I've told you before, you must trust me. There are things you must accept without proof."

They lapsed into a companionable silence. Kate watched a couple stroll past and felt a pang. Isolated and alone in a strange city worried her. She wondered how long Zvie would be with her. Would she make friends?

Zvie interrupted her melancholy thoughts. "You should acquaint yourself with the local grocer and the other services we'll need."

Kate's unspoken questions hung in the air. Still accustomed to Betty's world, she wondered what life with an angel would be like. How would they pay for services, for groceries—like a mortal, or would he use his *special* abilities?

"I've made financial arrangements," he said. "Harry will know where there's a merchant that specializes in ordering by telephone with delivery service."

After dinner, they strolled to the apartment. Kate excused herself to try the Jacuzzi. Afterward she sat on the terrace, mesmerized by the city lights. From the sunny climate and ordinary life of Betty Parker, to the wondrous Second Chance Academy and the bustling city of tall buildings that shaded its streets, Kate was unsure what was real or make-believe. Her mind and emotions churned as she tried to guess what her future held until she could stay awake no longer.

The next morning Kate dressed in black denims. Roses made of French knots and bronze beads ran up one leg from the hem to the knee and down from her waist to her knee on the opposite side. She paired a soft gray cashmere sweater and black ankle boots with the denims. After chatting with Harry, a treasury of information on shops and services in the neighborhood, Kate set out for the local grocery, deli, and liquor store. A hand-drawn map in her hand, their houseman had recommended the best places for her purposes.

From the street, the faded red brick two-story building resembled the other storefronts in the city block. Gilt-edged, stylized letters across the dingy window—Grocery and Deli—distinguished it from its neighbors. She guessed from its height that there might be an apartment above. Inside, an image of modern supermarkets surfaced. The smell of old wood mingled with the aroma of chickens on the rotisserie. The scuffed and worn floorboards creaked as she walked through the several rooms. As the store grew, the owner annexed neighboring buildings. Arched doorways cut through the walls connected the additions. Kate imagined a dark, smelly basement beneath the store and shivered.

A stock clerk pointed to the owner, doubling as the cashier.

"Hi. I'm Kate Dunning. Zvie and I moved to the neighborhood. Our doorman recommended your store to us."

"That right?" the balding, overweight man behind the counter said.

She leaned on the counter and gave him a charming smile to rivet his attention. Kate asked about their services, special orders, deliveries, and fees.

"We'll be entertaining a great deal so running an account and delivery service are important to us." She looked toward the back of the store. "I didn't see any cars in front. Is there a parking lot?"

"At the price of real estate in this city, lady?" He snorted. "Can't afford a parking lot without charging, and my customers wouldn't stand for that. I'll need the name of your bank. If your credit check shows you're reliable, there won't be a problem… Mrs. Dunning?"

"*Ms*. Dunning. Please call me Kate. I don't expect a problem." She removed the credit card and bank officer's business card from her wallet that Zvie had given her. She tore a check from the checkbook she'd found in her purse, a joint account with Betty Parker. She scrawled void across its face.

"I hope this is all right? We arrived yesterday afternoon." Kate shrugged to show their state of flux. "There's so much to do when you move, but we'll get it done. We'll pay with our credit card for a while. I suppose checks will take a few days. How long will a credit check take?"

"I'll have the results by the end of the day."

"Good. May I expect your call this afternoon?" She picked up a business card from the counter. "I'll just look around. We're entertaining this weekend."

Ceiling to floor shelves lined the walls and created aisles. Long fluorescent lights hung from chains in the pressed metal ceiling tiles. Freezers and coolers displayed produce, dairy, meat, and fish. Additional coolers and freezers contained convenience foods—ready-made entrees, salads, side dishes and desserts. One room housed a wine and liquor store, an entire wall dedicated to racks of wine bottles. Zvie will enjoy perusing and making selections from the inventory, she thought.

A man with roving eyes stocked shelves while several older men with boredom written on their faces tended the fresh meat and deli counters. She could see a processing area and rear entrance where a clerk pushed a loaded hand cart into a van.

Kate limited her shopping to what she could carry. Approaching the checkout line, the man at the register drew her attention. There was something familiar about him. Kate glanced at his hands, pleased to see the long slim fingers were bare. She knew that didn't mean a lot today. Many men and women did not proclaim their fettered state.

"*Kate,*" a voice in her head scolded. "*Another lapse in attitude?*"

She sighed. Zvie would lecture her when she returned to the apartment. She didn't understand why her cynical thoughts came under scrutiny while flippant or suggestive ones did not. Zvie didn't betray by so much as the twitch of an eyelash that he knew those.

Kate paid, gathered her carrier bag and hurried after the man who had preceded her at the register.

"Excuse me. Excuse me," she called.

He slowed, glancing over his shoulder, and she recognized Colin O'Brien.

"Excuse me," she repeated, a little breathless in her haste.

"Are you talking to me?" he asked, although there was no one else near.

"Yes, I am. Hi," she smiled as she reached him despite the scowl he directed at her.

"We just moved here. Would you answer a couple of questions?" She continued without waiting for his reply. "Do you shop here often? Do you use their delivery service?"

"Are you taking a survey?" Colin's mocking expression showed his annoyance, but he swept her trim figure before returning to her amber eyes. Something flickered in his eyes. She hoped it was approval.

Kate studied him too. His blue eyes were more striking in person than they had appeared on the screen or in publicity photos. His hair was lighter, a dark brown rather than black, as she had thought from the television episodes, and perhaps his hairline had receded a tad more. He looked older than he had in his previous series, a favorite of Betty's. She supposed filming had ended several years ago. He must be in his late thirties. Taller and leaner than she had imagined, he was still handsome. Kate felt a delicious tingle.

"On my honor, I don't have a hidden camera. I don't want an autograph or an audition. I promise not to disclose where you shop." *Jerk!*

"Occasionally. I use their delivery service occasionally," he repeated at her blank look. "I don't know of another store. This one is convenient so I haven't looked for another one."

"It's within walking distance for me too. We might be neighbors. Well, thank you."

He took a step backward and moved away from her.

She blurted, "Zvie told me he met you. I'm sure we'll meet again."

Kate turned to leave. She didn't see him reach out. Her heartbeat sped up as she looked at his hand on her arm. Then she raised her eyes. Colin released her. She faced him and waited for the question he so wanted to ask.

"Who? Who did you say met with me?" Colin said.

"Zvie. He told me you and he had dinner together a couple of weeks ago. He said he would contact you when we moved here."

"Do you know Zvie?"

She shifted her packages to fumble a business card from the outside pocket of her purse and extended it to him.

"How would I know his name otherwise? It isn't a common one, is it? I'll tell him I ran into you…. See you again soon." Kate turned to retrace her steps. She felt him watch her walk away.

Now she had his attention. Maybe this isn't a dream, she thought. *If it is, I hope Colin O'Brien plays an interactive part in it.* Her heart beat a wild rhythm in her chest. The rapid changes in her life and remnants of Betty's persona hadn't allowed Kate to fully accept her new identity.

Yesterday's newspaper featured a study confirming what women already knew. When choosing a mate, men chose good-looking women. Volunteers in a speed dating study chatted with prospective dates for three to seven minutes, then repeated the process with other prospects. Afterward, they indicated people they'd like to meet again, understanding that follow-up dates were possible. Although participants had completed a questionnaire stating characteristics and qualities they were looking for in a mate, the actual results of the study showed that the men opted for looks contrary to what they had disclosed in the form.

From the little information Zvie had shared, Colin O'Brien fit the article's conclusions. She was certain he would have ignored her if she had been Betty Parker.

CHAPTER -12-

Kate's mouth was dry, her hands clammy. She was quaking and trying not to show it. She had left the Academy with a new wardrobe, but Zvie had called in support. This would be her debut, not the dress rehearsals of the Academy.

"You can only make one first impression, Kate," but Zvie didn't tell her why tonight was so important.

Her sleeveless, forest green, silk dress enhanced her complexion and hair. It seemed very demure, slim skirt slit for walking ease that rewarded an observer with a glimpse of slim, shapely legs, and black sandals with a narrow heel.

Academy cosmeticians applied her makeup and swept her hair up off her graceful neck. Wispy strands curled about her face. She moistened her kiss-me red lips.

"Zvie, who are these people? Is there anyone I should know about?"

He raised his eyebrows to urge her to continue.

"You know, *the guy* who fits *the plan*?" she asked in the code she used to refer to her second chance partner.

"We've discussed this. You know I can't tell you if I invited *the guy*. I don't want to influence you," he said, smiling. "My restrictions, remember?"

"You engineered my meeting Colin at the food store, didn't you?"

He smiled his enigmatic smile and remained silent.

"Will he be here tonight? Is he the one? Is that the reason the Academy people prepped me for the party?

He answered her questions with one of his own. "Would you like him to be?"

"He's very handsome," she said, evading the question. *He makes me tingle, too, although he's a jerk.* Kate waited for Zvie's reaction, but he didn't comment.

Zvie gestured around the room. "Some of these sophisticated people are graduates of the Academy in the city tonight. Some of them are with their project angels. Many guests are *not* in the program so don't try to identify them. Relax and breathe." He draped an encouraging arm across her shoulders.

"You look so handsome tonight, Zvie. Why isn't it you? I'm so comfortable with you."

"Mingle like the Academy taught you." He gave her a nudge but tempered his command with a pleased smile.

Couples and singles arrived throughout the specified invitation time. Some guests stayed for only a few minutes while others sampled the buffet and lingered over drinks from the bar.

Kate had spent the greater part of the previous day confirming arrangements for the party. She had ordered appetizers from the deli and supplemented with dishes she learned to prepare at the Academy. She'd planned a variety of finger foods, petite-sized desserts, and a coffee service sat at the end of the table. A catering company supplied employees to circulate with appetizers. A bartender filled requests at the bar.

Kate reviewed her Academy lessons in a mental pep talk. *Remember, compliment the women's dresses, laugh at the men's jokes or if it's a serious discussion, listen and nod from time to time. Don't venture an opinion unless you know the subject. Above all, invite them to the buffet. Guests will remember the food when they may not remember your conversation.* She took a deep breath and approached a group of theater people discussing motion picture performances, nodded, murmured an occasional vague comment as she moved from group to group, urging them to sample the buffet or summoned a waiter to take drink requests. Opinionated critiques of plays and motion pictures amused her or shocked her at the stories or reputations discussed. She would ask Zvie to confirm or deny the tales. Kate surveyed the room, alternately performing her hostess duties with confidence or wondering if, like Alice, she'd fallen through a hole in the universe.

Throughout the evening, Zvie moved from group to group, exchanged a few words or listened to many more. She saw him give and receive business cards and accept invitations to meet for lunch. Other times, he agreed "to be in touch." *When did he get business cards?* Kate wondered what credentials or other information was on them.

A medley of show tunes provided a background to the buzz of conversation. They had selected the music for easy listening. She heard the strains of "Some Enchanted Evening" as Colin entered the room. He seemed to survey the guests before Zvie greeted him and waved her over.

"Colin O'Brien, I'd like you to meet my assistant, Kate Dunning."

"Kate Dunning," he repeated, savoring her name as if tasting it before committing it to memory.

"We've met… the Deli?" she reminded Zvie.

"May I get you a drink, Colin?" Zvie beckoned to a waiter then turned away to speak to a man standing nearby. Kate stood tongue-tied, searching for a topic of conversation and failing.

Colin raised his glass to several people but seemed unwilling to join them. Kate wondered if he was looking for the most influential or the most beautiful before he socialized. She gave herself a mental shake to clear her negativism.

Kate was feeling the effects of the hours of planning and anxiety that she had put into the preparations. She had wanted the party to be perfect, to make Zvie proud of her. At the moment she felt tired and a desire to be alone.

Kate quailed at the impression she was making—as interesting as mud.

"Please excuse me. I need to check with the staff coordinator," she said and retreated to the buffet table. She confirmed the food and liquor supplies were adequate and that the guests did not want for anything. She glanced back at Colin, who still stood alone.

He must have felt her eyes on him and raised his glass. When their eyes met, a jolt of recognition surprised her. Everything was running as she'd planned. She needed a few minutes of solitude. Kate made her way onto the terrace and welcomed the cool air after drawing in the cloying mix of perfumes and colognes.

"Are you hiding, Kate?" Colin asked.

She whirled around. He stood in the doorway. "No, just breathing. What about you? You just arrived and you've left the party."

"I paid my respects. I came to see Zvie… and you."

She shivered a little, running her hands up and down her crossed arms.

"Are you cold? Let me give you my jacket." He moved to take it off.

"Oh, no," she said. "If you do that, you'll shiver too."

He frowned. "I think I can handle it."

"Well, if you're sure…" Colin draped his jacket around her shoulders.

Hmm, nice. Almost like being in his arms. "I like your cologne. It reminds me of balmy tropical nights and Margaritas." *With a little Colin O'Brien mixed in.*

"I don't know about tropical nights… So, you're Zvie's assistant. Did you meet him here?"

"No, I moved with him."

"Oh? You must have a *close* relationship." His tone was suggestive.

"He's an interesting man. When you find a job you like doing, it's worth holding on to. So many people only tolerate their work. I love mine."

"I'd guess you have to be diplomatic. Some of your guests have earned a reputation for being difficult."

"That's true for Zvie, but I work behind the scenes. I'm inclined to be too candid, or so he tells me. If I were the ultimate diplomat, you and I wouldn't be standing here together." She shrugged. "I know you."

"Zvie introduced us a few minutes ago." Although Colin didn't move, she felt him withdraw.

Kate waved away his words. "I mean I know you from another life or another galaxy. We've met before or I knew we would meet. Does that sound crazy to you?"

"Are you putting me on, Kate? I don't believe in voodoo or magic. I've done some work in television. I'm sure you know that." Colin's lip lifted, his voice laden with cynicism.

Smug and conceited! Does he think I'm hitting on him? "Please don't patronize me. I'm not a star-struck teenager. Sometimes I meet someone and I know he'll be significant to me…" She murmured a response to his skeptical expression. "I lost that ability for a while, but that's a story for another time, when we've become friends."

"Will we become friends, Kate?"

"I think so. Did I upset you?"

"Let's say I'm wary," he replied and eased a step back.

"I swear I'm not certifiable. Ask Zvie. He'll vouch for me." Kate lifted her hand to affirm her oath as Zvie joined them.

"Everything okay, Kate? Colin?"

"Colin needs reassurance. Please tell him I'm not man-hungry with a unique approach. Excuse me. I'd better check with the staff. Thank you for loaning me your jacket."

*****

"What was that about?" Zvie asked as he watched her go.

"It was nothing. She didn't upset me. I thought she was teasing." Colin hesitated, reluctant to continue, but Zvie waited. "She told me she knew me on some cosmic level, that something predestined us to meet. I think she's a little peeved. You introduced us. So, yes, I agreed that she knew me. I suggested she had seen me on television."

"Kate is special," Zvie said. "Most people have difficulty accepting that gifted people have heightened perception. Please keep an open mind. She's a talented, warm, and delightful woman."

"She's a little fiery, too. No offense intended. Are you and she… Uh, I don't want to step on any toes or seem rude, but is there something between the two of you?"

"If you are asking, are we a couple, the answer is no. We do, however, enjoy a special bond."

"So, if I were to ask her out, I wouldn't offend you? If she'll speak to me, and if she will accept."

"Please do. My exclusive company has to bore her although after tonight I think we'll be busy."

"And what does Kate do in your counseling business?"

"She reads creative material and suggests performers who would fit the roles. She's drafting her first screenplay, and I'm impressed. I told you she's very talented."

"I might be too dull for her."

Zvie chuckled. "Come on. You have talents you're not even aware of, Colin. I knew that from the moment we met. Kate might be the one who will help you develop them."

CHAPTER-13-

"Hello, Kate?" Colin's voice greeted her when she answered the telephone.

"Hello, Colin. One moment, please, while I call Zvie." Kate said in a formal voice.

"Wait, please. I want to apologize for last night. My assumption was a mistake."

Kate hesitated for a heartbeat before she replied.

"Apology accepted. It isn't the first time someone thought I was a kook."

"I didn't. I thought you were teasing."

"Maybe we should start over, and I'll try to be more… ordinary. I haven't made a good impression, have I?"

"You've impressed me. I've never met anyone like you."

"That may be a good thing." She grimaced.

"Will you have dinner with me tonight, Kate? I know it's short notice, but I'd like to take you to one of my favorites. It's casual. Good food, music, they don't water the drinks, and the other patrons don't care what I do for a living."

"Does that happen often?"

"Too often when I'm with a date."

"It sounds like my kind of place. The food and music, I mean."

"Good. I'll come for you about eight."

"That's perfect," she said, thinking of what to wear.

"Remember, it's casual. See you later."

She turned to Zvie, the receiver still in her hand.

"Colin asked me to dinner. I'm surprised as he seems on guard with me. In fact, he admitted it. I thought I blew it after our conversation on the terrace," she said. "He's the one, isn't he, Zvie?"

He hesitated for a moment, weighing his options. There was no plausible reason to avoid answering, and he couldn't lie to her.

"Your intuition is alive and well, Kate. You've picked up on how skeptical he is too. He's commitment shy and reluctant to let anyone get too close."

"Colin's very attractive. The instant I saw him at the deli, I recognized him. I watched reruns of the television series. The first year was entertaining. In the second year I wondered how the writers could keep it going. I tried to imagine a new character to make it interesting, but the plot was tired and relied too much on seduction."

"He's dissatisfied with his career and thinks of this role only to pay his bills."

"Last night was strange, Zvie. When he came through the door and you waved me over, I experienced a thrill of recognition. It was more like a jolt. Later, on the terrace, I told him and offended him."

"Treat him with caution, Kate. He doesn't know who I am or that he's the reason we moved to this city."

"I guess he didn't need the Academy." She wrinkled her nose.

Kate was waiting when Harry announced Colin.

"Wish me luck," she called.

Zvie turned and approved her charcoal brown denim jeans, lace tee, and golden tan metallic jean jacket before he gave her a thumbs up. The Academy had accomplished its purpose. Kate's clothes sense complemented her. She would stand out.

CHAPTER -14-

"I hope you have news for me, Angel Second Chance." The Archangel Rafael had been waiting. "I need to update the Committee."

"Kate's time at the Academy was worthwhile. Her self-confidence is fragile, but we're working on that. We have been socializing and developing a client base. She's talented. If or when I leave her, she'll be able to carve a place for herself in the entertainment world as an agent or another capacity. Her instincts for potential projects and casting the various roles is impressive."

"So she's intelligent and possesses good instincts, but that's not the crux of your assignment. That is not what the Committee wants to hear, nor do I."

"I invited Colin to last night's entertainment. He sought Kate out on the terrace for a one-on-one conversation. Part of it went very well, but part of it did not. Kate recognized him as the other half of the project. She asked me to confirm that he is the one."

"How does she feel about Colin?"

"She's attracted to him. That she recognized him may complicate matters. Perhaps the Academy should not have encouraged Kate to be as outspoken as she is. You'll remember he is the more skeptical of the two. Her honesty may be too much for Colin right now. And he doesn't have the advantage of knowing my identity or that the Committee accepted his challenge. At some point I will have to tell him, but he is not ready." Zvie looked away from the Archangel and chased that scene away.

"I'll know more after tonight. Colin called Kate this afternoon, and they are on their first date as we speak."

"That *is* progress. I'm pleased, and the Committee will be too. Well done, Angel Second Chance."

CHAPTER -15-

Unsure of what casual meant to Colin, Kate had waffled over what she should wear. A quick glance at his leather coat and worn jeans, and she relaxed.

A ten-minute taxi ride delivered them to a two-story brick storefront with shuttered windows. The carved wooden sign tacked on the side of the building whispered *Bloooz*. A brief flight of steps led down to the entrance. A man in jeans opened the door to them.

Hmm. Jeans must be the uniform of choice, Kate thought.

She stopped inside the door while her eyes adjusted to the dim lighting. The aromas from the kitchen made her mouth water. Framed pin-up art popular decades ago in auto mechanics' garages and other male domains dotted the red walls—women with big breasts, tiny waists, curvy hips, and shapely legs. Their painted-on clothes left little to the imagination. The red walls, the posters of glamour girls in figure-revealing costumes alternating with mirrors made Kate think of pictures she'd seen of old-time bordellos. Small tables with red plush chairs edged a black-and-white tiled dance floor. An elevated second tier of tables afforded a view of the stage on the far end. The bar was busy, and she judged the club was a popular night spot.

A swarthy, dark-haired man with a bushy mustache greeted Colin by name.

"And this pretty lady is…?" he asked with gleaming black eyes.

"Kate, meet Leon. He manages this sorry excuse for a club."

"You add class to our poor establishment, Kate. How did this loser convince you to go out with him?"

"Just lucky," Colin replied before she could answer. "Are you going to make me watch you hit on my date, or do you have a table for us?"

"Testy, aren't you? It isn't often I get to chat with my guests," he said with a sigh. "But if you insist on keeping her to yourself, follow me." He led them to a table on the second tier. Kate slid across the red plush bench facing the dance floor, and Colin sat beside her. The subdued light and Colin's thigh brushing hers created an air of intimacy.

"Leon is an incorrigible flirt," Colin said. "It's one reason this place is popular."

"So, he acts that way with everyone is what you're saying."

"He may have given you a little more attention than usual."

A waitress took their drinks order and Kate browsed the menu.

"I've enjoyed everything I've ordered here, but these," Colin volunteered and pointed to several entrees, "were special."

A long-legged waitress in tight denim shorts and a stretchy T-shirt in keeping with the art on the walls took their order. Kate didn't envy her spending the evening in the three-inch espadrilles that completed her uniform.

She turned to the calendar art on the walls.

"I can see why you like to come here," she said with a smile.

"Do the posters offend you?"

"No, I've wondered why it took so long to put men on calendars. I assume it's because ad agencies didn't think women appreciated anatomy." She studied the nearest poster. "I think this calendar art is the forerunner of the Barbie doll. They have similar measurements."

"I've come here many times and never thought about it," he laughed. "What do you and Zvie do again?"

"He helps troubled productions get back on track. I remind him of appointments, miscellaneous office chores. I discuss creative materials he wants me to read and sometimes I suggest changes that might improve them."

They made small talk while they ate. At the bar below, Kate watched a man cup a woman's derriere as he embraced her. There always seems to be a couple whose blatant behavior is embarrassing or amusing. Women in tight clothing designed to draw attention strolled between bar and restroom, checking out the men who swiveled on bar stools, happy to watch the parade. Self-confident Casanovas eyed the unescorted women, appraised them and selected their targets.

"What's your approach?" Kate asked. "Enlist the bartender to introduce you, buy a complimentary drink, or the old, trite 'what's your sign' attention-grabber?"

"Not that hackneyed line for sure. I don't prowl and pick up strangers. I meet a lot of women in my work, but I prefer introductions by friends. And you?"

"It's safer to rely on introductions. This is my first date in..." She stopped mid-sentence, then continued, "a long time."

Colin's half smile and twinkling eyes challenged her. "You're putting me on, right?"

"No, I'm not. I was in a relationship that didn't work."

By the time they finished dinner, a four-piece band played soft rock. Couples drifted onto the floor. They listened to the music and watched the dancers over coffee.

"Would you dance with me, Kate?"

"I was hoping you'd ask." She shrugged out of her jacket, leaving it on the bench. Colin led her down the stairs to the dance floor.

A woman had been staring at them, her eyes never straying from Colin. At last, she gathered her courage and approached.

"You're Colin O'Brien, aren't you? From the show? I'm an avid fan. Would you dance with me? My friends won't believe I met you!" She was breathless and starry-eyed. When she whipped out a cell phone and snapped a picture, Colin grumbled under his breath.

Kate's eyes narrowed. She squeezed his hand. "Trust me," she murmured and turned to the girl.

"Excuse me. Am I invisible?" There was an edge to her voice, but she smiled. "Are you here with someone?"

"Why, yes, my date went to get drinks from the bar." She pointed at a man placing glasses on a nearby table. He searched the room, a frown and a puzzled look on his face. Then he spotted them.

"Here comes lover boy now," Kate said.

The girl flushed and nodded.

"What's his name?"

"Bob," she muttered. Her grim expression suggested a warrior preparing for a skirmish, unwilling to give up her chance to dance with a celebrity.

"Bobby boy," Kate said, with a wide smile. She pointed at the brash twenty-something woman. "Your friend offered me a dance with you. I love to dance. Let's do it."

"But… really?" he said.

"Yes," Kate replied as she grabbed his hand and pulled him away.

As they came together, Bob gave her a fatuous grin. Kate watched Colin turn to his fan without expression. He moved a step back and held her at arm's length.

"Bob, you've been great," Kate said, placing her hands on his chest to create space between them. "Is she special to you?" and Kate nodded toward his date.

"It's our first date." He shrugged. "Too early to tell."

"I came with Colin and I intend to leave with him. It's time to switch partners and you can find out. Thanks for playing along."

Bob grinned. "No problem, pretty lady. It's been real."

They danced their way over to the other couple. Kate tapped the woman's shoulder.

"My turn. You flattered Colin by your interest, didn't she, sweetheart?" She winked. "But tonight, he's with me, and I'm not good at sharing."

Colin grinned as she took his hand, and they moved away.

"Well, you handled her with finesse. I'll have you run interference more often."

"I might be available to help a friend in need," Kate teased. "She'll be a hit tomorrow when she shows the selfie to her friends."

As the evening wore on, the music changed to blues and slower ballads. Colin was smooth but not showy and they danced well together. He tucked her hand against his chest, drew her closer, and she melted against him. When the band broke for an intermission, they returned to their table.

"Do you want another drink, Kate?"

"No. I don't mind if you do, though."

"Are you ready to leave?"

She nodded.

Leon joined them as they waited for a cab. "I saw you on the dance floor. You made him look good. Too bad you're leaving, I wanted to ask you for a dance." Leon wiggled his eyebrows and slid a glance at Colin just as the doorman announced their ride.

Colin led Kate past the unattached men at the bar. He continued to hold her hand in the dim interior of the cab, drawing circles on her palm with his thumb. Their nearness in the night-darkened cab relieved only by street lights or the occasional neon sign ended too soon.

"Delivered safe and sound to your door without even a hair out of place," he remarked as he helped her from the cab.

"Want to come up for coffee or meditation on the terrace?" Kate said.

"Meditation?"

"I do my best thinking there. The view of the city relaxes me."

"We're meeting tomorrow about next season's show, but it's not an early morning meeting."

"What number season is this?"

"Too many."

The lights in the apartment were off but for the hall light. Kate turned on a lamp they passed on their way to the kitchen.

"Zvie must be out or asleep," she said as she brewed two cups of coffee, handed Colin a mug, and opened the terrace door. The cool, cloudless night made the stars seem brighter and closer than usual. Kate shook out the folds of an afghan and draped it around her. She curled in one corner of the rattan sofa. Colin hesitated before he sprawled in the matching chair.

"I never lived in an apartment or understood why living in a penthouse was attractive before. The city appears so clean and pretty from several stories above street level. I suppose that's why upper floor apartments are so expensive."

"Maybe," Colin replied.

"Sometimes my random thoughts just spill out. So, you don't seem very enthusiastic about the new season of your TV show."

"I'm ready to move on."

"Is your agent looking for something else for you? What about a motion picture either for theater or made for television?"

"I'd like that. Work for several months, then travel and hope another role comes along before the money runs out. Sam hasn't come up with anything. Sam Lewin is my agent," Colin explained. "He tells me I should stick with *Lost in Lust*."

"I don't know of any series that lasts forever. What will you do when you can't act anymore? I mean, when parts are harder to…" Kate broke off.

"You mean when I'm too old to entice an actress into bed? Or I'm gray, wrinkled, and paunchy?"

"That was clumsy, and I didn't mean it the way it sounded. What I meant to ask is if you have any goals other than acting."

"There are things I want to do, but nothing interests me enough to make me stop what I'm doing now."

"You have plenty of time. One day you'll have an epiphany and you'll know."

Kate leaned back and studied the sky.

"The stars look close tonight, don't they? Do you know anything about astronomy?"

"I don't star gaze."

"I do, but I've never been able to find any of the constellations. Maybe I'll visit a planetarium."

Colin set aside his cup and rose. He took Kate's hand and drew her to her feet.

"I need my beauty sleep so I can continue to act for a few more years." He winked, and Kate blushed, reminded of her awkward remarks. He reached for his cell phone and scrolled for the number of the cab company. "Let's call me a cab."

"Okay, you're a cab." She grinned, and he groaned.

"I guess you like old comedy movies."

"Old comedies, musicals, drama, but not sci-fi. The spectacular effects of today's films have spoiled it for me. The scenes in the old flicks are too unrealistic."

Kate walked with him to the elevator. "I enjoyed myself tonight, Colin. Thank you."

"I did too. We'll do it again soon."

The bell pinged, and the door slid open. Colin leaned against it to hold the elevator. He leaned toward her… giving her time to pull away before he kissed her, a light getting-to-know you kiss.

He ended the kiss and stepped into the elevator.

"Good night, Kate."

"Good night," Kate whispered and watched the door close. She circled her lips with her tongue, savoring his kiss.

CHAPTER -16-

After their date Colin became a frequent guest at the apartment and at Zvie's parties. The doorman would alert them that Colin was on his way up. They enjoyed refreshments on the terrace or at the small table in the kitchen. Sometimes he and Kate explored the city together — its parks, and the well-known art galleries, museums, and guidebook landmarks.

Zvie consented to accompany them only when they toured museums and art galleries. He had few interests beyond the intellectual. Even sharing an apartment revealed little about him. He didn't disclose any details. Zvie remained an enigma. She often wondered, but didn't ask, if he had memories of his life before he became an angel.

Kate recalled a line she had read that the city was an enchanted place for a couple. She acknowledged it was true even though she and Colin were Platonic friends. They cycled bike paths on rented bicycles and took walks along the city streets. She had to skip to match his long-legged stride.

"Hey, give a girl a break and slow down a little," she pleaded on one occasion. She typed street names and landmarks into her smart phone as they walked.

"What are you doing?" he asked.

"I don't have bread crumbs so I'm noting street names in case I fall too far behind. I'm new to this area, and I want to make it back to my apartment."

"No worries, Kate. I got your message."

They strolled in a comfortable silence, each lost in thought. Movies with the city as a backdrop and scenes scrolled in front of Kate.

"Do you like old musicals?" she asked.

"Do I get points if I do?"

"Don't be so defensive. I'm not analyzing you." She hid an amused smile. "I like musicals. Walking along this street reminded me of one set in a city like this. Have you ever wanted to sing and dance on the stage or in movies?"

"No, I can't say I ever did. My voice is best suited for singing in the shower. Did you ever want to sing and dance in movies?"

"Not really. Am I too curious?"

"Not really," he echoed. His lips quirked in a beginning smile.

"You might be a tad too tall for the lead in a musical. Most of the dancers in the old movies were average height or short." She smiled to take any implied sting out of her remark. An old song occurred to her, and she sang "You Were Meant for Me" in a husky voice.

Colin looked askance at her but slowed his pace. She caught up with him and linked her arm through his. Her boot heels struck the cadence of the song running through her memory.

"Can you picture it? I saw a Gene Kelly movie once. He didn't have a terrific voice, but he was a fantastic dancer. I knew by one look at him he was in love with the film's female lead. Her mere expression showed how much she adored him. And they conveyed all that while strolling to the beat of the song with an occasional dance step thrown in before he performed his solo."

Colin faltered but soon matched her steps. Two gray-haired women toting shopping bags walked toward them and stopped to watch, sighing as they passed. Kate could almost hear their hearts flutter. Colin hadn't dashed cold water on her fantasy.

She slowed her pace on the last line of the lyrics and looked at him as she sang. *Zvie!* She scolded. *I wouldn't have remembered that song with the angel line in it on my own.*

"If you're looking for a career boost, I can't help you," Colin said, with a laugh.

"With this voice, you think I would audition? Well, in the movies the male lead dancer looked at his partner like he either wanted to kiss her senseless or treat her like she was made of porcelain. At the very least he would have smiled at her. You failed on both counts, so I guess neither of us qualifies for a career in musicals." She made a face and sidestepped a suspicious puddle. "The dancers in the movies didn't have to step over slime in the street. Yuck!"

He didn't comment, but a smile teased his sensuous mouth.

"Don't you ever act a little zany because it's a new day, and no one has spoiled it for you yet?" Kate asked.

"Sometimes you strike me as a little crazy. And I mean that in the nicest way. If I wasn't bigger than you, you might scare me."

She fought the urge to smooth his frown with her fingertips.

"What's your angle, Kate? Who are you really?"

He looked so puzzled that she took pity on him. "I'm Kate Dunning, Zvie's assistant, the woman walking beside you."

"Somehow I don't think so."

They walked in a companionable silence past unremarkable red brick and granite buildings, unlike the landmark skyscrapers of the downtown area of the city. The streets weren't crowded, although one had to avoid the litter and occasional evidence of careless pet owners.

When Kate first came to the city, the size of the buildings and the crowds had overwhelmed her. She'd always thought of it as one vast city that covered acres and acres populated by millions of people. Now, her explorations made her realize the city comprised smaller neighborhoods with apartments, shops and customer service businesses that abutted an invisible boundary, repeating to the next one until the neighborhoods ended and so did the metropolis.

Kate watched the residents of the city weave the fabric of their lives, but she had no part in that tapestry. She grew restless and wondered if she would ever find her place.

Zvie produced complimentary tickets to plays and movie premiers, and the three of them attended together. They dined at the best restaurants and gossip columns linked Colin, Kate and Zvie. They appeared in the society and entertainment news, and news hounds speculated on their friendship. One columnist suggested Colin might be shopping for a new agent.

Sam Lewin read the article.

CHAPTER -17-

The mornings that had held the warmth of late summer slipped into the chill of early winter. Perhaps, because the season suggested loss, Kate grew restless as the fall colors faded to a brown, barren landscape, and activities in the parks gave way to emptiness. She expected something or someone, but what or who?

Zvie sat at the breakfast table, dressed in his pressed khakis, white polo shirt, and polished brown loafers. He was sans socks, his one concession to at-home casual.

"Kate, you've been pacing all morning," he said "Want to talk?"

"I have this feeling something's out of synch or I've forgotten something important. I can't explain it. Something's different today, I'm not sure..." Her voice trailed away, and she looked pensive.

Zvie answered the doorbell and Colin breezed in. The brisk bite of autumn accompanied him.

"Let's go for a walk, Kate. It's perfect weather for walking. Would you care to join us, Zvie?"

"No, thanks, I can tour the parks from the apartment where I have access to food, drink, and comfort," he said pointing to his laptop where he spent most of his day. "Please take Kate before she wears a groove in the floor." Zvie turned to her. "You'll feel better after a walk, my dear."

She rinsed her cup and turned to leave, feeling Zvie's eyes on her.

Colin and Kate favored a park nearby with footpaths, bordered by trees, and a shallow pond in the center. They walked the perimeter, found a bench with an unobstructed view of the water and people watched. Nannies frequented the park and gathered at nearby picnic tables. They exchanged gossip and advice while their charges crept ever closer to the pond. After a set number of admonitions, they collected the children and left.

Farther from the nanny table, pet owners threw Frisbees and tossed balls with a variety of dogs. The barks and wagging tails teased the recesses of Kate's memory. A young woman and an old dog with a white muzzle ambled toward the pet area. She talked to the dog as they walked, the Lab close by her side. Kate felt a twinge of sadness at the dog's slow steps and couldn't look away.

"Kate? Earth to Kate." Colin tugged at her sleeve.

"I'm sorry," she said, dragging her gaze to him. "What did you say?"

"Where are you? What is it?"

"There's something about them," she pointed, "the young lady with the Lab. Something familiar."

"We've probably seen them here," Colin dismissed them with a wave of his hand. "Are you ready to leave? I could go for a coffee."

When they rose from the bench, the dog raised its head and looked their way. Whining and wagging, the dog surged forward. At the unexpected tug, the dog bounded across the field trailing the leash, the owner in pursuit.

"Maggie. Maggie, come here! What's got into you?"

The dog ran to Kate and circled her with happy little yips, then sat and offered her paw.

Kate knelt on one knee and took the dog's paw in her hand. She hugged her and felt her fur.

"Hello, sweetheart. Whose pretty lady, are you? Do you think I'm someone you know?" Kate stroked the dog and shivered. She looked closer. *Is this? Could it be? Maggie! The young woman would have to be Chloe. Impossible! Chloe's in Florida with James. She could be visiting. Would she bring Maggie with her?*

The young woman rushed up to them. "I'm so sorry. Maggie has never run away from me. She never runs period."

Kate drew a ragged breath and let it out before she climbed to her feet. She swayed and Colin steadied her.

"Are you okay?" he asked.

"Just got up too fast, I think." Kate turned. Her eyes widened. Her heart hammered and threatened to explode. She struggled to breathe. Chloe! She looked the same, yet she was different. There was a maturity and a suggestion of sadness about her. When Kate spoke, her words were stilted, her voice unnatural.

"You don't have to apologize. I love dogs. She probably sensed it."

"Her owner died recently and," Chloe looked away, her eyes misty. "I think Maggie's searching for her, but this is the first time she's ever approached anyone with this much enthusiasm."

The young woman tilted her head, scrunched her brow, puzzled. She stared at Kate. "Have we met before? I feel like I should know you."

"No," Kate blurted. "I mean, I would have remembered you and Maggie if we had. I often come to this park. It's my retreat from the busyness of the city." Maggie pressed against Kate's legs, and she continued to stroke her.

"I just discovered this little pocket of open space. This is our first time here, Maggie and me." Chloe pointed at the dog. "My husband had to come for some advance training, and we came with him. I'm Chloe." She held out her hand.

"I'm . . . Kate." She reached for Chloe's hand. When they touched, her body tingled with a static shock, and she pulled her hand away. For a moment she saw Chloe and Maggie as they had been when she drove away from them.

"This is Colin…um…O'Brien." Kate stumbled over his name, barely completing the introduction. Her breathing was labored and painful. She had to get away before she burst into tears or blurted her former identity.

Kate took a step back. She longed to embrace Chloe, to ask about her marriage, her life. A crushing sense of loss and despair swamped Kate once again.

"Oh," Kate's fist pressed against her mouth to stifle a wail. She wanted to beat her fists against something for what she'd lost. She hung on to her composure only by a thread.

"Well, enjoy the park. We were just leaving. Colin's chilly." Kate forced a smile and clasped Chloe's hand. "It was wonderful meeting you, Chloe and Maggie. Perhaps I'll see you here again."

Kate bent over the dog and fought back tears. "I miss you so much. I'm so sorry. Bye Maggie," she whispered in Maggie's old ear. Then she straightened and strode away without looking back. She heard the dog whimper, then Chloe said, "Maggie. What is it with you? That wasn't Mom. Let's go home. I'll find you a cookie."

"Kate, what's going on?" Colin asked.

She'd almost forgotten he was there. She brushed at her tears. "Nothing's going on. What makes you think that?"

"Maybe it's because you're practically running. And you're crying."

He pulled her to a stop and turned her to face him. He brushed his thumbs under her eyes.

"She reminds me of someone, and I had a dog like Maggie." Her voice failed. *I thought the past was behind me.*

CHAPTER -18-

When Colin next came to the apartment, Kate lay on her yoga mat in the great room. Her clothes were damp, and her forehead beaded with perspiration. She felt his eyes on her, but she continued to breathe and relax. When the DVD ended, she rolled to a sitting position and brushed back stray strands of hair that had escaped from an elastic headband. She waved a greeting, reached for her bottle of water, and held it against her flushed face while she studied him.

"Take your coat off and sit down," she said. "Would you like a drink?"

"No, thanks." He sat on the edge of a chair.

"You look tense. Anything wrong?"

"I came straight from the studio, a taping session, and it didn't go well."

"Hello, Colin. What happened?" Zvie asked as he joined them.

"The female lead…we can't get through the scene." He turned to Zvie. "Would you come by tomorrow morning and see if you can suggest something?"

Zvie nodded his agreement.

"Why don't you come along, Kate? Have you ever watched the filming of a television show?" Colin asked.

"No, I haven't. It sounds interesting." She watched him fidget and rose to her feet. "That's a problem for tomorrow; for right now come over here. Take off your jacket, lie down on my mat, and close your eyes."

"I don't think…"

Zvie glanced at Kate and eased out of the room.

"That's the general idea. Don't think. Close your eyes. Empty your mind." She stood, eased the jacket from his shoulders, and slid in a new disk. He eyed her with suspicion but complied. When she removed his shoes, his eyes flipped open, and he frowned.

"It's only your shoes, Colin. You're safe with me. Close your eyes." Her voice was low and soft.

She massaged his feet and murmured instructions for him to relax his ankles, knees, thighs, his hips, continuing up his body. Her hands hovered as she spoke, not quite touching. She moved to his head and her fingertips smoothed away his frown. She pressed his shoulders into the mat and eased back, listened to his even breathing and knew he had fallen asleep.

Kate hurried to the shower. Afterward, she changed into a casual knit shirt and drawstring pants. She sat reading until Colin opened his eyes. He looked dazed as though he couldn't remember where he was.

"Feel better?" she asked, her voice soft, just above a whisper.

Colin focused and nodded. "I'm sorry. I must have dozed off."

"You did. Take your time sitting up and lean against the sofa. How about some water?" She placed a bottle near him.

"What did you do? I remember you took my shoes off and did something to my feet." He uncapped the bottle and drank.

"I suggested that you relax. You needed to unwind. Are you tired?"

"I am." He leaned against the sofa and closed his eyes again. "I think I'll have an early night." He found his shoes, slipped into them, stood and shrugged into his jacket. Clearing his throat, he rubbed the back of his neck. He seemed unsure what to say before he walked to the door. "See you at the studio tomorrow?"

"I'm looking forward to it." She closed the door behind him.

*****

The next day was too cool to sit on the terrace. Kate and Zvie had coffee and juice in the kitchen. Kate browsed the morning paper and turned to their favorite columnist. Bernard was a regular at Zvie's parties. Colin and a beautiful brunette stared up at her from the page.

Morning News

Colin O'Brien and Flora Kidd were cozy at a table for two in LaRoma last night. Ms. Kidd is a guest on Colin's series, Lost in Lust. Could art be imitating life? If so, the scenes between them should sizzle.

"That lying worm!" Kate exploded. "I thought we were friends. I trusted him. He lied to me. 'Early night' my royal fanny. I'm not going to the studio. I don't want to see him again."

"Kate, *I want* you to go with me. You know the press blows things out of proportion and makes them into something different from what they are. I'm sure there's a reasonable explanation."

"How can you defend him? Almost the last thing he said to me before he left was 'I think I'll have an early night.' He did not." She paused, sobering as she looked at the picture beside the column. "Maybe he had an early night. Maybe they were in bed before ten."

She spun away, but not before Zvie saw her distress.

"Calm down. You're over reacting. Get ready to go. And, Kate? Promise you'll be polite."

"I hear you. But if he gives me an opening, I'll tell him I know he lied."

"Kate..." Zvie shook his head. "I'll have Harry call a taxi."

After a short, silent ride they arrived at an unpretentious block of unremarkable buildings. Their cab slowed before what could have passed as a down-at-the-heels retail building. The facade did not reveal the glamorous fantasy business housed inside.

"Remember, Kate. I'm here to help. You're here to watch... in silence." He cautioned her as the cab eased to the curb. "I met the director two weeks ago, and he has a very contentious personality. That may be one reason they're having problems. Let's try to maintain a low profile."

"*I* wouldn't *presume* to interfere. I've even dressed to blend into the shadows." Kate wore form-fitting brown suede pants, a matching knee-length coat, with a white silk shirt.

Zvie hid a smile. It was part of Kate's charm that she was unaware her coloring and her beauty made it impossible to overlook her. She would have to wear a sack over her head to be inconspicuous.

CHAPTER -19-

Colin was pacing outside the building. When the driver opened the door, he hurried over.

"I'm glad you could make it." He shook hands with Zvie. Kate stepped back to avoid his touch. Her nod was frosty, and she raised her chin a notch.

"Zane called for a break, and the caterer is setting up brunch. I walked out to watch for you on the pretext of getting some fresh air. We may as well eat while I tell you about the morning."

Zvie and Kate's entrance attracted attention as they filled plates from a buffet set out for the cast and crew. They selected a table in the corner, and the men waited to sit while Kate removed her coat.

Colin inclined his head toward another table near the serving line. "That's Flora Kidd with my agent, Sam Lewin." An attractive brunette sat with a stocky man in a garish purple-and-black striped jacket.

Kate glanced over. Sam's coarse features and hooded eyes made her think of Edward G. Robinson. She tried and failed to suppress a shiver when his glittering gaze met hers.

She turned her attention to the woman in the morning press photo, tried to guess her age and gave it up. It was hard to tell with show business types.

Kate's thoughts turned to Colin's career while he and Zvie discussed the current problem. During a lull in their conversation, she asked. "There are things about acting that I'm curious about. Do you mind clearing some of them up for me, Colin?"

"Ask away."

"You seem tagged as a shallow charmer with a roving eye and unhappy endings. In *Lovers and Liars,* you cheated, and you died. This series is different only that you're alive, but you're still a womanizer. Is that a natural role for you?"

"I don't know what you mean by *natural* role. Our audience seems to like it. I get fan mail all the time. Some guys write who wish they were me."

"I'm sure they'd like to *enjoy* as much variety as you do in the program. But this character is drifting without an anchor. He moves from one woman to another like he's searching for something. Is it a coincidence, do you think, that you're cast in this role?"

"Kate, remember why we're here," Zvie reproved. "These are products of someone's imagination. Colin is pretending what some writer put into words."

Kate continued. "Are these the only parts Sam considers for you? Is he living his life through your roles and the publicity he arranges for you?"

"Sam knows I couldn't do a musical and you should ask Sam what he imagines."

"Is it difficult to separate your life from pretense? Would you kiss a woman you date the same way you kiss on the set? Is there a difference between a stage kiss and a real one?"

Colin set his coffee cup down with a splash. "Well, yes, there's a difference. Screen kisses are planned and—"

"You plan off-screen kisses too. You don't go around kissing just anyone, do you? If you're attracted to someone, at some point you *plan* to kiss her, don't you?"

"Kate, it's not the same. I have a script, a story line, and I'm told when to kiss someone. It's the character I'm playing, not me. The kiss means nothing."

"I don't see how you can separate the two. A kiss is a kiss is a kiss. Do they teach kissing 101 in acting school? Is there a class on technique, a particular angle so you avoid bumping noses? And, does the script call for a chaste kiss, one with tongue, or is that up to you? And how could a woman ever be sure you aren't pretending?"

"I think Colin means one is mechanical on command, and the other is because he feels an attraction and wants to pursue that attraction by kissing a specific woman," Zvie offered.

"Thank you, Zvie. That's exactly what I mean," Colin nodded.

Kate turned to Zvie with a peevish, stay-out-of-this look. "I wanted Colin to answer."

Then she turned back to Colin. "Is it reasonable, for instance, if a reporter sees you kiss a woman off the set, to assume it means something? Or is every woman an opportunity to practice your technique?"

Colin pursed his lips. His eyes were icy. "Where's this going, Kate? Are you writing an article? *You* may assume if I kiss someone away from the set it's not a stage kiss. Any more questions?"

So, what does that chaste goodnight kiss we shared mean? Kate ignored his attitude.

"Well, yes. I'm familiar with the show, and there are many sexy scenes. Do actors wear something to suppress a revealing reaction?" She paused and leaned forward. "I guess there isn't a chastity belt for a guy, is there?"

Colin choked and grabbed a napkin.

"Kate!" Zvie groaned and rolled his eyes to the ceiling.

"I'm not being facetious, Zvie. The instructors at the Academy told me—"

"The Academy?" Colin clung to the words.

He noticed the occupants of the closest tables straining to listen to their conversation.

"Could you lower your voice please?" Colin said.

"You said it was okay to ask anything. Are you shushing me?" but she lowered her voice.

"I didn't expect you to grill me like this. What's up with you?"

"Consider it research for a part in a crime show. Is there a class on faking love in advanced acting class?"

Colin exhaled with a whoosh. "There's something about a room full of people watching that turns me off," Colin insisted. "I'm not an exhibitionist, nor am I a porn star."

Kate snorted her disbelief. She leaned close, trailed her fingers up his arm, and asked in a sultry voice suggesting bedroom secrets. "How do you keep from showing your enthusiasm with all that cleavage and warm skin sliding against skin?"

Colin gaped at her, at a loss to answer, before collecting himself. A crew member at the nearest table snickered.

"Kate, that's more than enough," Zvie scolded.

Colin shook his head at Zvie, tilted Kate's face to his, and kissed her. A stage hand at the closest table let out a low whistle. The room grew silent.

"There seems to be only one way to shut you up," he murmured and smoothed her lips with his thumb. "Anything else you'd like to ask?"

She started to speak.

"Another, Kate?" Colin leaned close and whispered. "We'll continue this discussion in private. I have to go to work."

"Work? You call that work!" Kate huffed.

Colin walked away to speculative looks, cat calls, and knowing grins, except for Sam. He glared at Kate and crushed his coffee cup, the brown liquid dribbling onto the table.

When filming resumed, Zvie and Kate watched from the back of the room.

Zvie turned to her. "Please try to be invisible until they've finished. I'm sure Colin's composure is a little ragged."

"Poor baby," she snipped, but she pressed her fingers against her tingling lips and wondered if their private discussion would include kissing.

Someone commanded, "Quiet," and Colin and Flora moved to the music. Kate surmised they'd end in a clinch. If the script proceeded as usual, he would dance her to the bed, and they'd fall into it, blah, blah. She yawned at its predictability.

"Flora!" the director yelled, startling Kate. Colin and the actress broke apart. "You want this guy. You've been coming on to him all evening. He got the message. He's in the mood right where you want him. Go for it." Zane threw up his hands.

Flora stomped off the set. Kate watched as Sam sauntered to her side. He draped his arm around her shoulders and nodded at the torrent of words spilling from her mouth.

Zvie greeted the director, listened to his complaints, and commiserated with him. Makeup people swarmed over Colin and the actress, blotting, brushing, while wardrobe adjusted clothing. Kate turned so she couldn't see either Flora or Colin and add to the problem.

When she heard footsteps approach, she turned to face Zvie and the director.

"Kate, you're about the same size as the female lead. I suggested that you walk through the scene with Colin. Flora is ready to burst into tears. She's threatening to walk out. I thought if she could see the scene, she could recreate it."

"What, are you nuts?" Sam shouted as he stormed over to join them. "This broad's got no boobs. The differences between melons and, well, they're obvious. Look at her hair." He reached for a lock, but Kate stepped away. "You're out of your friggin' mind!"

Zvie pinned Colin's agent with blazing blue eyes.

"You ditching the shots from this morning?" Sam ranted. He pointed a stubby finger at Kate. "She knows nothin' about nothin'. Give me an effin' break."

"You made your point, Sam," Zane acknowledged, and turned back to Zvie.

"I'm not an actress. I wouldn't know the first thing about doing that scene," Kate said.

"When you break it down, it's a dance… only a dance. You've danced with Colin, haven't you? Try it for me?" Zvie said.

"No cameras," Kate clarified, "just a walk-through, right? And just as I'm dressed?"

"Well, no. Zane wants you in costume for realism. It'll only take a minute."

Sam threw his hands up. He voiced his objections in a voice he wanted overheard as he rejoined Flora.

Five minutes later, Kate emerged from the dressing room with the gown tucked and basted to fit her slimmer figure. She moved with caution to avoid pin pricks. Colin approached with an insolent smile and a wicked light in his eyes.

He leaned toward her. "You'll be able to do your own research, Kate."

"I'm doing this only because Zvie asked me to," she muttered. "The director might turn his head and allow me to cop a feel in the interests of dramatic license, Colin, but I doubt that it would get past everyone else's watching eyes."

He burst into laughter. "How can I fake romance after that?"

"You're so experienced; figure it out. What happened, Colin? Did you and Flora rehearse so much last night she hasn't enough stamina to do the scene?"

He narrowed his eyes. "What do you mean?"

"'I think I'll have an early night.'" She mimicked, and her eyes sparked.

"What are you suggesting?"

"Suggesting? Your picture is in Bernard's column this morning. I don't know why you lied to me or why I'm in the middle of this… this filming problem. Zvie insisted I come with him. I didn't want to. I wanted honest answers to my questions too."

Colin's retort died unspoken. The director called for quiet, and the music began. Kate moved into Colin's arms, and he drew her close. She held herself stiffly until their eyes met. His reflected laughter. She lowered her lashes. *Able to do my research.* She lifted her arms, and her breasts brushed against him. She twirled the hair at his nape. He stiffened and stifled his surprise. Her hand inched down the front of his shirt, and she toyed with the buttons before slipping one, another, and then another from the buttonholes.

"What are you doing, Kate?" he murmured.

"This is a seduction scene, isn't it? I must be doing something very wrong if you can't guess I'm seducing you," she whispered as she slipped her hand inside his shirt and stroked his chest. They moved toward the bed until his legs were against it, and he sat. Kate stood between his knees, gazed into his eyes, and pushed him onto his back. She raised one knee, rested it on the bed and leaned over him.

Colin's hands brushed her breasts as he pulled her down. Then he rolled, pinning her to the bed under him. He searched her eyes and moved lower until his lips met hers. She heard the director yell and pushed at Colin's chest, but he deepened the kiss. When he drew away, he blinked several times and ran his hand through his hair.

"Was that a stage kiss, Colin?"

He pushed to sit up, his breathing rapid. "What game are you playing, Kate?"

Zvie and Zane walked to them.

"That was great, Colin. Spot on." Zane enthused. A smile lit his face. "We'll substitute Flora's face on the film. Zvie, a marvelous idea."

Kate noticed Sam's mouth tighten as though sucking a lemon, and his hateful glare made her uneasy.

"You filmed that? You said you wouldn't." Kate stared at the director, then at Zvie. She felt betrayed as she accepted his hand to stand and return to wardrobe to change into her own clothes.

Zvie and Colin were talking together when she rejoined them.

"Here she is. No harmful after effects, I assume?" Zvie asked.

"Only a few scratches from the pins, but I'll survive."

"I think Zane wants to shoot another scene today. I'll take Kate away so she doesn't cause any more distractions."

Kate looked up into Colin's captivating blue eyes, and he leaned close. "You lied to me, too, Kate. I'm not safe with you."

CHAPTER -20-

Back at the apartment Zvie gave Kate a searching look. "You gave Colin something to think about, didn't you?"

"That wasn't why I asked those questions. Flora reminded me of his career. The gossip columns have linked him with several beautiful women. I wanted to know if all the years of make believe have numbed him. Does he even have feelings anymore? Would he know the difference between actual love and fake? Maybe there's another man for me… somewhere."

"Are you having second thoughts?"

She hesitated, looked thoughtful. "I am. Betty made poor choices, serious mistakes—lust that burned out and left her empty. Ralph might have loved Betty, but I'd bet he couldn't tell you the color of her eyes. She was like an old shoe, comfortable but replaceable."

Zvie waited, unwilling to break her chain of thought. It was Kate's day for disclosures.

"I'll concede that love is real. What's that old saying? Lucky in cards, unlucky in love? Maybe I should play poker." She rolled her eyes.

"It's too early in our timetable to decide that, my dear."

"I don't think so, Zvie. Colin treats me like his maiden aunt, if he has one. I want a man who wants me, who'll call me because he misses me, not give me a weather report."

"I don't think Colin would kiss his aunt like he kissed you today," Zvie said.

"If Colin isn't capable of love, I have to distance myself from him. I don't want stage love or lust that burns out, and I don't want comfortable this time. I want to burn in passion's fire. I want to feel alive. Is that asking too much?"

"You should know it isn't the norm. Love requires dedication and effort to keep a raging fire stoked. Over time fires cool unless both parties work to keep it going. You may have to decide how much or how little you're willing to give or receive."

"That's my point, Zvie. I don't want to waste my love."

"Colin has similar desires and needs or the Celestial Appeals Committee would not have matched you. He was also unhappy. His career makes it harder for him to accept what you could be to him. We have time to bring him around. Faith, my dear. He can't be complacent after this morning."

Kate dwelled on her second chance and the complication of Colin's career and found no acceptable answers. She went for a walk with her doubts and returned with them. She tried to escape in her favorite author's latest novel, tried to translate the futuristic detective series to the screen. Both the female and male leads were strong and sexy with unique supporting characters. Colin would be a great choice for the male lead. When the phone rang, she was still casting the screenplay.

"Hello, Kate. Did you recover from your acting debut?"

Colin? "I'm surprised to hear from you. Are you finished for the day?"

"The rest of the session went like it should. It's short notice again, but would you like to come out for dinner tonight?"

She hesitated.

"Reluctant, Kate? What happened to this morning's bravado?"

"I'm more than a little embarrassed, not reluctant. I'm sorry if I caused you any problems."

"No worries. Zane thought your additions made the scene better than scripted. And you raised my standing with the crew. About dinner?" he prompted.

"I'd like that. What time?"

"How about seven, casual, at my place?"

His apartment?

"I'm not a gourmet cook, but I know my way around a kitchen." He evaded her unspoken question.

"What should I bring?"

"Just you."

Kate was frowning at her phone when Zvie walked into the room.

"That was Colin. I'm invited to dinner at his place tonight."

"Good. He isn't wasting any time. I assume an intimate dinner for two?"

"I thought about us all afternoon, Zvie. I don't think this relationship is going anywhere. Maybe I should cancel."

"You should go, Kate. If you have questions, get answers." He wrinkled his forehead. "Let me see. Most men prepare simple meals. You do whatever women do before a date, and I'll visit that wine and spirit room at the market. I'll get something special for you to take."

Zvie could be so transparent. She smiled at his excuse to browse the store, taste the samples, and buy his personal favorites.

Kate turned the taps to the Jacuzzi, selected her favorite bath salts, and eased into the bath. When she dried off, she wrapped her hair in a towel and applied makeup. After wielding a blow dryer and a roller brush, her hair lay loose around her shoulders.

"Not too shabby," she complimented her image in the mirror. *Casual,* he'd said, but jeans didn't appeal to her. She pulled on black pants with an iridescent bronze mock-wrap shirt, then searched her closet for the black cape with black leather piping, an impulse purchase.

Zvie waited for her in the living room.

"You look lovely, Kate." He draped her cape over her shoulders, lifted a lock of hair from inside the collar, then handed her purse to her. "Wait while I call down for a taxi. Do you have your key? And the bottle of wine?"

"Zvie, why are you fussing like a mother hen with her chick?"

"Am I?" He walked with her to the elevator, pressed the call button. As the doors closed, Zvie smiled. "Enjoy your evening."

Kate dismissed the taxi in front of Colin's apartment building a few minutes past seven. She pressed the buzzer beside the door, cradling the bottle of wine. "It's Kate," she replied when he answered.

"Take the elevator to the fourth floor, and I'll meet you."

When the elevator doors slid open, the hall was empty. She debated between two apartments when one door opened.

A stocky man backed into the hall. A young blonde woman in a lipstick red mini dress followed him out of the apartment. When he turned Kate recognized Colin's agent. Sam scowled, ran a hand through thinning shoe-black hair and said something unintelligible to Colin.

"I have plans tonight. You should have called, Sam."

"But this won't take long," Sam wheedled.

"I don't care if it's a minute or five minutes. You should have called before coming over. Evening Kate." Colin nodded before leading his unwelcome visitors toward the elevator.

"Hold the elevator," Sam barked. Kate reached for the door as it closed. Sam brushed past her and slammed the door with his palm, retracting it. His companion stumbled into the elevator, unstable on the absurdly high heels of her strappy shoes.

"Kate," Sam grunted, piercing her with small black eyes before the elevator doors closed.

"Am I interrupting?" Kate asked. "He wasn't happy to see me."

"His visit was unexpected. I told him I had plans, and he could just drop out. Let's start over." Colin kissed her cheek. "Hello, Kate. You look lovely as always. I like the cape."

"Thank you. I brought you a peace offering. Zvie told me it's an excellent vintage." She handed the bottle to him and unbuttoned her cape.

"Thank you." He took her cape and gestured toward the doorway. "Come out to the kitchen."

Kate looked around the masculine living room decorated in muted colors. A chocolate leather sectional dominated the room. A multicolored area rug covered the floor before it and a modern floor lamp with multiple chrome arms supporting globes arced over the corner of the sofa. Lamp tables, an occasional chair, and a TV mounted on the opposite wall completed the furnishings.

Colin had meant casual. His washed-out jeans rode low on his hips. A flannel shirt hung open over a white T-shirt and he scuffed in a pair of worn leather mules.

An island cart where Colin had been working displayed a variety of implements and assorted vegetables on its butcher-block top.

"What can I do to help?" Kate asked.

"I have everything under control. Let's have a glass of wine. The glasses are hanging under the cabinet. I've already opened the bottle." He gestured toward the countertop.

Kate poured for both of them and sipped while she watched him chop vegetables and brush them with olive oil and herbs. She smelled a hint of garlic before he slid the baking dish into the oven. He measured pasta and set it aside to add to a pot of water coming to a boil. Kate saw the tall candles and place setting for two on a small table at the dining end of the kitchen. He walked over to stand opposite her at the breakfast bar.

"I hope you like pasta. We're having roasted vegetables with pasta and a tossed salad. I'm not an expert, but I can do several simple dishes."

"I like anything that someone else prepares."

"For someone who doesn't like to cook, the fare at your apartment is darn good."

"I didn't say I don't like to cook. I like to putter in the kitchen, but I prefer simpler meals that I don't have to agonize over. A buffet for twenty or more, even if we cater some selections, is stressful. We seem to always feed a crew, or Zvie wants to try the latest restaurant he's heard about.

The opportunity to experiment gets lost. And it's always nice to try something someone else has prepared."

Colin added the pasta to the boiling water, then carried salad and bread sticks to the table. He lit the candles, dimmed the overhead light, but left a light on over the range.

"If I have this timed right, the main dish will be ready to come out of the oven when we've finished the salad." The greens were crisp, and the dressing did not drown the salad ingredients. He cleared, then served the pasta dish topped with grated cheese.

After dinner, they worked together to clear the dishes. Kate turned to Colin. "My compliments to the chef."

"I told you I know my way around the kitchen. Eating out gets monotonous. I often cook for myself."

"Judging by how often your name appears in newspaper columns, I assumed you ate out every night. Want help with the washing up?"

"No. My cleaning lady comes tomorrow. Let's take the wine into the living room." Colin picked up a remote, and easy listening music filled the room. Kate strolled around and examined the paintings, books, and art objects.

"No family pictures or young Colin snapshots?" She asked.

"All in photo albums." When he didn't offer to show her, Kate didn't pursue it. She slipped out of her shoes and curled up in the sectional's curve.

"This is a comfortable room."

"It's a furnished rental, Kate. I accepted the part in this show at the time my marriage ended, and I needed a place to live. This was the first apartment the rental agent showed me. I've added a few things, but I didn't think I would be here this long. I expected the series would run a season or two, and I'd transition into motion pictures." He shrugged and topped off her wine glass.

"Wine makes me sleepy. I think…"

"Don't think." Colin interrupted. "I have something to show you." He muted the music and inserted a disk into the DVD player.

"Ready? The engineer gave me a copy of this morning's shoot. I thought you might like to see your film debut."

Kate groaned and closed her eyes to blot out the screen.

"Open your eyes, Kate." He sat beside her and pressed the remote in his hand. "We look good together. Your height and mine are complementary; I can rest my chin against your hair. At this point I would have let my hand slide down your hip a little, but it was the female lead's scene." Colin gave a running commentary while the images filled the screen. "We eliminated some sound bites. See my look of surprise? It's real; that's when you played with my hair. Here, you told me you were seducing me. The cameraman caught you opening my shirt and slipping your hand inside." He paused the action, took the wine glass from her hand and set it on the table. The play resumed.

"See how you pushed me and leaned over?" He stopped the film again, eased her down, and arranged pillows under her head.

The sequence resumed. "You're showing a bit of cleavage although Wardrobe did a suitable job of sewing you into that dress. See how sexy and real it looks when I roll over and press you to the bed? The cameraman stopped filming here. We filmed a retake from this point after you left. They'll splice the tape so Flora will look up at me."

"Ah, yes, your *early night* date."

Colin rolled his eyes. "You asked me if that was a stage kiss." His voice resonated through her as he brushed his lips across hers. She closed her eyes.

"Hmm. Is this a stage kiss?" Kate murmured.

"No, this is real. I want you, Kate." He traced her neckline to the fastening at her side.

"What are you doing, Colin?"

"That's my line." He grinned. "I must be doing something wrong, if you don't know I'm seducing you," he murmured, adjusting the volume of the music.

He pulled her to her feet and into his arms. The music was slow and dreamy, and they moved to its rhythm. Kate looped her arms around his neck and again played with the hair at his nape, wondering if Colin was following the show's script or his own.

"See? No reaction. I expected it this time." Colin nuzzled her neck while he stroked her back. His hand slid to her hip, and he drew her to him. He tucked her hand to his chest, and she relaxed against him.

"Feel my heart pounding, Kate? If you don't want this, don't want me, tell me now."

"I told you the first time I saw you that something predetermined we meet." Kate reminded him.

"I don't want to hear about predestination. Not tonight. I want to hear that you want me as much as I want you."

"I want you," she whispered.

He danced with her into his bedroom until she felt the edge of the bed against her legs. She lost her balance and sat. Colin eased her against the pillows and followed her down.

"You have beautiful hair." He picked up a lock and let it slide through his fingers. "I'd know you in the dark by your perfume. You have unusual eyes—cat's eyes. I've seen them light with laughter, watched them gleam and tease. They spark when you're angry and lose their luster when you're upset. Will they glow with passion? What do you think, Kate?" His voice was low, his face close to hers.

"I don't know," she whispered. Kate raised her hand and cupped his cheek. Then she stroked his lips with her thumb.

He reached out, and she heard a click. The bedside lamp cast a soft glow over the room. He propped himself on one elbow.

"I want to see you," he said. He brushed his lips over hers, then to each side of her mouth before kissing her. "Open for me, Kate." His tongue slid between her lips and hers met and danced with his. He tasted of wine and spices.

His hand slid under her blouse and crept toward her breast. He smoothed his thumb over her nipple. She shivered at his touch. He moved his palm to her other breast and brushed his palm over its peak. He raised her blouse over her breasts and lowered his head. She felt his tongue circle her nipple through the lace of her bra, and she squirmed.

"Do you like that?" He moved to her other breast.

"Hmm," she ran her fingers through his hair. He lifted the blouse over her head, released the clasp of her bra, and pushed it away. He tossed her clothes to the floor. Kate trembled; heat building inside her vied with the cool of the room.

He looked at her for a moment, his predatory smile promising pleasure, before he lowered his head to her breast and rolled his tongue around the nipple. Then he blew on it. Kate pulsed, wanting more. Heat pooled in her core. Pleasure crawled through her, and she pulled his T-shirt from the waistband of his jeans. Her hands smoothed his back and moved around to his chest. She stroked her palms over his nipples, felt them pucker and grow hard. Colin sat up, discarded his shirt and peeled off her pants and a black lace thong.

He devoured her with his eyes. "I imagined you'd look like this. Soft and feminine. You're beautiful, Kate."

She tugged on the snap at his waistband and fumbled with his zipper. "One of us isn't playing fair. He's wearing way too many clothes."

"I can remedy that," and he removed his jeans and T-shirt. "This is the difference between faking and feeling it, Kate. There's a huge difference."

"Are you bragging, Colin?" and she reached between them, running her hand down his belly and around his arousal. Part of her remembered the Academy lectures, but instinct guided her as she roamed and touched, indulging her feelings.

Colin kissed his way over her body and then reclaimed her lips. Sensitive nipples reacted to the coarse hair sprinkled on his bare chest. He stroked her thighs, found the sensitive mound between. Kate smoothed her hands over him, imprinting him in her brain. She thought she would burst into flames and heard him groan.

"Colin," she urged.

He drew away for an instant before he inched inside her. He hesitated until she relaxed around him and then thrust deeper. She tightened around him, and he jerked. Finding their rhythm, he thrust deeper, faster, until they exploded in passion's fire.

*****

Sated, Colin drew Kate close, her head on his shoulder, her arm across his chest. Kate's eyes closed, and she slept, but

Colin's mind buzzed, warding off sleep. He lay awake, rehashing the day and the evening's climax. *Kate is beautiful… and talented, if I can believe Zvie. The sex was… fantastic… but am I in love with her? Zvie said I would know if this is real.* He frowned. As pleasurable as the night had been, the incredible sex hadn't convinced him. He drew the sheet over them and closed his eyes.

Colin woke with morning peeking through the sheer draperies at the window. Memories of the night before stirred him, and he reached out to kiss and coax Kate awake, but the bed was empty.

"What the hell!" Did she leave, and he didn't hear her go? The thought like a spray of chilly water brought him wide awake. Throwing aside the covers, Colin sat on the edge of the bed, running his fingers through his hair. He had not counted on waking alone. What was that about? He'd drowsed between sleep and wakefulness, feeling Kate beside him, expecting to make love to her again. Her fragrance, the musky smell of sex and coffee enticed him. *Coffee?* Colin pulled on sweatpants and padded to the kitchen. His mood improved when he saw Kate leaning against the breakfast counter looking out at the city.

"Good morning," he said. "You're up early."

Kate turned to him, a coffee mug in her hand.

"Not so early," she replied. She wore his robe, had rolled the sleeves several times, and the hem brushed the floor, hiding her bare feet. She had tied the belt in a bow to close it.

Colin reached for a mug and poured coffee. He sat at the counter and rested a bare foot on the rail of a stool.

"Regrets?" He tried to read her expression.

"I'm good. Woke up in the strange bed and couldn't go back to sleep."

"Sure that's all? I was disappointed you weren't there. I thought—"

"Let me guess." She wrinkled her nose. You're miffed, maybe a shade angry. You concluded I left without thanking you for dinner and…"

"And?" Colin urged.

"The good sex." She smiled at him. Her hair mussed and her face devoid of makeup, the sunlight that lit his kitchen enhanced her beauty. He wanted her back in his bed.

"Good, huh? I thought it was better than good and sort of hoped you would too." He raised his eyebrows.

"I enjoyed what we shared last night… for a first time."

"Okay, I feel better."

"Remember the comparative forms of good? Good, better, best?"

"A grammar lesson, Kate? Go on." He encouraged, puzzled how it could relate to sex.

Kate drank coffee, set her cup down, and crossed to him. She brushed his knees.

"When you wake up next to a man with a pleasant tingle because of what you shared the night before, you hope there might be something between you, something more than satisfied lust. That's *good* sex. When the night before made you want to make love again the morning after? That's *better* sex."

"And best?"

She put her hands on his shoulders, leaned toward him, and brushed his lips with hers. She whispered. "Let's work on better before we explore that."

Colin kissed the pulse pounding in her throat and noticed the chafing from his whiskers.

"I should shave," he said, standing, but his fingers found the edge of his robe. He gave the belt a tug, and the edges parted. Pushing the robe from her shoulders, he lifted her against him. She wrapped her legs around him, and he carried her to the bedroom. All thoughts of shaving vanished as they tumbled onto the bed. He nibbled at her neck, her ear, and the corner of her mouth, finding her lips. The kiss deepened, and they began the pleasurable dance of rediscovering their passion. Kate's hands and mouth were busy, demanding, and Colin's groin tightened, seeking the satisfaction denied him when he woke. He was hard and ready. Kate straddled him, looked into his eyes and lowered to touch and tease.

Buzzzzzz! Buzzzzzz! Buzzzzzz!

"Are you expecting someone?" Kate asked, her voice husky.

"Damn!" Colin cursed the doorbell's continued buzz. He lay indecisive, but the mood and his arousal slipped away with the grating noise. Kate moved aside, and he shrugged into his robe.

She heard Colin answer the door, followed by voices.

"Sam! What the bloody hell are you doing here? Didn't I tell you to call before you come over?"

"It's morning." Sam growled. "Since when do I need an appointment?"

"Since I have a private life, and why is she here?"

"I told you I wanted you to meet her and—"

"You brought her last night. I met her. Go away and take her with you."

Colin ushered his uninvited guests into the hall, then vented his frustration in the hostile slamming of the door.

Kate was in the bathroom when he returned. He threw a pillow at the wall. It didn't erase his irritation. Kate had dressed when she emerged.

"I'm sorry, Kate." He put his arms around her and touched his brow to hers.

"No need to apologize, Colin. I'm sorry too, but *things* happen." She shrugged. "I wonder…" and left the rest unsaid. She was certain Sam came to find out if she had spent the night, if she was still there. "Our discovery of better will have to wait."

CHAPTER -21-

"Tell me about Colin's apartment. You can learn a lot about a man by his home."

"It was masculine, neat, neutral colors—no family or publicity photos, no early snapshots. I thought that was odd. And Sam was there when I arrived."

"Sam? Surely not by invitation."

Kate shrugged, skirting around discussing the night she had spent with Colin. She knew Zvie had been about to ask where Colin was hiding, or if they'd argued, when she handed him the newspaper. Bernard's morning column reported a Colin sighting.

Morning News

CO was at Hot Spot with yet another blonde ingénue, a clone of the last one in a lengthy line of fleeting lovelies. Ho hum. Sam Lewin was with them.

The Flame opened last night. Evan Ritchard, Serena Burton, and Harry Watson were among the A-listers attending the upscale restaurant's premiere. Kate Dunning and Zvie arrived late and Claudio, the owner, met them at curbside. The opening was an unqualified success, and Zvie shared his opinion that The Flame is an experience that discriminating diners should not miss.

Kate's surprise at Bernard's column was not as great as Zvie's. Once a frequent visitor to their apartment, Colin had not been there since Kate had dinner at his place. He had telephoned several times, claiming work, commitments, and *something* Sam had in the works.

Bernard's report confirmed what Kate suspected: Colin had planned her seduction with patience and charm, no doubt perfected by his career roles. She blushed at the memory, how easy she'd surrendered, her former pleasure turning to embarrassment, then to cynicism. She wanted to confront him, demand an explanation, but she wouldn't risk further humiliation. Would he ease out of her life now that she was another notch on his bedpost?

CHAPTER -22-

At Zvie's social that evening, Kate greeted their guests with one eye fixed on the door. Colin had never been this late to any of their receptions, or whatever Zvie was calling them. Perhaps he wouldn't come. The last time he called, he asked for Zvie after a stilted exchange punctuated by silences. He was aloof and withdrawn with her.

At the sound of the doorbell, Kate started toward the door, but one of the catering staff reached it before she did. A young blonde clung to his arm; the same one she had seen at Colin's apartment with Sam. Kate stopped mid-stride amazed at her apparel—tights to her ankles and four-inch heels. Her breasts threatened to fall out of the neckline of a smock that could have passed for maternity wear. Its hem brushed her knees. If she wore striped tights, she would have looked like Raggedy Ann in velvet. A complacent Sam followed.

Kate heard titters behind her, but she wasn't certain they were for the ingénue's outlandish dress and her tottering attempt to walk in the ridiculously high heels—or directed at her.

Kate spun and strode to her bedroom. She locked the bathroom door and stared into the mirror.

"Fool. Fool. Fool! How could you think he was falling in love with you?" she asked her image. "Because you wanted him to care; you wanted to believe it," she answered, wiping tears from her cheeks. "He gave a super performance. Fooled you with that seduction scene, didn't he? He must have laughed long and loud at how easy you were. He paid you back in spades, his playboy reputation still secure."

Kate pressed a cool washcloth to her reddened eyes and freshened her makeup. "Put some starch in your spine, because Zvie will not allow you to hide in here." She straightened her shoulders and tried a smile. "You must do better than that." She scolded her image in the mirror and left her sanctum.

She felt like a wind-up toy, her key wound one too many times. Kate greeted acquaintances, spoke to friends, and welcomed first-time guests. Fulfilling her role as Zvie's hostess, she urged everyone to sample the buffet or visit the bar. She smiled—a mere stretch of her lips—as she worked her way around the room, avoiding Colin. When she had circled the room, she entered the kitchen and onto the terrace. She leaned on the balcony rail, welcoming the cool breeze on her feverish face.

Something brushed against her legs. "Maggie! What are you doing here? How did you find…" She went to her knees, was still kneeling, holding onto the railing when Zvie found her.

"Kate! What happened? Are you ill?" He rushed to her side.

"Maggie was here. How did she…"

He regarded her in silence. She returned his compassionate gaze and understood. Tears blurred her vision.

"She died, didn't she? And I wasn't there for her after all the times she comforted me. What a self-centered fool Betty was to make that wish. She should have stayed with Maggie and Chloe… They loved her."

Zvie made shushing noises and helped her to her feet.

Maggie's death triggered painful memories—Betty's memories—Maggie as a furry armful, as an old dog sitting at her feet on the patio, their walks together, and evenings when she was Betty's sole companion. She pictured the vacant seat that would have been hers at Chloe's wedding, remembered her daughter's sad eyes and Maggie's joy when they'd met at the park. Chloe and Maggie together when she drove away… forever etched in her virtual photo album.

Zvie chose his words with care. "She was old, Kate; it was time. There wasn't anything you could do."

"Nothing I could do? I could have held her, thanked her for her companionship and loyalty, told her I loved her."

"She knew, Kate. That's why she came to tell you goodbye—"

"It's my night, isn't it?" Kate interrupted, her voice low and ragged. "Like Betty, I'm a fool, a trusting, naïve fool. Colin was so convincing. I believed he was falling in love with me. Now I feel used and foolish."

"Kate." He held out his arms.

She put her head on his shoulder. "I won't let you down, but we have to talk after everyone leaves."

Kate felt Zvie's eyes assessing her. Crushed and humiliated, her eyes held tears she struggled not to shed.

Scenes of her former life and this one mocked her. *If I could only go back…*

"I'd better go inside. Our guests will wonder where we are," Zvie said. "I've called the Academy for reinforcements. Remember Roman?"

"The Latin dance instructor?"

"That's the one. He'll be here soon. I want you to give him a warm welcome, follow his lead. The two of you will give a short dance recital and then go clubbing to the best and most popular places."

"I don't feel like dancing. What will that prove? I want to…"

He placed a finger over her lips. "I want you and Roman seen together. Sam's scheming is all too plain. If it's publicity he's after, we'll give him and Colin a lesson. Publicity, indeed! I will not let him ruin my project." He raised her chin so she could no longer avoid his gaze.

Zvie's icy eyes matched his stern expression. "Listen to me. Believe in me. Sam is no match for a project angel."

Kate tried to smile but could not. "I need a minute, Zvie."

"Did I tell you that your dress is lovely?" his statement both a compliment and a criticism of Colin's companion.

"No, but thank you." Kate's black sleeveless dress showed a hint of cleavage through its deep V-neck, and the cocktail length skirt swirled around her legs. She had added a black lace shawl.

She still stood in Zvie's arms as the kitchen door slid open.

"It's too chilly to linger. Don't be long." Zvie released her and gave Colin a curt nod as he rejoined his guests.

"Escaping again, Kate?" Colin asked as he ambled to the railing.

Kate sniffed and swiped at her tears with the back of her hand before she faced him.

"What's wrong?" he asked.

"Nothing that concerns you. Why are you here? Shouldn't you glue yourself to the side of Ms. Ghastly Dress?"

He coughed. "Ms. Ghastly Dress?"

"Maybe I should call her Raggedy Ann in Velvet."

"Jealous, Kate?" Colin chuckled.

"Of her poor taste? Don't be absurd."

"Kitti assured us it's the latest fashion."

"It might be the latest of some misogynist designer who convinces gullible fashion slaves it's chic. I'll bet he shares a hearty laugh with friends whenever anyone buys it. No one should wear that unless they're auditioning for a revival of Annie… or a kid's cartoon."

"Don't be snide, Kate. It doesn't become you. Sam asked me to bring her. It's good publicity."

"That's a hoot! Publicity for whom, Colin?"

"Why, for me."

"Get real. I thought I was naïve, but you've been around long enough to have learned a thing or two. This is another example of Sam's treachery."

"You aren't fair to him."

"Oh, *puh*-lease. Tell me what she can do for you. Is she famous? Does anyone know her? Does she have name recognition?"

"Well…"

"Has she reached the grand old age of eighteen, Colin? Ah," she nodded as though it had just occurred to her. "*Sam* thinks I'm too old for you. Does being with me ruin your image? Does she make your testosterone surge like you *say* your leading ladies don't? Be careful. Being linked with her could label you a cradle robber."

"Come on, Kate. You know how important publicity is in my business."

Kate offered a nasty smile. "I know what I know. Try to follow this if you can. You are the stallion in the stable."

"Stallion? Why, thank you," he grinned.

"Yes, *stallion*," she stressed. "And stop with that silly patronizing smile like you're placating some child."

His smile receded as his eyes turned stormy. She poked his chest with her index finger.

"*You* have the name recognition. Sam collects fees from *your* work, which commissions pay the maintenance, the mortgage, and the expenses for his stable. Sam's the owner, in case you hadn't figured that out. Raggedy Ann in Velvet is an unrated filly. She hasn't won her maiden race yet, but she has good conformation. She may have potential, but she's unproven until she wins her first race." Kate paced back and forth with an exaggerated sway of her hips. "If the stallion shows interest in her, she might attract attention even if she can't run a lick. Their relationship might get her in the right races."

Kate paused for effect and took a breath.

Colin's tight-lipped smile was strained, and his eyes, cold. "You're very entertaining. Go on with your fairy tale."

"Sam doesn't care about your career or your image. He only cares about getting his purse. Maybe you'll retire to the ranch, but not to the stud barn. Are you getting the picture yet? You're giving her the boost of publicity, not the other way around." Her eyes widened with a new thought, an ugly one. "Sam's only keeping you in the series so he can be around beautiful, half-naked women. It's his brand of pornography."

Colin's eyes narrowed to slits; his face taut with anger. "Are you through? You have such a way with words, Kate. Why don't you write a novel?"

She shook her head. "You can't see past your macho ego, can you? I thought you were tired of being a sex object. I thought you wanted roles to show your talent. Did you just use me to get free advice? Compared to Zvie, I was a bargain, wasn't I? All you had to do was take me to dinner and sleep with me. It didn't cost you anything but time."

"Kate, it wasn't like that."

"You gave a wonderful performance, Colin. I misjudged you," she continued. "You're first, foremost, and *only* an actor. I'm sure you noticed there are reporters here tonight. If Raggedy Ann in Velvet is such a significant publicity opportunity, join her." Kate spun and left him on the terrace.

Her confrontation with Colin left Kate drained, and she welcomed the hand Zvie held out to her.

"Roman arrived," Zvie said. "Remember to follow his lead."

Zvie greeted the handsome young Latin with enthusiasm. "Roman, my friend. We're so happy you could come tonight. Kate and I have missed your company."

Kate nodded. Roman's chocolate brown eyes warmed with his smile. "Darling, we're together again." He kissed her and whispered with every appearance of intimacy. "Are you ready to dance?"

"I don't know," Kate hedged. "What will you have to drink? Are you hungry?"

"Only for you. Let's toast our reunion." The bartender handed Roman a squat glass with amber liquid in ice. Kate lifted a glass of punch from a passing waiter. Roman leaned close to whisper. "Relax. Everyone will focus on me, wonder who I am. We'll give them something to discuss."

Zvie walked to the center of the room and raised his voice.

"Attention, my friends. Roman has asked Kate to enter the Dancing Stars program with him. I asked them to entertain you. Please step back to give them some space."

Roman drained his drink, took Kate's glass, and set it aside.

The conversation rose to a heightened buzz as Zvie pushed a disk into the player.

Roman's warm smile raised Kate's confidence as they waited for the music. Guiding her through the precise steps and turns of the tango, Kate responded to his flirtatious manner with lowered lashes and a teasing smile. He moved with sinuous ease, his tailored black pants and snowy white, open-necked shirt emphasized his broad shoulders and tapered hips. During the dance Kate set her sorrow and unhappiness aside, captivated by Roman's mesmerizing dark eyes.

"I love your hair, but you should set it free," he whispered, scattering pins as he ran his fingers through Kate's hair. The tempo of the music changed, and she followed his lead to a salsa beat. When the music ended, a moment of stunned silence preceded scattered applause and murmurs of approval.

"That was better than an aerobic workout, Roman, and more fun." Kate smoothed a lock of hair from her brow and fanned her flushed face.

Zvie hooked Kate's arm and whispered, "Very well done. If I didn't know better, I would swear the two of you had practiced." He escorted them to where Sam stood with Colin and Kitti.

"How about it, Sam? You're *rumored* to be an expert judge of talent. Do they have the pizzazz to qualify for the competition?"

Before he could answer, Zvie turned to the child-woman. "Honey, the man in the gray suit by the bar would like to meet you. Why don't you totter over and oblige him?" When she had gone, Zvie spoke to Sam. "Your client is a pretty *child*, albeit a precocious one. No one who sees her, however, would accept that she's a seductress. More likely the press will conclude Colin is encouraging a child in a game of make-believe or trying to recapture his youth." Zvie's eyes drilled Sam. "*I know* what you're doing."

Sam sputtered, "I don't know—"

"If you deluded Colin into thinking that girl would be good for his image," he turned to include Colin, "and you agreed, it was a serious mistake. You would do well to find another agent."

"Now see here," Sam began, but Zvie turned his back, resuming a conversation with Roman and Kate.

"Run along. I know you want to make up for lost time. I'll make your excuses. And I won't wait up for you," he said in a stage whisper.

CHAPTER -23-

Kate and Roman swept through several of the popular nightspots, pausing only long enough to be recognized. Throughout the evening Kate spoke to reporters she had met at Zvie's apartment and introduced Roman, who held her close, playing his part well, while his eyes sent her intimate messages that brought color to her cheeks.

In the predawn, Roman and Kate returned to the apartment where Zvie waited for them. They rehashed the evening together while nibbling on leftovers from the party.

"Roman was a hot topic. Several of our friends asked where you've been hiding him," he told Kate. "Bernard thought he recognized him. It's possible, although it's been years since he was at the Academy."

Kate gave him a sharp look.

"Yes, Bernard needed the Academy, although I wasn't his project angel. Sam and his friend left soon after you and Roman, as did Colin." At last he asked what was foremost on his mind. "Did you enjoy the evening?"

"I can't speak for Kate, but I did," Roman said. "After tonight your friends might be convinced we'll audition for that program."

"You can imagine, Zvie. We drew the spotlight. You made me look good," Kate complimented Roman.

"You are a striking couple—grace and strength," Zvie responded. "You play off one another. Did you see anyone you knew?"

"We spoke with several reporters who have been your guests," Kate said.

"Excellent. Sam will be bilious when he reads the gossip columns tomorrow."

"I suppose. Thank you, Roman. I appreciate your coming tonight." Kate yawned. "Will you excuse me? I'm exhausted." She rose and left the kitchen.

"Kate may have enjoyed *some* of the evening," Roman said, "even if her smiles didn't reach her eyes. You can be proud of her."

"I'm pleased you were available. Tonight could have been humiliating for her."

"I can't imagine any man preferring that girl, but there's no explaining taste, is there?

"No. Do you have classes tomorrow?"

"Yes."

"You'd best be on your way. Thank you again."

"My pleasure. Please call me if you need any further help."

*****

Kate hung her dress in the back of the closet. She wouldn't wear it any time soon, if ever. "Ouch," she stubbed her bare toe on the corner of a carton against the back wall. Staring at the offending box, she pulled it and a smaller one into the light.

"Why now, Kate, when you should go to bed and pull the covers over your head?" She shivered as she recognized her handwriting. Working the sealing tape loose with her nails, she stripped it off and lifted the lid of the larger box. She stirred the contents, then sank to the floor.

She shuffled through photographs. "Sassy," she whispered at the snapshot of a dog that had been her special favorite as old memories surfaced. She recognized Ralph, Chloe, her parents and her sister. Her forehead puckered. *Who are these people?*

Kate read the book titles and fanned the pages. Betty's mother had scrawled her name in the front of several old paperbacks with dog-eared covers and yellowed pages. She scanned the covers of CD and DVD collections. When she had emptied both boxes, reminders of Betty's life surrounded Kate. She sat back on her heels, saddened by the meager pile of belongings that had held meaning for Betty, although at that moment she doubted Betty could have been unhappier than Kate Dunning.

Sifting through the contents once again, Kate discarded unidentified photos and old paperbacks. She read letters between Betty and her family after her move to Florida, reliving Betty's loneliness. Then she tossed them to the discard pile along with the classified ads where Betty had circled rental apartments. Kate shelved the CDs and repacked the smaller carton with the DVD collections and photo albums of Chloe and Betty's pets. She wrote her name and address across the top, stowed her laptop into a carrying case.

Kate changed into jeans and a knit shirt and bundled her hair into a clasp at her nape. Then she left her bedroom to confront Zvie.

Although the past week's events had been troubling, last night had crowned her growing suspicion that her second chance would not have a happy ending. She approached Zvie with resolve. He would expect her to burst into tears or rant, her usual practice, and he'd had sufficient time to plan how best to pacify her.

"Has Roman gone?" Kate asked.

"Yes, he returned to the Academy."

"Too bad he isn't here more often. I enjoyed dancing with him."

"Will you join me in a glass of wine?"

"No, thank you. I would rather have tea."

They moved to the kitchen, and Kate made her favorite brew. When she finished, they took their drinks to the small table by the terrace door.

"I'm eager to read the paper tomorrow morning. Bernard will give you and Roman a sentence or two."

"That's not what I want to talk about."

"I didn't suppose it was. Start wherever and whenever you're ready."

"Thank you for everything you've done for me and thank whoever sent you. The Second Chance Academy was fantastic. I love my new look, my body, living the life that Betty only dreamed of. Even meeting Colin," she said in a murmur.

Zvie sipped his wine and waited.

"I still regret losing Chloe… and Maggie. The Archangel and his cohorts might not understand a dog could mean so much to me." She brushed away a tear. "I wish I could have had my second chance by eliminating Ralph from my life. I don't mean I wanted him to die. I was the unhappy one who prayed for another chance, who wanted to find love. It's doubtful Ralph ever thought about whether he had love or wanted it. He seemed content as long as his dresser drawer held clean underwear, his socks matched, and his meals were fit to eat. I think he's content with his life, or maybe he was better at accepting it. Betty could not have enjoyed her second chance at his expense." Kate sipped from her cup.

Still Zvie said nothing.

"The people who report events in the city—the ones we know—knew of Colin's attention. They assumed we were a couple… so did I. They expected something more permanent. He hurt more than my pride. You can tell the Archangel half of your assignment is a success. I believe love is real, but not everyone finds love. I hoped in my second life I would be one of the lucky ones."

"It's too early to make that judgment," Zvie said.

"You said that before… It isn't too early. Colin got too close for his comfort, and Sam bailed him out. He seized that publicity ploy like… like a man on fire would jump into a puddle to put out the flames. He could have refused. You've wielded that old free will stick at me often enough. Sam is a conniving, nasty…" Kate searched for an adequate description without resorting to profanity and gave up. "Sam needs Colin, but Colin doesn't need Sam. Why can't he see that? I made my past mistakes with Colin even worse tonight after I told him what I thought of Sam and their professional relationship. I accused him of sleeping with me so he wouldn't have to pay your fees. He was furious."

"Oh, Kate!"

"I know. My temper controlled my tongue. So, I have spoken and so it is done, to paraphrase the King of Siam." She tried to smile and failed.

"I wouldn't have asked to find love if I'd known it would be so painful... that it would make me more miserable than being alone and lonely." She offered a wan smile. "I know what comes next."

Zvie stiffened, waiting for her to elaborate.

"Going back is impossible. It's beyond belief that Betty could have survived the accident. I couldn't live with Ralph, not after my experiences here. Betty's life would make me more miserable than before my second chance. I'd go crazy reading about Colin with other women, so I can't stay here. You said we have a time limit, and I'm reasonably certain the Archangel won't let you be with me forever." She waited, hoping she might be wrong.

Zvie shrugged.

"That leaves one alternative," Kate whispered. "When the time on the clock expires, I will die." She bent to look at her hands as though she would find another solution there. She regarded Zvie with misty eyes. "I hope you will guide me through that process as you have everything else." She set aside the teacup. Drawing a big breath, she told him her decision.

"I want to go back while I still have time. I know the drill; I cannot contact Chloe. She wouldn't know me anyway, so there's no point to it. I have to revisit where Betty lived. Or maybe I need to see where I lived? I'm confused," Kate massaged her temples. "Perhaps I can get my head and my thoughts in order before my time is up. I promise I won't do anything to discredit you. I just want to make sense of my life… *lives*. I want to know where Betty… and I… went wrong, why neither of us found love."

"Kate, there is *nothing* wrong with you. You are beautiful, sensitive, and talented. Colin is running scared. He—"

She shushed him. "You're sweet, Zvie. I told you before I wish it could have been you or someone like you, but I don't have good taste in men. There is something that draws me to the outlaws and not the lawmen, pardner." She joked unsuccessfully. "I pass over the loving, agreeable guys for the handsome, sexy, self-centered men. I'm not describing them well, but you know what I mean. How much time do I have?"

"I'll let you know after I see the Archangel again."

"I want to go right away. I don't want to see Colin. Please don't tell anyone where I am. I want to go with your blessing, to find myself and… peace."

"Are you *sure*? I think you should give Colin a chance to come to his senses."

"No, I'm not sure, but I don't want to stay. If Colin changes his mind, maybe I'll have changed mine too. You'll know where I am."

"Running away isn't going to…" he sighed. "Go pack. I'll talk to the Archangel, but you can't stay away indefinitely. As you say, we'll be in touch. I will let you know when you must be back, or if there is a critical development."

"Thank you." She rose, kissed his cheek, and shuffled from the room, drooping and moving like the old Betty Parker.

Kate packed, gathered her credit cards, and pulled her leather jacket from the closet. Her energy flagged in the early morning light.

"I've called a taxi," Zvie said. "It should be waiting. If you leave now, you won't have to face Harry and his questions. I'll tell everyone you're on vacation. If you have too much time on your hands, call that screenwriter who contacted you. I see you're taking your laptop."

"If I can get my head together...."

"I'll miss you. If I miss you too much, I may have to drop in on you again."

"Like you did in Betty's car? Just be sure I'm alone." Her attempted humor fell flat.

Zvie carried her bags to the elevator. They were silent on the ride to the lobby. When the doors slid open, he faced her.

"Last chance to change your mind. I don't want you to go. Sometimes free will is a blasted nuisance!"

Kate nodded.

The cabbie was standing by his car. Zvie opened the door and helped load her belongings. Kate shivered and shrugged into her jacket. Shouldering her computer bag and clutching her purse, she walked to the taxi.

"To the airport," Zvie told the driver as he handed him some bills. He turned to Kate, and she hugged him.

"I love you," she whispered and climbed into the car. She did not wave or look at him as the car pulled away from the curb.

*****

Kate joined the line at the airline counter. She chose the earliest flight nearest her destination, bought her ticket, and checked her suitcase and the box. At that early hour the lines through the security checkpoint were short. She sighed with relief when she reached the gate. She would breathe even easier when she left the city behind.

After boarding, she found a pillow and blanket, and settled for the flight. Kate turned her face to the window as tears leaked from her eyes. The engines whined; the aircraft rolled, picked up speed and raced down the runway. Kate closed her eyes as the airplane lifted; the city slid away.

Chapter -24-

"Angel Second Chance, this is unexpected," the Archangel Rafael said. "You are looking prosperous. Are you enjoying your assignment?"

"This *is* one of my more pleasing projects. The city is known for its fine gustatory establishments."

"We're aware of your penchant for fine wine and choice food. We're also aware you consider yourself something of a gourmet. May I remind you, however, that your primary aim is not to write a five-star dining guide. Do you have something significant to report? A breakthrough, perhaps?"

"Significant, but I do not believe you will be pleased, nor am I. By chance, Kate encountered Chloe and Maggie in one of the local parks. The dog came to her last night; it distressed her. She realized Maggie had died. I expect the vision will revive memories of her former life."

"Her sensory talents are strengthening then."

"Yes, and this could not have happened on a worse night. Colin's agent is doing his utmost to come between Kate and Colin. Sam recognizes Kate is a threat to his control over Colin and to his lifestyle. I believe he's determined to prevent

Colin from having any relationship other than the ones he dictates. I suspect he's at the root of Colin's two previous failures. After last night, Sam knows he and I have opposing views. I will *not* allow him further access to my connections or the apartment."

The Archangel leaned forward. "And why may I ask?"

"I must credit Sam with the ability to get into someone else's psyche although he misuses the talent. Colin escorted an ingénue to my reception last night. The community we have cultivated assumed Kate and Colin were a couple. Human nature…" Zvie hesitated and rephrased. "As a result, Kate, Colin, and the aspiring actress were hot topics of gossip. The evening was humiliating for Kate until Roman arrived. He played the role of Kate's long-lost lover. I expect Sam will seethe when he reads the newspaper reports."

The Archangel seemed dubious. "An interesting strategy, Zvie, but what will it accomplish?"

"Publicity is vital in the arena in which Sam wants to be ringmaster. Colin has to see his agent's true character and be strong enough to withstand his manipulations, or he will waste his second chance opportunities and I will have failed. I expect I'll hear from Colin tomorrow." Zvie glanced at the Great Clock. "Correction. I should hear from him today."

"Kate knows of the time limit attached to her second chance," Zvie continued. "With what she pieced together at the Second Chance Academy and the strengthening of her intuition, our Kate has perceived what will happen if the project fails. She asked to be alone to straighten out her thoughts. I couldn't forbid her… free will, you know."

The Archangel studied Zvie from under raised brows.

"Kate is vulnerable now," Zvie continued. "She plans to revisit the area where Betty lived. I request that a celestial bodyguard monitor her while she's on her journey. I'd like to accompany her…"

The Archangel ruffled his fringe of hair and waved his hand to silence Zvie. "The Committee is concerned. And, I confess, I have some qualms too. You realize Kate is part of an assignment? Are you becoming too fond of her, too attached? You will advise me if I need to reassign you and substitute another?"

Zvie tried to conceal his surprise. "Of all my projects Kate is special. I want her to be happy."

"Perhaps you are impeding progress by your feelings. Are you conveying something more than project angel to your charge?"

"I have not lost sight that I am an angel, and Kate is mortal. I recognize a deeper relationship between us is… impossible."

"Extraordinary, Zvie, but not impossible. There are historical instances of relationships between mortals and angels. The bigger question is whether you would want one if it were permissible."

"The relationships you speak of were unique. I do not believe Kate qualifies, and I have no illusions of my stature. Unlike Armaros, I do not have sexual feelings for Kate or any other mortal woman. I admit; however, I love her. I feel closer to her than any of my prior projects, but I *will* carry out my assignment."

"I had to advise you of the Committee's concerns. We cannot sacrifice you for the sake of this mission. Kate's absence is perhaps a matter of good timing. You need to distance yourself and regain your perspective, or we may consider alternatives."

"I understand, Archangel."

"I believe it is time to reveal your identity to Colin. You must not forget that he has desires and needs. This project must move along despite its more pleasant aspects."

"I have introduced Colin to several influential people, and I am pursuing promising leads," Zvie continued. "One of them should contact me soon about a career development for him." Zvie took a deep breath. "I need to stay close. I cannot leave him to Sam's manipulations, and I will reveal my identity."

"Request granted, Zvie. We will assign a guardian angel to your Kate. He or she will report to you if you need to intervene."

"Will the Committee grant an extension if Colin proves immune to the shock treatment, or if he shows any sign of coming to our side?"

"I doubt the Committee will grant an extension, but I will pose your question. I believe we have a few months remaining. Kate could go back to the Academy." The Archangel paused, but Zvie didn't comment. "Zvie? God speed."

Chapter -25-

Zvie strolled to the corner newsstand to collect the morning newspapers. Then, lured by the enticing aromas from the bakery as the first trays came out of the ovens, he selected his favorites. He returned to the silent apartment and brewed coffee. Ordinarily, the aroma of fresh coffee would wake Kate. Not at her best in the morning until after her first cup, she would yawn and speak little, but there would be no Kate today.

Opening the newspaper, he read Bernard's column.

Morning News

Besides the sumptuous buffet and interesting guests at Zvie and Kate Dunning's entertainments, we met Kate's handsome friend, Roman. Is he Kate's new beau or a former one resurrected? This writer thought, as did my colleagues, that Colin O'Brien and Kate Dunning were more than friends. Last night, however, O'Brien arrived with a woman wearing a remarkable dress by a new designer.

Zvie smiled at his subtle criticism.

The Daily Telegraph

Patrons at Casa Blanca watched Kate Dunning and Roman's sensual performance of the tango, the dance of love. Ah Kate, if I were younger, I would learn to tango with you.

The Daily Mirror

Last night the temperature at Hot Salsa soared courtesy of Kate Dunning and Roman's sensuous moves and flirtatious exchanges to the rhythms of Hot Salsa's combo. Salsa lessons, anyone?

Zvie read similar complimentary reviews in the remaining papers. Coffee cup in hand, he strolled to the window. An airplane's contrail prompted thoughts of Kate. She had promised to call when she reached the hotel. He reached for his phone, but the intercom's buzz interrupted him.

"Mr. Zvie. It's Harry. Colin O'Brien is here. You want I should send him up?"

"Is he alone?"

"Yes, sir."

"Thank you, Harry." Zvie applauded the doorman's perception. He must have been on duty last night. Zvie folded the papers to the reports of Kate and Roman's club appearances. When the doorbell rang, he took his time answering the door.

"Good morning, my friend." Zvie glanced down the empty hall. "You're in time for coffee and fresh bakery. You look tired, Colin. Rough night?"

"I didn't sleep," he said, following Zvie to the kitchen.

"I surmised that." He eyed Colin's unshaven, rumpled appearance. "As we age, it's difficult to keep up with younger women. I learned my lesson on that score long ago."

"I left right after Kate and Roman."

"Kiki—is that her name?—seemed *very* affectionate." Zvie's expression was bland.

"I wasn't with her last night. Why did Harry call you? He always waved me up before."

"Harry was on duty last night. He must have seen you arrive. Colin, Sam is no longer welcome here. It would save embarrassment to all of us if you told him."

"Not welcome? Why?"

"He planned to humiliate Kate last night. No one hurts her and continues to be welcome. *No one!*" Zvie's stern voice and matching expression lasted only a moment before his customary pleasant demeanor reappeared. He poured Colin's coffee and gestured to the plates and assorted bakery. "Let's sit in the kitchen. It's too cool for the terrace."

Colin saw Bernard's column. After a glance he pushed it aside and skimmed the remaining reports.

"I stepped in a nasty puddle last night, didn't I, Zvie? Kate's angry. Sam's angry. I told him I wanted no part of his plan, but he ambushed me. Kitti latched onto me like a leech. I couldn't shake her off without causing a scene."

"Come now, Colin. Bernard reported that he saw you together at a restaurant. Why not admit you're... *dating*?" Zvie's implication was unmistakable.

"That's not the way it is!"

Zvie gauged Colin's response to his veiled suggestion.

"What a fiasco. I tried explaining to Kate, but she told me some unpleasant truths I should have seen for myself."

"She did?" Zvie feigned surprise.

"I saw Kate in your arms last night."

"Did you?"

"Are you sure there's nothing between the two of you?"

"Kate is lovely, but I'm not romantically involved with her or any woman." Zvie raised his hand to ward off any misunderstanding. "I'm not attracted to any *man* either. I won't deny that I love Kate, but I am not *in* love with her. You know the difference, don't you, Colin?"

"I think so," he mumbled. "Something happened before I came out, didn't it?"

"Yes, she received sad and unsettling news, but Kate didn't want to bow out of the party when I told her Roman would be a guest."

Colin went on as if he hadn't heard Zvie. "She'd been crying… told me she wasn't my concern. That was a splash of icy water. I thought we were friends."

"Friends! I can understand your spending time with friends to ward off loneliness, but do you satisfy your sexual urges with them as well?"

"No! Sam asked me to bring Kitti. Kate told me Sam was using me to launch his other clients' careers, and I was a fool to trust him."

"She's right. Sam will keep you in *Lost in Lust* until they cancel the show." Zvie shrugged. "I think you know and resent it. As a result, your professional and personal life suffers."

Colin shredded a roll and sipped his coffee. From time to time he glanced at the doorway. "It's quiet in the apartment.

Is Kate still asleep? She must have been out late." He gestured to the newspapers. "I'd like to talk to her."

"That's not possible. Kate left early this morning."

"Kate left?" Colin echoed. "Did she go with Roman?"

"No, she is not with Roman. She went alone."

"Left," he repeated. "Where did she go?"

"Her trip was unplanned. When she reaches her destination, she'll call me. At least, I hope she will."

"You let her go?"

"She's an adult, Colin. I couldn't stop her."

Colin's eyes narrowed. "Are you being straight with me?"

"I don't have a reason not to be. My *code* will not allow me to lie."

"What code and why did Kate leave?"

"Kate thought you cared for her, as did many others." Zvie gestured at the newspapers. "Kate isn't a woman who engages in casual sex. She believes you seduced her to get even for the scene at the taping session."

"She told you that?"

"You disappeared after you slept with her. What was she to think?"

"Is *that* why she went away?"

"Don't flatter yourself, Colin. You contributed to her decision in a small way. Kate wants to find her identity."

"You're putting me on! Kate is the most self-confident person I've ever met."

"Appearances are not always what they seem. Some people seem self-confident and clever when they're the direct opposite," Zvie said. "Kate has…concerns. She wants to be part of life not observe it. She wants to belong."

"But she belongs here, with you, doesn't she? When will she be back?"

"Soon, I hope. She left only a few hours ago and I miss her humor, her observations, her thoughtfulness." Zvie's expression softened. "She does so many things to make my life pleasant and comfortable. You sensed the emptiness, the silence in the apartment."

"You told me there's nothing romantic between you and Kate."

Zvie's mouth quirked at Colin's turmoil. "It's time you and I have a serious talk, my friend."

"I thought that's what we were doing."

Zvie smiled and asked. "Do you recall when we met?"

"Mogul Productions hosted a reception for a producer. I stopped in. We went to dinner at my favorite restaurant."

"I came to town that night to meet you."

"How could you know I'd be there?" Colin scoffed. "I *heard* about the event by chance. Going there was a spur-of-the-moment decision. Sam didn't know about it."

"How could Sam know? He doesn't move in A-list circles. Without you…but I digress. Do you remember this?" Zvie snapped his fingers, and a rippling air curtain solidified into Colin's image.

"How did you do that?" He looked to Zvie and back to his image.

Instead of answering, Zvie said, "You were going through a tough time. I believe your wife had left you, but I'm not clear on the details at the moment. You escaped to the terrace to be alone. 'I have to know if love is real, or if it's an illusion, a scam perpetrated by the entertainment media. If it exists, help me find it or give me the good sense to remain alone. Don't let me play the fool again.' It is you speaking, isn't it?"

He tensed, turning to Zvie. "What kind of parlor trick is this? How…"

"I know *you*, Colin. You were a lonely little boy. From the window of your room at boarding school, you watched your parents drive away." A young Colin's face pressed against the window.

"No one knows that. I never told anyone. You're guessing."

Zvie stiffened. "Even if I were, it's accurate, isn't it? When you were growing up, you had lots of acquaintances but few friends."

Colin discounted the images with a wave of his hand. "I must have told you all this when we had dinner."

"Think, my friend. We talked about your career and your disillusionment. You told me about your marriages, but you did not mention anyone else."

"Then how? There's a projector hidden somewhere, right?" Colin stood, ran his hand under the cabinets, and opened doors.

"There are no projectors, but if there were, ask me how I got the film. I do not produce movies. You told me you drifted into your first marriage. You don't regret sleeping with her, but you regret *marrying* her. Sound familiar?"

"Stated like that, it sounds like a bigger mistake than I thought." Colin's lip curled. "This is ancient history. What's your point?"

"You claim your second wife used you to further her career, that it was a cold, loveless affair."

Colin nodded. "I told you about her."

"You did," Zvie agreed. "You seem to believe several people have used you to further their interests, but you trust Sam, a master puppeteer."

"Kate thinks so."

"Sam isn't keen on your association with Kate. She told me Sam called on you very early the morning after she had dinner with you at your apartment. He hoped to find out if Kate was still there and if you were serious about her. If you were, he would have to step in so he could continue to use you to promote the women he earmarks as budding talents."

"Kate said Sam doesn't like her. He's been abrupt the few times they met, and the night at my apartment."

"And yet, you follow his advice?" Zvie shook his head.

"Look, let me know where Kate is. I know I can make her understand about Kitti."

"Are you so full of yourself you think if you add an endearment, she'll believe anything you tell her? If you do, you don't know Kate. I don't tell lies. I don't know where she is."

Colin and Zvie exchanged steady eye contact—one skeptical, the other offended.

"I asked Kate who she was soon after I met her. She said she was just Kate Dunning, but who is Kate? Who are you?" Colin gestured toward the kitchen cabinets. "How did you..."

"Are you ready to accept what I'm about to tell you without affidavits and witnesses?"

Colin smirked. "Nice bit of theater."

Zvie's blue eyes flashed. "My name *is* Zvie, but in another dimension I am Angel Second Chance, a project angel. After your challenge, the Archangel Rafael assigned me to prove to you that love exists, help you find it."

Colin gaped. He stared bug-eyed for a tick or two, then laughed. "You're putting me on. You set me up. When is Kate going to pop out and shout gotcha?"

"I'm forbidden to produce a bolt of lightning or mix a potion for you to drink so you'll believe. If it were only that easy," he added under his breath. "I've never met anyone more determined to throw away the greatest opportunity of his life." Zvie walked to the terrace window, frustrated and impatient. He looked toward heaven for inspiration.

"So, you say you're here to help me." Colin said behind him. "Why me?"

"I do not make those decisions nor do I debate them," Zvie replied without turning. "My guess is your desperation reached the sympathetic ear of a member of the Celestial Appeals Committee who convinced the entire panel." He heaved a sigh and faced Colin. "That group hears petitions, grants pleas and second chances. My superior, Archangel Rafael, did not approve of the ruling, but it is binding. Do you know how fortunate you are?"

Colin shrugged.

"There are over six billion people in the world. The number grows daily. Think of that and consider how many prayers and requests the Committee receives every day. It grants only a few. That's how rare second chances are. If you accept what I've told you, you will find love and the fulfillment you have only dreamed of." Zvie saw Colin's amazement. "Yes, we know of your dissatisfaction with your career. Without experiencing love, you can't portray it. When Kate asked you those probing questions, she focused on actual issues you need to resolve."

"Just suppose I believe you. Where does Kate figure in this?"

"Kate is also a second chance project. She scoffed at love like you. Unlike you, she gave up everything to find it—family, friends, her identity. Don't look at me like I'm a lunatic," Zvie said. "I'm lucid. Do you want to see more scenes and hear specifics about yourself and your past life?"

"Yes… No… I need to think. What I know is there's something weird about you, or you couldn't live with Kate and not have an affair with her."

"I suppose that's a start. Why do you want to find Kate? What difference does it make whether she believes you?"

"I don't…" Running his hand through his tousled hair, Colin blurted, "Kate makes me feel better when I have a terrible day. She frustrates me, yet makes me laugh. I'm never bored or lonely with her." He added in a low voice. "She makes me feel special. Whoa! I've never thought of another woman this way."

"And?"

"Look, I don't want to make another mistake and read about it in the tabloids or the gossip columns, okay?" Colin frowned, then confided. "I'm worried. Maybe I'll never see her again. Did I screw up—big time?"

"Give Kate a little space," Zvie advised with a slight smile. "If she doesn't call soon, I'll find her."

Chapter -26-

Kate trailed off the plane and claimed her bags, the only ones remaining on the carousel. After signing the rental car agency forms, a porter loaded her belongings on the agency shuttle. She collected the car and followed the programmed directions in the GPS to I-95. Cautiously, Kate merged onto the north-south expressway. A vague sense of a traffic disaster channeled her to the slow lane. After a tense forty-five-minute drive, she exited, exhaled, and uncurled her fingers from the steering wheel.

Kate had traveled to Florida to revisit the events leading to Betty's second chance. She had to know if Betty's choice had been the right one. Only then could she embrace her identity and put the past behind her.

Driving through streets that teased her memories of another time and place, she found the neighborhood supermarket where Betty had shopped. Unused to the variety and abundance, Kate gave in to temptation. A variety of snacks and convenience foods were in the bags stowed in the trunk of her rental car.

Instinct guided her to Betty's neighborhood. She parked and stared at the dark windows and unkempt lawn of Betty's house. *Was it as forlorn inside? Would she feel Betty's unhappiness?* Emboldened by the realty sign, she peered in the windows and tried the knob on the front door—locked.

Kate dialed the realtor and left a message with the answering service. Forty minutes later she arrived at the small hotel where Zvie had stayed when Betty met him. She registered and unloaded the car. Hanging the do-not-disturb sign on her door, she crawled into bed, emotionally and physically exhausted.

When Kate woke, the face of her watch glowed on the bedside table. She read the time and placed it face down. *What did time matter?* She turned her face into the pillow and wept for Betty's shattered life and Kate's heartache. When she next awoke and hauled herself out of bed, she pushed the drapes aside. The sky was a postcard blue. *Why did the sun have to shine?* Gloom and rain would better suit her mood.

Kate slipped the first disk of *Lovers and Liars* into the DVD player, the TV series she'd brought with her. She focused on a younger Colin, his face and body more youthful. Cynicism had not yet etched his features. She munched on snacks while she watched all the episodes. After the credits, Kate snapped each disk, dropping the pieces into the wastebasket. She swiped at a tear. Colin had been so convincing. She'd wanted him to love her.

She toyed with calling Zvie but put off speaking with him… or anyone. Kate stared at the television, uncaring what filled the screen so long as she wasn't alone with her thoughts.

*****

Kate couldn't ignore the compulsion any longer. "Zvie?"

"Kate! You said you would call when you checked in to the hotel. Surely you haven't been in the airport these last three days."

"I don't have to tell you where I am, do I?" she replied, an edge in her voice.

"No. Still, I'd like to hear from you. The apartment is too quiet without you. What have you been doing?"

"Watching television. I haven't been out of the hotel room. Well… I've told myself a hundred times what a fool I've been."

"That doesn't sound like it was a good idea for you to go away alone. Perhaps you should come home."

"Home? Where is home? I don't know who I am."

"Don't be silly. You're Kate Dunning. Dredging up old baggage will accomplish nothing." *How many memories had the familiar surroundings revived?* Zvie broke the silence when it stretched too long. "Colin asked about you. He said he tried to explain about Kitti, and you wouldn't listen. Is that right?"

"He made up that feeble excuse on the spot. Colin made his choice. If he cared for me, he'd have said no to Sam."

"He says he said no, but they ambushed him. He wants to know where you are."

"That's old history, Zvie."

"So soon, Kate? Colin misses you and wants to see you. What should I tell him?"

"See Sam about a replacement," she muttered. "Wait. Give him the Julie London CD in my room. Tell him to listen to "Cry Me a River.""

"That's harsh. You told me you loved him. If that were so, you would forgive him or give him a chance to explain."

"I don't want to talk about him.… I'll be in touch."

*****

The listing realtor had not responded, and she called again. "This is Kate Dunning. I called you about a house on Crescent… Tomorrow morning at ten… I'll meet you there."

Kate strolled along the boardwalk until she spotted the beach where Betty and Chloe had met Zvie. The scent of suntan lotion mingled with the sea breeze as she watched the ocean waves play with the shore. Remembering, Chloe had believed Betty needed a friend, had noticed the unknown guy, and encouraged her mother to 'make nice.'

Awareness of Florida's heat and humidity urged Kate to a tiny restaurant sandwiched between two bars. She forced herself to eat half of the seafood special and drink a tall glass of ice water. Returning to the hotel, she showered away the grit from the beach. She asked for a wake-up call and turned out the lights, but sleep eluded her. Her mind churned with what she might face tomorrow.

With a groan, Kate swung her feet to the floor, dressed, and drove to the beach. She located the café where Betty, Chloe and Zvie had gone after the beach yoga class. The aroma of hamburgers on the grill made her mouth water. A noisy, twenty-something group crowded the bar. Kate circled them and chose a table by the window.

A boyish man left the party at the bar. Kate watched his reflection in the window as he approached.

"Hi. You look lonely," he said. His toothy smile dominated his tanned face. He pulled out a chair and straddled it. "What's your name?"

Kate frowned, sending him a *go away* message. "Betty."

"I'm Jayson."

She nodded.

"I'm a lifeguard on the beach across the street."

"Bet she wants to meet you." She gestured to a woman, sending him flirty smiles.

He turned and brushed her off with a glance.

The waitress set Kate's plate in front of her, nodding to Jayson. He helped himself to a French fry and popped it in his mouth.

"A kid on a raft drifted too far out today. I had to tow her in."

Kate bit into her sandwich without comment.

Jayson signaled the waitress to bring him another beer. Kate watched two women cast mute appeals to the guys at the bar as they gyrated to the music of a small combo.

"Want to dance?" Jayson asked.

"No, thank you."

"Oh, come on, you're not *that* old."

"No… thank… you." *Jerk!*

"You're not very friendly."

When the combo broke for an intermission, Kate motioned to the waitress and paid her check.

"Goodnight, Jayson." She started for the door.

He drained his beer and bolted after her. "Not so fast. It's too late for a pretty lady to go walking on the beach alone."

"I'm not going walking on the beach. I'm going to my car."

"Whatever." Jayson gripped her arm.

"Take your hand off me," Kate hissed. The bartender looked up.

"I'm just walking you to your car, Betty." Jayson tightened his grip; his smile held no warmth. He saluted the bartender as he hustled her out the door. Her car stood alone.

Kate fumbled for pepper spray and pressed the panic button on the key fob. The security alarm shrilled as Jayson pushed her against the door. His arms and torso trapped her. He pressed a wet, open-mouth kiss on her neck. Kate shuddered and elbowed him.

Jayson grunted. His guttural voice reeked of stale beer. "Stuck-up bitch. You don't fool me. You old broads come to the beach looking for this." He forced a hand inside her blouse, popping the buttons and tearing the fabric.

Kate's scream accompanied the car's alarm. Throwing her head back, she struck his nose. Jayson cursed and leaned heavily against her. He was strong, fit, and determined.

"You shouldna done that." Jayson growled, wiping his nose on her shoulder. She felt his growing excitement, tasted bile.

"Excuse me," a voice behind them said. "Is there a problem here?"

"Butt out," Jayson snarled.

"Call the police!" she yelled to the slender man reflected in the car window.

Jayson groaned and fell to his knees.

"That won't be necessary. Get in the car and leave, Kate," the stranger ordered.

"I said, butt out," Jayson slurred as he lurched to his feet. "Who the hell is Kate? She's Betty."

The stranger stepped between them. Forcing Jayson's arm behind his back, Jayson staggered.

"Do I know you?" Kate asked. "How—"

"Leave," the stranger repeated and frog marched Jayson across the street.

Kate climbed into the car. She stabbed at the ignition several times with a shaky hand before she inserted the key. Back in her hotel room, she rubbed her arm, reddened from Jayson's grip. She searched for Tylenol but would have welcomed mini-liquor bottles. She dropped her ruined blouse in the wastebasket and showered away Jayson's unwanted attentions.

In bed, Kate shuddered anew and thanked her Samaritan, whoever he might be. That restaurant had been friendlier when Betty, Chloe, and Zvie had eaten there. Betty had been unaware her second chance began that night.

Chapter -27-

"Zvie? Ezra here."

"Good morning." Zvie greeted the celestial bodyguard looking after Kate. "Is Kate all right?"

"Her experience with Jayson shook her and should have taught her caution."

"Jayson?"

Ezra sketched the incident from the night before.

Zvie groaned. "I knew she shouldn't have gone off alone."

"Rest easy, Zvie. I'll keep Kate safe."

"Stay with her, Ezra. She was young and naïve when she married. Although divorced and remarried, she's had little dating experience. Like tigers who target the young and the weak, predators like Jayson sense her inexperience. It attracts them. Call me if you need my help."

Chapter -28-

Kate punched the pillow. Daylight creeping through the drapes and sounds of departing guests awakened her. Visions of Betty's marriage danced against her closed eyelids. Ralph had provided for Betty and Chloe, but he'd been weak in parenting and sharing household responsibilities.

Betty had resented his out-of-town assignments. He said they paid more; she thought he was escaping. Her resentment cooled her passion, which further strained their relationship until they were two strangers bound by a piece of paper.

Kate! Let it go.

She rolled her eyes. She hadn't received a reprimand from Zvie in months.

Her phone's Mozart ring tone broke her reverie.

"Zvie? Is anything wrong?"

"Can't I call because I miss you?"

"I...."

"I heard you had trouble on the beach, Kate. I hope you weren't planning anything foolish."

"How did you find out about that?"

"Promise me you won't pick up any strangers. You won't find any answers that way," Zvie said, ignoring her question.

"For the record, I didn't pick him up. He forced his attentions on me. Am I being followed?"

"Kate, Kate," he chided. "Did you suppose we would allow someone selected for a special blessing to drop off the celestial radar?"

She groaned.

"Colin and I are going to that little Italian restaurant he likes," Zvie said, changing the subject. "I remember the pasta there was very good."

"Is it time for dinner?"

Zvie clucked at his chick like a mother hen. "Are you eating?"

"Don't fuss at me, Zvie."

"I'd like you to come back, Kate. Everyone is asking for you."

"Everyone? That's a broad statement. Who is everyone?"

"Harry, for one, and Bernard, and Colin calls every day. He's worried about you. The producers want to write him out of the show. It may be permanent."

"That might be good for him. Perhaps he'll focus on what he wants in his life instead of letting Sam dictate to him."

"You're very judgmental, Kate. You of all people should know how easy it is to let someone else make your life decisions. Colin wants to talk to you. I think you should call him."

She was silent for several seconds. The disloyal thought surfaced that Zvie had offered Colin a reward if he revived their relationship. Their rift would hinder the success of Zvie's assignment. She tried to push it away, but the thought persisted. "I have to know why Betty made the choices she made."

"Anyone could make similar decisions. Relationships require cooperation and effort." She could hear that she was trying his patience.

"Yes, but other people make mistakes and they live with them. Betty didn't."

"Most people don't have a second chance offered to them. Sensitives and intuitive people live by their emotions. Their depth of feeling allows them to create—write, compose, paint, whatever. Left brain and right brain people think and act differently. Ralph is one and Betty was the other."

"So, if Betty and Ralph had taken analytical tests before they married, they'd have discovered their incompatibility?" Kate jabbed at Zvie. "Why are opposites allowed to attract if their failure is predictable and the rate is so high?"

"What's this foolishness about allowing attraction? Chemistry plays an important part in selecting a mate, but please remember free will. If the individuals are not at the extreme ends of the scale, opposites complement each other. You and Colin are very much alike—creative, afraid to show your feelings, or to trust. Stop fighting your destiny, Kate."

"I'll talk to you soon, Zvie." She hoped he'd get the hint that she didn't want to continue their discussion.

"Come home, Kate," Zvie said. Then she heard him mumble, "She's still ambivalent."

Kate looked at the phone in her hand. Colin must have been there. Listening. Zvie just didn't understand her conflict. She wasn't a rebellious teenager. She was more than a piece of the mission he wanted to succeed. She had to know if her transformation would lead her to a happier life. She was a success in so many areas, but was she a success as a woman?

And was she doomed if she found love, but it wasn't returned?

Her solitude wore on her. She needed to be around people, even if only as an observer. Kate showered and sifted through the clothes she had brought. She would find a place with gaiety, laughter, and life. She sighed. *If only Roman were here.*

Throngs of people crowded the sidewalks fronting the beach in Chloe's old neighborhood. Couples strolled the boardwalk. She valet parked, crossed to the beckoning lights, and scanned the menus posted outside restaurants, drawn to a club advertising a trio.

Kate listed for a table and ordered a glass of wine in the bar. Unobtrusively, with the help of a menu, she considered the men. She didn't see anyone she wanted to meet. *Damn Colin!* Her drink arrived as the hostess beckoned her to a table. She scanned the area nearest her and, again, didn't see anyone she wanted to encourage.

"Would you mind if this man shared your table?" The hostess gave her a bright smile. "The only vacancies we have seat four, and we hold those for larger parties. You appear to be alone?"

Kate looked up at the man standing beside her chair. Dressed in casual clothes, he wouldn't stand out in a crowd. Other than the obvious—not old, but not young—she couldn't read him, and Jayson had made her wary. His mouth quirked as she considered him.

"Do I pass?" He smiled, but his voice held an edge, as if insulted that she hadn't welcomed him.

"I… all right," Kate agreed. The hostess signaled a busboy, and he hurried over to lay another place setting. A waitress followed in his wake.

The hostess gave her another bright smile and left.

"I came to enjoy dinner and the entertainment, not *to be* the entertainment." She smiled to take the sting from her words. "Are you okay with that?"

"I hear the message. Am I allowed to talk until the act takes the stage?"

Smart Aleck. "What do you want to talk about?"

"Who are you? You're a pretty lady. Why are you here alone?"

"My name is Betty, and I'm here by myself because my guy is filming a television show out of the city." That should discourage him, and she felt justified using Colin.

"Television show! I'm impressed. Anybody I might recognize?"

"It's a weekly series, but he's more popular with women. Who are you? Why are you here by yourself?"

"My name is Don." He extended his hand. "I'm on a field trip for my company."

"Hello, Don. Why do I feel you rarely do this?" She gestured at the club scene and their table.

He leaned back in his chair. "I'm married. Is it branded on my forehead?"

"No, but if you're looking to hook up, you should sit at the bar. There are several unaccompanied women there."

"I'll remember that if I want to have an affair."

Too smooth. Kate wondered if he'd met women like this before.

He talked about his job and the company he worked for and that his wife stayed home with their two children while he traveled. "I have the requisite boring pictures," he said, as he extracted his wallet.

She took the photos he offered, made appropriate compliments.

Don bent her ear with stories of his kids and travel but with few mentions of his wife.

The waitress served Kate as the house lights dimmed for the show. She breathed a sigh of relief and ate, grateful that her dinner and the trio discouraged further conversation. She was nearly finished when the waitress brought Don's dinner.

"Would you like another drink?" he asked.

"No, but thank you. I'm driving."

At the intermission the waitress brought her check, and Don held out his hand. "Allow me. It's the least I can do for sharing your table and boring you with my stories."

"You don't have to do that," Kate protested.

"It would be my pleasure."

"Thank you. I hope your trip is a success." She pushed back her chair.

"Why don't you stay? The evening's young. We could find out if I can still dance, or there must be other entertainment in a touristy town like this. I haven't been clubbing in quite a while."

"Thank you, Don, but Colin expects me to call." *Does it count as a lie if you cross your fingers?* Don might have been open about his marriage and children, but she was sure he would cheat if given the chance. *Is he typical?* She fished her parking receipt from her purse before she stood and avoided contact with any appraising eyes as she waited for her car.

Chapter -29-

"Zvie? Ezra reporting."

"Kate…" Zvie pulled out a chair and sat. "Has there been another incident?"

"Although innocent, her brief encounter with Don disillusioned her. I fear she is more cynical about men and their fidelity now."

"Don?" Zvie wanted clarification.

"Kate dined out last night. There was a waiting list for tables at the establishment. The hostess at the restaurant asked her to share her table. I believe Don requested it, and money changed hands. Don is a married man with two small children. On the surface it was innocent until he invited her to go clubbing with him. Had she accepted, I'm certain I would have had to intervene."

"She must reconcile with her past soon or, as Archangel Rafael suggested, she must go back to the Academy. Keep me informed, Ezra."

Chapter -30-

Kate leaned against her car sipping coffee from a to-go cup, wavering between impatience and dread as she waited for the real estate agent. An occasional bird searched the overgrown yard for an overlooked morsel, then scolded from the empty bird feeder.

"Hi there. Have you been waiting long?" A well-groomed brunette said, flashing a practiced smile from the open door of her white sedan.

Kate straightened, joining the agent on the front sidewalk of Betty's house. "I didn't know how to judge the traffic, so I left early."

"I'm Sarita Gibson." The agent held out her hand.

"Kate Dunning."

Kate dismissed the agent's chatter as she led her to the front door. She tensed while Sarita worked the combination to the lockbox and extracted the key. Stale air and ghosts from Betty's past embraced Kate and drew her inside. Betty's suitcase, the one she'd packed for her trip to her sister's house, still stood by the front door like a watchman guarding the entry.

"The house has been closed for several weeks."

Ralph must have put the house up for sale soon after the accident.

"The owner is away. He's had an offer or two, but nothing he considered." Sarita turned on lights, chatting up the house features as they walked through.

Kate stepped back in time, almost able to touch Betty's unhappiness. The master bedroom and bath were just as Betty had left them. She opened the closet where Betty's clothes still hung, slid hangers along the rod, fingered fabrics and looked at labels, somber colors, conservative, serviceable styles. Kate wrinkled her nose.

Nothing to see but signs of wear in Chloe's empty bedroom. In the third bedroom, Betty had stacked boxes inside the closet. She had filled them for a potential move or to give to the Good Will store, undecided whether to stay or accept her second chance.

"What do you think?" Sarita asked. "It needs updating, but it's a good neighborhood, convenient to shopping and schools. Shall I write up an offer?"

"I'm not interested in buying," Kate said. "I told you in my phone message I want to rent for two weeks. I have… *commitments* and can't stay longer."

Sarita pursed her lips, consulted the listing for a few seconds, and named an inflated number.

Kate rolled her eyes. "Really? That's a little high."

"I won't be able to show the house while you're in it. A hotel room would be less costly, but you'll have more privacy here, almost like being home, and our weather—where did you say you were from?"

"Up north." Kate turned to the patio. She needed to be here to find her answers. She nodded, and Sarita produced a rental agreement. Kate skimmed it, discussed certain paragraphs with the agent before crossing out a word or phrase, initialed the changes and signed. Sarita entered a date and notation on her pda before adding her signature. Kate exchanged her check for the keys.

Sarita raised her eyebrows at the names on the check. "Betty Parker… Any relation to the owner?"

"Coincidence," Kate replied.

"Before the two weeks are up, I'll call you to arrange a time to inspect for damages." Sarita told Kate.

"You *will* let the owner know that I rented the house, won't you? I don't want to be bothered by an unexpected visit."

"No worries. Mr. Parker is on an extended cruise. I don't remember the details. His daughter took what she wanted months ago. She isn't in the area anymore." Sarita hesitated as though goodbye was awkward for her. "Well, enjoy your stay."

Kate switched lights on and off as she revisited the rooms, ending in the third bedroom. Spotting a CD, she read the title and put it in her purse, planning to listen to it in the car. She returned to the kitchen, searched the cupboards for a canister of coffee and washed the dirty coffeemaker before she brewed a cup. *Typical Ralph to use it and leave it.*

The house was silent like the television opposite Ralph's worn recliner, hushed as if holding its breath, hibernating, waiting for another family to bring it to life again. Shivers ran up her spine at the quiet. She opened the sliding glass door to the patio to let in fresh air. Betty's favorite wicker chair beckoned. She found a mug and took her coffee to the patio.

"Maggie, I'm home," she whispered in a quivering voice, but there was no response.

Kate swallowed with difficulty. *That was fanciful and foolish.* This house would be even lonelier without the dog. She finished her coffee, then drove to the hotel to check out.

"Zvie? I've rented Betty's house," she reported to his answering machine. "My phone is on if you have to reach me."

The next day, after a restive night at the house, Kate continued tracing Betty's life. She resurrected business clothes and drove the main north-south artery to Miami. Leaving her car in a parking garage, she walked to the downtown building where Betty had worked. After consulting the directory, she watched the lights flash above the elevator door as she rode to the forty-first floor. When the car stopped, she looked around the lobby — same black-and-white tile, dark paneled walls, same smell of old files memorializing conflicts.

Kate approached the receptionist and fabricated a name. "Is Mr. Watkins in?"

With a smile, the receptionist consulted her directory. "No one here by that name."

"I didn't think this office looked familiar," she said with what she hoped was a self-deprecating laugh. "Could I meet with the office manager? I'm Kate Dunning."

After a few minutes, a stocky, gray-haired woman strode through the glass doors.

"Kate Dunning? How do you do? I'm Barbara Paulson." Her smile did not cover her annoyance. "If you're a sales rep, you're wasting your time. Our principal office in St. Louis does all the purchasing."

"This isn't a sales call."

"What can I do for you?"

"Betty Parker is my friend. She's not returning my emails and last time I spoke with her, this is where she worked. I hoped you could help me contact her."

Ms. Paulson's eyes widened, and she gaped before stammering, "Betty hasn't worked here for months." She flopped into a chair. Kate sat across from her without an invitation.

"Oh? What happened? I thought Betty was happy here."

"The firm downsized and the attorney they paired her with took a position in another firm. We didn't have another opening."

"Hmm." She raised her eyebrows. "I've come a long way, and it's noon. Maybe a woman she worked with…?"

"I'm sorry to be the one to tell you, but Betty had a serious automobile accident. She didn't survive."

"Didn't survive?" She looked at the floor, furrowed her brow before speaking. "Betty had a husband and a daughter. Could you give me their contact information?"

"Our firm has a policy not to give out personal information."

"I hoped, considering the circumstances, you might relax your rules."

"I can't. I'm sorry that I had to tell you the sad news."

Kate stood and Ms. Paulson walked with her to the elevator. Kate experienced the same dreary atmosphere that had added to Betty's depression. She left the building and crossed the street to another office high-rise.

She took the elevator to the eighteenth floor and asked for Nancy Donald, Betty's attorney friend. After a few moments, a blonde woman in a conservative dress came out of the inner offices. Kate braced to meet her.

"Perhaps you could make an appointment for later this week?" Nancy paused with a professional smile. "I'm sorry, but I'm late for a luncheon date." Glancing at her watch, Nancy brushed past her. Unsure if Nancy had disappointed or offended her, Kate watched Betty's friend board the elevator. Nancy hadn't recognized her.

With slow steps Kate returned to her car, then to Betty's house. She changed and sat on the patio. Confused and depressed, she had reached another fork in the road. She must exorcise Betty or Kate. They could not coexist.

Chapter -31-

Kate missed the tantalizing aromas and fresh pastries from the neighborhood bakery near Zvie's apartment as she considered the meager contents of the refrigerator. After a boring breakfast, she adjourned to the patio with her coffee.

The backyard was empty, the play equipment gone. It had been time. Chloe had been out of that stage ages ago.

Watching the birds glide onto the back fence brought back memories. A green parakeet had landed at Ralph's feet. He had picked it up seconds before their dog reached it. Betty had driven to the pet store to buy a cage and bird food, slipping through the door as they were closing. The bird had walked on Chloe's back or pulled at her hair while she did homework. On mild days, they hung the birdcage on the patio. One day, Betty forgot to tie the cage door. Peep lifted it and flew away, vanishing from their lives as she had come. Days later, Betty still beat herself up for not securing the door. Chloe was sad but philosophical. She thought Peep had gone to find another little girl who needed her.

A lizard, a miniature dinosaur, performed push-ups on the screen. Several varieties populated South Florida and skittered or lazed along the fence rails in the sun or hid among the foliage. When challenged, an orange pouch in the lizard's throat would expand and contract like a small balloon. Chloe had called them "Lizzies." Before her bedtime she and Betty would search the vines on the fence for sleeping Lizzies so Chloe could touch one. This became a ritual until Chloe outgrew it.

Kate discovered Betty's neighborhood was growing younger. Uniformed school children passed the house carrying book bags, but the same self-appointed monitor of the neighborhood still lived next door.

Kate heard a child shriek and pushed open the screen door. Mrs. Watson's inquisitive stare compelled her to the fence.

"Did you buy the house?" Mrs. Watson blurted.

"No, I'll be leaving soon. Did you know the people who lived here?"

"I knew Betty on sight, talked to her a few times, but she was always in a hurry to get to her car or into the house. She had a job. I suppose she didn't have time to chat."

"Did you know her husband too?"

"Ralph? He wasn't here much. I seem to recall he worked out of town somewhere. I didn't see a "Sold" sign. I wondered if he'd gotten married again." Mrs. Watson's arch glance looked for a response.

"Oh? Did you expect that?"

"Let's say it wouldn't surprise me." The toddler in the yard diverted her attention. "My grandson," she nodded and smiled with pride. "I have to watch him like a hawk. He's a lively one."

"He's a good-looking boy." Kate edged away. "It's been nice talking to you."

She lost interest in the book she was reading and brought her computer to the kitchen. Distracted, she gave her project only a desultory effort before her attention drifted.

When Ralph and Betty and Chloe had moved here, the patio had been open. A pair of doves had built a nest in one of Betty's hanging plants. The plant hadn't survived the doves living there while they incubated the eggs. When the baby birds hatched, the plant swung violently when the parents fed the babies, alarming Betty.

"Damn, Betty, you're putting pillows on the patio floor?" Ralph groused, "They won't be worth two cents after the birds shit on them."

"But Ralph, the patio floor is so hard. It's only until they leave the nest so a baby won't get hurt if it falls."

After the birds flew away, Ralph screened the patio. Strange, she could remember that and yet she couldn't name the people in the photographs in that box at Zvie's apartment.

Chapter -32-

During that night, Kate woke, startled. *Was that a noise?* She froze. Holding her breath, she strained to listen. The hallway was dim, but the house had been dark when she went to bed. She fumbled for her phone and dialed 911, speaking to the dispatcher. Sliding to her feet, she stole down the hall to avoid being trapped in the bedroom. Kate heard laughter in the kitchen. Whoever was in the house didn't fear discovery. She peered around the corner. Ralph Parker lay in the recliner, a travel bag by his side.

"Ralph! What are you doing here?" Kate asked, walking over to confront him. He turned a startled face to her. *Oops! I shouldn't have said that.*

"Who the hell are you?" he demanded, jumping to his feet. "And how did you know my name?"

Ralph looked older and tired.

"I'm Kate Dunning."

"Why are you here in my house?" He glared at her from his superior height, then leered as he came toward her. "Did Walt put you up to this?"

"I don't know Walt. Is he in the habit of providing surprises in the form of women to you?"

"Walt likes to play tricks. He knows I— It's none of your damn business what my friends do. Answer me. Why are you here?"

"Your realtor rented this house to me for two weeks."

"She *what*?"

"Your realtor assured me no one would disturb me. Obviously, she was wrong. I paid an outrageous sum, I might add."

A knock at the door interrupted them. When Ralph opened the door, a policeman focused on Ralph, his mag light gripped in his hand. Strobe lights from his squad car whirled and lit the front of the house.

"Somebody called in an intruder at this address," he said.

"Yeah, the *intruder* is standing over there." Ralph pointed at Kate.

"Officer, I made the call. I was asleep in the bedroom when lights from the kitchen and sound from the television woke me. When I investigated, *he*," she pointed, "was sitting over there watching TV. I have a rental agreement that gives me exclusive occupancy and a receipt for the rental fee."

"Hold it." With a weary sigh, the patrolman raised his hand when they yammered. "Let's see some identification."

Ralph got his wallet from the kitchen drawer. After asking permission, Kate walked to the bedroom for her driver's license, her copy of the rental agreement, and the realtor's card. She pulled on sweatpants before she returned. The policeman studied their documents and called the station while Kate and Ralph continued to grumble accusations.

"Look, the night is almost over," Kate volunteered when the officer turned back to them. "I can move out in the morning *if* he'll refund the rest of my rental. I'll go to a hotel and *he*," again she pointed at Ralph, "can take it up with his real estate agent."

"What do you say, Mr. Parker? Sounds reasonable. I can see this… uh incident escalating, not to mention becoming expensive and complicated, if either of you press charges. The court docket is full. It could take weeks before a hearing to sort this out." The officer looked at Ralph, then at Kate with a stern, no-nonsense demeanor. "Or, I can run you both to the station. You can call your lawyers and let them work it out." His communicator squawked, and he reached for it with impatience. Kate heard the dispatcher report more urgent matters requiring his attention.

"All right, all right," Ralph agreed. "I came back earlier than I intended."

Kate rolled her eyes and huffed. He glared at her but didn't comment. "I'd like your card, Officer, in case there's a problem."

After the officer left, sleep was out of the question. Kate made a pot of coffee and took a cup to the patio. After a few minutes, Ralph joined her.

"Betty and her mutt spent a lot of time out here," he said.

"I know. She wrote about her observations from the patio. It was her favorite place."

"Chloe and me… we didn't know about you. Betty never mentioned you. It was weird she had a secret friend. How *did* you two know each other?"

"We worked together a long time ago. Wait a minute! What are you asking? You and Betty lived together. Surely you knew her."

"I *thought* I did. Still, it's damned odd she never mentioned you."

"Not so strange. Didn't you work and live out of town for several years? Betty said you lived separate lives."

"I guess we did."

"I wondered about your marriage. Were you in love with her?"

"I thought a lot about us after the accident." He stroked his bristled chin. "Yeah, I was crazy about her when we got married, but she changed."

If you only knew how much, Kate thought.

"Betty wanted to be perfect, like June Cleaver—super clean house, laundry just so, bills paid before they were due. She got in a snit if I was a few minutes late for dinner. We weren't married very long before I wondered if she was making her grocery list while we did it. After Chloe was born, she didn't have time for me. She forgot how to have fun."

"Could you have helped her have free time?"

"Listen. Betty enjoyed being a martyr. She had to do everything herself. Nobody could do it good enough to suit her. Betty's savings didn't surprise me. She was so into the future that she didn't have time to live in the present."

Ralph heard Kate's indignant huff. "Yeah, I could have helped more; I know that now. I wish…"

Ralph sagged, blinking his eyes, and looked away from Kate. "Maybe if she'd talked to me, our life could have been better, but Betty never let on how she felt. We became two strangers with nothing in common but Chloe."

Kate had to admit there was truth in Ralph's words and she felt sad for Betty. Ralph wasn't the monster Betty had imagined. If they had only talked to each other.

The sense of responsibility and thrift drilled into Betty in her childhood had followed her into adulthood. The work ethic was so strong that she had felt guilty when she enjoyed herself. Betty had been working toward retirement, for the future, and then, ironically, she didn't have one. If only she could warn Chloe not to make the same mistake.

Let it go, Kate.

She jerked at *Zvie's* reprimand.

Ralph rambled about Betty, Chloe and his plans, happy to have someone to talk to. Kate listened with half an ear. He wouldn't have any problem finding someone to share his life again if he wanted--if he didn't talk the woman to death first. Attractive widowers were always in demand. The night turned into predawn, and Kate yawned.

"If you'll excuse me, I'll go dress. I have a few things to gather up, and I'll load the car. I've been here for ten days and I paid for two weeks. How do you want to handle the refund?" Kate doubted she could have stayed in the house the rest of the rental term even without Ralph's unexpected appearance. The house and its memories depressed her. That was why she had spent so much time on the patio, and she suspected it had been Betty's reason too.

"I'm curious, Ralph. When you saw the rental car in the driveway, didn't you question that someone might be inside?"

"I've been traveling for almost twenty-four hours straight to get home. I didn't even *see* the car in the drive until the cop knocked on the door."

Ralph handed her a check. Kate glanced at it and stuffed it into her bag. She walked out to the patio, took a quick look around and said a silent goodbye. *I'll do my best to make your second chance worthwhile, and I'll do my best by Chloe if she ever needs you.*

Kate did a quick walk-through to make sure she had everything. Ralph carried her bags to the car.

"Goodbye, Ralph." Kate held out her hand. "It was… interesting." She slid under the wheel, turned the key, and backed out of the drive.

Chapter -33-

Kate left Betty's neighborhood and checked into a hotel on Biscayne Boulevard. Betty's memories still troubled her, even after a shower, room service, and a nap.

Haven't you wallowed in Betty's emotional wreckage long enough, Kate? a voice chastised her.

Zvie, Kate acknowledged, dabbing at her eyes.

Chloe gave Betty's life purpose but Chloe matured and sought her own life. She couldn't fill Betty's need forever.

"I know, but—"

Forgive the insecure, lonely little girl who wanted to belong, to find love.

Kate acknowledged Betty's childhood and her quest for approval had made her too diligent, too serious.

Yes, Ralph seemed indifferent. Yes, her first husband was immature and cruel, but Betty needed so much from her friends and lovers she stifled their affection before it could ripen into love.

Kate realized Betty had tried to ease her loneliness with outgoing friendly types; it had governed her choices in the men she married. Ralph's attractive looks and amiable manner drew her to him, although she came to resent him.

Early in their marriage Betty refused his invitations to enjoy leisure with him, instead taking care of chores and duties. Her festering resentment chilled their relationship until Ralph became indifferent. With her realization, Kate could leave Betty's failed marriages in the past where they belonged. She also understood why a second chance appealed to Betty.

Betty's house and its associations enforced your negative view of Betty's second chance, an event that isn't going well at the moment. I cautioned you that memories must not interfere with your recent life. Learn from Betty's mistakes, Kate. Cherish her memories of Chloe but don't let them diminish the gift granted her. Chloe is a casualty of Betty's plea for love. You may always regret her loss, but you must believe James will care for her.

"Zvie, saying goodbye hurts so much." Muffled sobs followed her words.

*****

Kate filled her days so she would not revisit Betty's memories—yoga classes, the hotel's workout facilities, performing each exercise station at a local park. She borrowed books and DVDs from the hotel library to fill her evenings.

Sporting events on the multiple television screens of a local restaurant made eating alone comfortable. The local sports enthusiasts paid her scant attention as they rode bar stools and followed their favorite teams.

With a lighter spirit at last, Kate scheduled a day at the spa to revive and relax.

"Zvie? It's Kate," she said with confidence, phoning him.

"Kate! You sound… different."

"I'm good. Um, Zvie? I talked with Ralph."

"Kate, you didn't—"

"I didn't break the rules. It was by accident." She touched on their conversation. Meeting Betty's husband had helped her see Betty in a fresh light.

Just as she had at the Second Chance Academy, Betty's persona was fading while Kate grew stronger. She was ready to deal with Colin.

Chapter -34-

"Hello?"

"Colin? It's Kate. Zvie said you wanted me to call?"

"Kate! I was about to accept you'd never talk to me again. Are you in town?"

"No, I'm in Florida. The sun is shining. I'm going for a swim in the pool and a walk on the beach. Eat your heart out in the frozen north."

He chuckled. "I've missed you, Kate. I'd like to see you. Would you like company?"

"You're not working? Zvie said something about the show."

"They've written me out of *Lost in Lust*—at my request. I don't want to talk about the show or Zvie. Did you hear me? I miss you. What would you say to my coming there?"

"Dare I read between the lines? Do you miss my scintillating conversation, or are you tired of winter?"

"You have a way with words, but I want to talk about us. And I don't want it to be over a cell phone."

"*Us*! I didn't think you and me were *us*. You've never shown I was anything but a companion or a diversion."

"I screwed up, all right? Give me a chance to get it right."

"I don't know…"

"Give me a break. You only *think* you know what happened."

"I suppose I owe you that much. Zvie mentioned you and he had a long talk. I'm guessing he told you his secret?"

"We should talk about that too. How about getting together, just you and me, without Zvie?"

"Only if it's without Sam."

"Deal. I'll call you with my itinerary. Is that all right?"

"I… Yes, I'll wait for your call."

*****

Kate was antsy. Colin would arrive that afternoon. She went for a walk on the beach, but it didn't soothe her. Returning to her room, she considered her limited wardrobe. She called the concierge to arrange a ride to the airport. She didn't want to appear too eager, but she didn't want to miss Colin.

At the airport, Kate scanned the overhead monitors displaying arrivals and departures. She bought coffee and chose a bench where she could see the barrier separating the incoming passengers from the terminal hub.

The caption on a discarded magazine captured her attention—*How to Date with Success*. She turned to the article and scanned the headings: Take Your Time, Life Is Stressful, Please Yourself, Date with a Future.

After a multi-year study and follow-up interviews, the results of a university study recommended dating for at least two years before marriage to improve the chance of success. Kate uttered an unladylike snort. *If I follow that advice, I'll be one of Colin's memories.* The article further suggested couples spend time together until they knew each other. *Well duh!* The writer discouraged passionate encounters because they cloud reason. *No sex. Where did he find couples to date that long without intimacy?*

Confront character flaws or unwelcome traits; don't sweep them under the rug. That seemed too simple, but it had been a major factor in the failure of Betty and Ralph's marriage.

Please Yourself. Kate nodded. *Zvie says the Committee destined Colin and me to be together, but is he my only choice? What about that old free will card Zvie draws out of his magic deck?*

Kate glanced at the monitors. Colin's flight number blinked; the plane had landed. She lay aside the magazine and walked toward the barrier. She spotted Colin weaving through the first passengers ambling down the concourse. Her heart beat faster as he came nearer. He seemed thinner and tired since she'd last seen him. Unsmiling, he searched the people gathered at the gate.

Kate waved as she stepped forward. "Colin! Over here."

Two women pointed as he changed course, dropping his carry-on bag by her feet. "You're here. I thought you'd change your mind. I spent the entire flight wondering if you'd show." He reached out.

"I'm here," she confirmed and walked into his embrace. They stood with arms around each other. Kate sighed. This was where she wanted to be, if only she could trust him. A stream of passengers heading for baggage claim and exits jostled them.

"I should have a car waiting." He located a stocky, dark-haired man in a short-sleeve guayabera holding a sign for O'Brien. "There."

After claiming Colin's luggage, Kate gave the driver the name and address of the hotel.

"It always amazes me the weather is so different between cities," Colin said. The tropical sun shone in a movie-set blue sky. Palm trees, white and pastel buildings contrasted with the gray cityscape he had left that morning.

"You look thinner, Colin."

"I was about to say the same to you, Kate."

"This has been a tough trip for me, although yesterday was pleasant. What have you been doing?"

Colin elaborated on the script changes that had allowed him to leave the show. "Sam argued against it. He said once I'm out of sight, the producers, directors, and casting people will forget me. According to him, I can kiss my career goodbye."

"Sam blames me, doesn't he?" Kate said.

"You're not one of his personal favorites, but I've moved down the list too. Sam and I have parted ways, Kate. He no longer represents me. Zvie is contacting people he knows on the West Coast, and he'll put me in touch with them. If I have to do guest appearances or another series, I will, but I hope to move in a different direction. So, as of last week, I'm unemployed."

"I moved into a suite. I hope that wasn't presumptuous?" She watched to see his reaction. "It seemed like the thing to do if we need a serious talk to resolve *us*."

"Good idea." He yawned. "Sorry.

Their route left the airport expressway, wound through the city streets skirting the Bay, then to the curved drive of the hotel. Colin signed the ticket for the driver while the bellhop managed his luggage.

They were silent as the elevator rose. When the door of the suite closed behind them, Kate crossed to the windows and opened the drapes. She was unsure how to act or what to say now that they were alone. She watched the traffic below, anxious about telling of her experiences, wondering how Colin would react.

"I didn't believe Zvie when he said you left," Colin said. "When I realized he was serious, I thought you went with Roman. It hit me like a brick. I thought I blew my chance."

"Roman taught me to dance." She turned to him. "We're friends."

"It looked like a lot more than that. Our… night together spooked me. I needed space to think. You know my history. I don't want to make another mistake, but I don't want you out of my life."

"In my mind, we were more than friends." Kate gave a curt laugh. "When I saw you and Kitti—"

"That was a setup," Colin interrupted. "Sam talked me into taking her to dinner, acting a part. I sugarcoated it that night you lectured me. You made me so mad I walked around most of the night. When I thought over what you said, I had to admit you made sense."

"I shouldn't have come on so strong. The whispers, amused looks I got, and Sam's smug face embarrassed me." She hesitated before whispering, "Seeing you with *her* hurt me."

"I'm sorry. I wish I could rub it out like it never happened. You made me realize Sam has done nothing for my career in a long time. When he looked at me, he saw dollar signs. He wanted me to stay in the show until the network canceled it."

Kate held her tongue. She'd said it all that disastrous night.

"Zvie told me you have things to work out. I don't want to add to your problems." He hesitated. "I think I'm in love with you, Kate. I came to find out if this is real, to see if you feel anything for me."

"I haven't separated *you* from Colin O'Brien, the actor. Your fans have seen as much or more of you than I have. Hundreds of women have seen you pretending to have sex on their TV screens." She paced, coming ever nearer to him, drawn like a magnet to iron. "You must think I'm a prude, but I haven't come to terms with that. When we're out together, I've seen a woman beckon you with her eyes like I'm invisible, and I wonder if it will go further… if it already has."

"I'm not a player, Kate, despite the publicity. When I'm working, I follow the script, then I walk away. I don't have casual sex with my co-stars. My body is a tool of my profession."

"Have you used that tool so often that your feelings are the same on and off the set?"

"Kate! When we made love, I wasn't pretending."

"It's my problem, Colin. I have to resolve it. I'm trying, but I'm not there yet."

"It's funny. I was more nervous taking my clothes off in front of you than on the set." He uttered a self-deprecating laugh. "Those *other* people are significant only because they affect my career and my bank account."

She framed his face with her hands, searched his eyes. "I don't want to make a mistake either. Let's not make any promises or commitments. Let's get to know each other in the next few days and see what happens."

"Define getting to know each other."

"If we *like* each other after we're alone together, that will be a plus. If we're still *attracted* after being with each other twenty-four/seven, that's another positive. If you have any annoying habits—monopolize the bathroom, if you're a neat freak or a slob, if you snore, talk incessantly, for example—those things are meaningful over a lifetime. And they should concern you too."

"I'll hire a maid. Tell me what you can't stand, Kate."

"I'm serious, Colin. The brochures in the lobby advertise a lot to see and do. I'm sure we'll be able to find *something* to occupy our time besides deciding if we want to be roommates," she teased. "Let's discover if this place is all neon and flash or a romantic getaway."

When their eyes met, Kate felt the warm pull of attraction. She still wanted him.

"I've missed you a lot, Kate. I want us to spend time alone."

"Come sit down." She crossed to the sofa and patted the cushions.

He sank down with a sigh, closed his eyes, and reached for her hand. "I can't remember ever being this tired."

"Zvie's revelations are exhausting. There was a woman who lived close by. She's a crucial part of me."

"How is she important to us?"

"My second chance began with her. I'm not sure how it happened. What I'm trying to say is Kate Dunning came to exist from Betty's second chance. Betty Parker—that's her name—met Zvie, confessed she wanted a second chance, and Zvie took control. That's when he entered my life. He supervised Betty's transformation into Kate Dunning." She pointed to herself. "That's the closest to an explanation I've found. This woman didn't know how her second chance would play out or I doubt she'd have taken it." Saying the words aloud clarified her thoughts. Betty *hadn't* known what she would give up.

"That day in the park," Kate said, "I recognized Chloe and the dog."

"I knew something upset you, although you tried to hide it."

"She's Betty's daughter. Maggie was Betty's dog. Maggie knew me. I have intuitive thoughts and feelings I can't explain. Is that creepy?" She shifted the conversation. "Did Zvie disclose his identity?"

"Yeah, I accused him of putting me on."

"I can relate." She searched his eyes. "Do you believe him?"

"Maybe... I suspected you and Zvie of staging a con to get back at me—your absence, his claim—but Zvie swore it's true. It's weird he knows so much about me, things known only to me. I asked him why he chose me for special attention."

"I'd like to know too. Betty gave up her daughter, her identity, and her life. What did you sacrifice?" her voice hard, accusing.

"Are you angry, Kate?"

"Not angry, but it seems unfair." She conceded Betty had not wanted another thirty years of her static life with Ralph, but if she had been assertive, stronger, she would have Chloe. *Did Colin deserve a reward without sacrifice, with no pain?*

"Zvie said a Committee listens to appeals and, with the Archangel, decides which ones to grant. Take it up with him or them." Colin frowned and sat up. "I saw myself demanding proof that love exists. There wasn't anybody else around. It blows my mind how he came by that. He showed me as a kid too. I'd like to know how he got *those* images. And the way he projected them is unbelievable. I thought I'd seen the latest in projection equipment."

"I met Roman at the celestial Academy-slash-finishing school. He's an instructor there. I went in as Betty Parker and came out as Kate Dunning. Sometimes I feel like I'm half one person and half another. Zvie told me Betty's memories will fade. Thinking about my life, this complete experience…" Her voice faded.

Colin yawned. Head resting on the sofa back again, he encouraged her, "Go on."

"I'm tired… tired of trying to understand. When I ask Zvie to explain, he tells me there are things I have to take on faith. I think the only way I can live with what happened is to do that—just accept it. If you see the report of Betty's accident, no one could survive without celestial intervention."

"Zvie told me you're linked to somebody else."

"I know. That intuition thing again."

"You know? Who is it?"

"I can't tell you. Zvie says I have to trust we'll find each other before it's too late."

His quizzical expression urged her to reply to his unspoken question.

"My future is tenuous if Zvie's mission doesn't succeed within a time limit."

They rehashed their disclosures in silence. Colin appeared to take Kate's explanations in stride. The make-believe world he inhabited made acceptance easier than if he'd had another career.

"Let's go for a walk," Kate said. "I've had enough of Betty Parker, Kate, and Zvie. Do you want to change into something less likely to identify you as Colin O'Brien? When we get back, we can order room service, watch a movie, or… would you rather go out?"

"No, it sounds like a plan. Do you suppose we could work in some snuggling, maybe even get naked?" He leered and wagged his eyebrows.

"Go change," she ordered, but she smiled.

They walked hand in hand. A soft breeze carried the tang of Biscayne Bay. The sun was setting the water on fire when they returned to the hotel. Colin fixed drinks from the mini bar. Kate read the blurb following titles of the movie selections. They ordered a romantic comedy. Somehow an action flick or a thriller had not seemed right for their reunion.

Colin pushed the food cart into the hall; Kate brought pillows from the nearest bedroom. "We may as well watch the movie in comfort." She piled pillows on the sofa and coffee table, then opened the doors of the armoire to reveal the television.

"I'm disappointed the hotel doesn't carry the nostalgia channel. We could have watched an old musical." She hid her grin at his groan. "Here, you're in charge of the remote."

"It must be love if you're giving up control of the remote," he said.

They relaxed while the cast in the movie scrolled. The plot was predictable, and the dialogue tired. Midway into the movie, Colin's breathing slowed and deepened. Kate realized she was watching alone. She took the remote, lowered the volume, and fast forwarded through the film. When the movie was over, she covered Colin with a light blanket and dimmed the lights.

Kate walked to the bedroom she'd claimed, followed her nightly ritual, and slipped into bed. She considered the irony in her last waking moments: one of television's sexiest actors was sharing her suite, and she was in bed alone.

During the night Kate surfaced, aware of Colin's arm draped across her hip. She sighed and went back to sleep.

A weak sunlight was creeping through the draperies when Colin stirred. He swept her hair aside, kissed her neck, and cradled her breast.

"Good morning, Kate," he whispered. "This is the way I wanted to wake up the morning after we made love, but you weren't in my bed."

"Would it have made a difference?" She turned to face him.

"I can only guess." He nuzzled her ear and pulled her closer." I enjoy waking up next to you."

"Hmm." Kate inched back. "You attracted me from the day we first met. I didn't hide it. That was a mistake."

"But?" he questioned.

"Remember our discussion yesterday? I want us to get to know each other. Sex will only complicate our feelings. We have enough shadows to clear. I want a monogamous, forever kind of guy—no one-night stands, no competing with the flavor of the month, no trying each other on to see if we fit. If you're not interested in that, we should say goodbye."

Colin sat up, adjusted the pillow behind him. "Did you think I came down here for sex?"

"You didn't say *what* you expect from me."

"I said I wanted to discuss *us*, find out what we mean to each other. I still want that. I can be patient, but it doesn't rule out touching and kissing."

She smoothed his frown, then kissed him. "I'll shower and dress. Why don't you order coffee and something to go with it?"

Kate came out of the bathroom and packed her belongings while Colin showered and dressed.

"I have a rental car," Kate said. "The valet parked it in front. It should make our sightseeing thingy easier. All right?"

"I definitely think we should do the tourist *thingy*." Colin smiled, recovering his good humor. "Do you have a destination in mind?"

"Let's start with where Zvie came into Betty's life. After that, we'll take it day by day."

Chapter -35-

Zvie reviewed the progress of his mission with mixed emotions. He had not thought being a project angel could be a disadvantage. He would miss Kate's companionship, the restaurants, and the parties. He enjoyed working in the entertainment industry. The respect and admiration accorded him when he provided solutions pleased him. He doubted there would ever be another mission as interesting as Kate and Colin. This project would be a glowing addition to his chronicle of successes. He braced for his report.

"Ah, Angel Second Chance. So good of you to come. I understand Kate is more tractable after her recent escapades. Does she appreciate that you requested a backup angel to watch over her?"

"I haven't discussed Ezra with her. There was to be no contact with her former life, but it may have served the greater purpose."

"On another note, how did Colin react to your revelations?"

"Better than I expected. In his profession, illusions are common. I showed him images to reinforce my claim. He searched for a hidden projector. Eventually he'll realize that a projector alone could not have produced the images I showed him."

"What are your plans?"

"I believe Kate has resolved her identity struggle. Colin has joined her in Florida. I will continue to monitor their activities… discreetly. If they need a nudge, I'll provide it. I expect they will reach an understanding."

"Excellent. I will look for an appropriate assignment for you. It seems you will be available soon."

"I still have one segment of the project to accomplish, Archangel."

The Archangel rolled his eyes. "And that is?"

"The redirection of Colin's career," Zvie reminded his superior. "I must get Colin an audition for a role that will change the focus of his career, the last piece of the project."

"How long will that take?"

"I should know soon. I hope Kate and Colin commit before the audition takes place. If Colin goes to California alone, it could be disastrous. Sam Lewin surrendered too easily, considering Colin's importance to him. I don't think we've seen the last of him."

"The project is so close to fruition. Take care that nothing ruinous happens. We are relying on you."

Chapter -36-

Colin and Kate drove north along the beach road until they reached the suburb where Betty had lived. With Kate's guidance, they wound their way through the neighborhood. Realty sign still in place in the yard, empty driveway and drawn shades—the house was lifeless and forlorn. Mrs. Watson, ever vigilant, sat on her porch, and Kate wondered, not for the first time, how the woman ever got any chores done. *Was there a Mr. Watson?* She didn't know.

They resumed their drive to the beach where Betty had taken yoga classes and lunched at a beachfront restaurant. Then Kate directed Colin to the hotel where Zvie had stayed and she had cried out her pain. After registering, they spent the afternoon swimming and sunbathing. When their thoughts turned to dinner, Kate looked for the restaurant where she had met Don.

"That leaves several hours before our reservation. Whatever should we do?" Colin drew her close. "You smell like sunblock."

"You say the sweetest things. Your cologne has a similar scent…. We could surf the TV channels for reruns of *Lovers and Liars*," she suggested.

"Oh Lord, no! I don't want to see how young and green I was, or the screwups captured on film."

"I thought it was better than *Lost in Lust*. I used to think that show survived only because the fans were voyeurs who got off on buff bodies."

"Buff, huh?" He ignored her critical review and struck a pose. She ran her fingertips down his arm.

"Oh, baby, such wonderful muscles." She fluttered her eyelashes.

Colin laughed, but lost his teasing air. "Kate—."

"I know. Let's go shopping. I'm sick of the clothes I brought with me."

Colin sighed his disappointment.

They followed the signs to the mall. Kate splurged on a dress, too-dear-to-pass-up casual clothes, and accessories. Colin drew stares and whispers behind shielded lips. One woman gave Kate a pointed once-over, reminding her he was a celebrity while she was a nobody. Several faces popped up too often for a coincidence. When they returned to the car, she remarked on it.

"At that last store, I saw the same man too many times before for it to be chance. Did you notice him? Short, dark, thin mustache, flamboyant shirt and white pants?"

"I wasn't paying a lot of attention to anyone."

"He almost brushed against me when we were looking in the jeweler's window."

"That guy? I thought he might try to snatch your purse."

"That didn't occur to me. I think we'll see him again," she said with feeling.

They changed, drove to the restaurant, and left the car with a valet. Colin spoke to the greeter, autographed a menu, and she guided them to their table. They were enjoying appetizers when Kate felt someone brush her shoulder.

"Betty? It is you, isn't it?"

She looked at his hand, then to the man by their table.

"Hello, Don. Still here, or back again?"

"Still here. The project is taking on a life of its own." He turned to Colin.

"Don, meet Colin," Kate said. "Colin, Don and I shared a table last time I was here. He's on company business."

Colin pushed back his chair and straightened his six-foot two-inch frame. The two men took each other's measure. Don's eyes widened. Colin's grip was firmer than necessary as they shook hands.

"Television, isn't it?" Don remarked. "I think that's what Betty told me."

"That's right."

Recognizing the need to steer the conversation, Kate said, "It must be hard on your wife for you to be away for such an extended period."

"She's used to it." Don said.

"Well, it was… interesting meeting you, Dan." Colin sat and replaced his napkin.

"Don… my name is Don," he corrected.

"Dan, Don… you'll excuse us? Two's company and…" Colin waved his hand. The incomplete adage hung in the air between them.

Don flushed; Kate's lips twitched.

"Sorry. Didn't mean to intrude. I hope I see you again, Betty." He walked away.

"You weren't very polite," Kate observed.

"He wanted to join us, and I damn well would not invite him.… An admirer?"

"I told you. We shared a table. He showed me pictures of his kids, told me about his job, and bought dinner."

"Kate, wife and kids or not, he wanted to get you in bed. You know it too."

"Well, it didn't happen. But, if it had, I wouldn't have been betraying anyone, would I?" she challenged.

"Only his wife and kids." Colin lifted his hands in surrender. "Let's leave it. Would you like to dance?" He held out his hand. Holding her close, he scanned the club as they moved on the dance floor, but he didn't see Don. When the number ended, they returned to their table as the waitress brought their entrees.

"Good choice, Kate. Enjoyable place, decent entertainment," Colin said. "Have you thought what you want to do tomorrow?" He leaned back in his chair. The man in the shopping mall stood by the bar—no longer coincidence.

"Continue sightseeing? This pace must agree with you. You look younger than when you arrived, and you're less tense."

"I could lose all of my tension if you'd encourage me."

"Patience, Colin. 'All things come round to him who will but wait'."

"Another cliché, Kate?"

"Longfellow. Remember my penchant with words?"

"I remember. My college lit wasn't very interesting. I prefer action and mysteries. Do you want an after-dinner drink? Or dessert?"

"No, I'll have coffee. And you? Are you going to splurge on something decadent?"

"I have to watch my figure so I can work a while longer." He wagged his eyebrows, and Kate flushed at the remembered conversation.

"Coffee," he confirmed to the waitress. "Let's drive along the beach before we head back."

Colin glanced in the rearview mirror as he drove. When they were at the hotel, he told Kate the man from the shopping mall was at the restaurant.

"That restaurant is a popular place. He might be a fan, or paparazzi, but I didn't see a camera. What other reason could there be?" She yawned. "I'm sorry. I've been so stressed the last few weeks that it's catching up with me."

"That's okay. I'll check email and browse the internet. Kiss me goodnight. You'll be asleep by the time I turn in."

The next day they discovered a secluded beach and unique shops. They stayed at a cozy bed-and-breakfast. Colin's unshaven, scruffy appearance was an effective disguise, or the residents were too polite to acknowledge him.

"What's on the agenda?" He glanced at the road map.

"There's a seafood festival in a coastal town… there." Kate pointed to a bold-faced name. "I thought we would wend our way there and check it out. Okay with you?"

"'Wend our way'?" he gibed with a grin that increased her heart rate. "Anything you want is okay with me. You're the tour guide."

Chapter -37-

Signs advertising the event greeted them miles from the site. They parked where attendants directed and walked to the festival grounds. Several of the city's restaurants sponsored tents where they served their specialties. Booths displaying artwork and handicrafts lined their path as they made their way to the midway of a small carnival.

"Look, Colin," Kate pointed to a sign. "A fortune teller!"

"Surely you don't believe in that bunkum."

"Hey, who am I to scoff at anything after my experiences. Let's go in. You can be first." She pulled him into the tent.

Kate inhaled, recognizing the scent of patchouli even before she saw a thin line of smoke curling in the air from the incense sticks. The darkened tent and her voluminous robe nearly hid the woman seated at the table. Her black hair was sprinkled with gray and wiry strands escaped the careless bun she'd fashioned. Her weathered skin made her look ancient, but her eyes were sharp and clear. She appraised them before motioning to the two chairs in front of her table.

"So, you want me to tell your future. Everybody wants to know until I tell them what I see. You are sure you want to know?"

Kate nodded. Her excitement was tangible. Pointing at Colin, she said, "He'll go first."

"Clear your mind, relax." She took Colin's hands in hers and looked at his palms, then turned them over to rest on the table. The old woman closed her eyes, brushing the back of his hands with her fingertips.

"You have been lonely. This is a fateful time for you. A woman from your past wants back in your life. She will bring trouble. A wicked man will try to come between you and your woman. He is not your friend. You will move from the gray city to one that sparkles in the sun, a city of illusions and temptations. Be careful you do not lose yourself there. You are struggling with uncertainty. Happiness, success, fortune—everything depends on the answer. Do not wait too long, or she will go away… forever. She is the one. Love is a gift."

She opened her eyes, inclined her head. "To be chosen is a great honor. Trust the angel. You understand?" She stared into his eyes.

Colin sat back, startled.

"Now you, lady." Kate extended her hands. The fortuneteller closed her eyes. "You have come through a great change, loss, and heartache to a life of discovery. One who loves you accepts it can never be. He will leave you. Another holds your life…" The fortuneteller's eyes flew open. She passed her hand across her face. "I will not speak of this."

The warmth of the day and the fun of the reading dissipated. Kate's hands trembled; she felt lightheaded, nauseous.

The old woman gave her a pitying look and continued. "You question if he's the only one. You want to trust, but he hurt you, disappointed you. Your fears are genuine, but he loves you. You will leave the gray city." The fortuneteller shrugged. "The road forks, but the choice is not yours. It depends on the other. You will have success."

"Celestial powers have chosen you too, but you paid a great price." She patted Kate's hand and slumped, exhaustion in the slope of her shoulders and her half-closed eyes. "Trust the angel. Believe. He will take care of you."

Kate stared at the table. Colin paid the fortuneteller, and thanked her.

When Kate didn't stand, he touched her. "Kate?"

She flinched and stood. Colin led her from the tent.

She squinted in the sun. "How did she know about the angel?" Kate said. "She saw something troubling in my future she didn't want to tell me." Kate shivered, and Colin draped his arm across her shoulders."

"Kate, you listened to the ramblings of an old woman. She knows nothing for sure. Relax. It was that hocus-pocus atmosphere in there. Look around you. *This* is real."

They retraced their steps in silence. Then, Colin said, "Zvie's trying to arrange an audition for me in California, that's the land of *shine*. I'd like to believe she's tuned in to the future.... I don't get the bit of being careful not to lose myself. How can you get lost with a GPS? If you accept her *rambling*, the trouble man is—"

"Sam," Kate finished. "He dislikes me. He'll turn up again soon."

"Let's get out of here," Colin suggested. "This is too weird."

*****

"Let's go to the dance, Colin." Kate pointed at a placard advertising a Dance at the Young at Heart Club in front of the refreshment tent—Relive the Music of the Forties by the Kenny James Orchestra. "That was the era of big bands and wonderful dance music. We may be the youngest ones there, but we can people watch. Let's find a motel and get directions to the club."

In their room, Kate curled on the bed, her arm across her eyes. The fortune-teller had unnerved her. *Should I believe her or is she a fake? Am I running out of time? How long, Zvie?* The bed dipped as Colin sat down.

"Are you all right, Kate?" He moved her arm away from her eyes and studied her.

"I'm all right. Thank you for asking." She rose to walk away, but Colin drew her down onto his lap.

"We don't have to go to this dance if you're not up to it. We can have a quiet evening. I'll pick up something for dinner, and we'll stay in."

"I think I need noise and people tonight."

"Okay. If you want to go to this dance, we should get ready."

Kate wore the dress she bought at the mall on their shopping expedition.

"Very nice," Colin said.

"And you, sir." She smoothed the collar of the white silk shirt he wore with cocoa brown linen pants, a beige herringbone sports coat draped over his arm.

"I jotted down the directions. You be the navigator and watch the street signs."

Colin turned into the lot beside the Town Hall, shrugged into his jacket, and they followed the stream of couples to the door. He paid their admission, answering questions about how they had heard of the event.

Women entering the hall ranged from platinum blondes with wrinkled cheeks or faces planed by surgery; faded beauties with gray hair; and women with pink-tinted coiffures who refused to accept aging. They varied in shapes and sizes, dressed in sequins, crepe, and silk. Their partners wore white or light blue shirts and business suits. They were balding, sans hair or turning gray or white, paunchy from a comfortable lifestyle or lean and spare. Some men, like the women with titian hair, were handsome, aging versions of their youth. Unlike most of their contemporaries, they wore dinner jackets or evening wear. All enjoyed the music of their glory days.

Kate and Colin danced the first set, then sat with drinks, munching on peanuts provided at their table, and watched the couples on the dance floor when the orchestra began again. Adventurous pairs performed a sedate version of the foxtrot and jitterbug cadences of their youth. One of the more dashing men approached, first asking Colin if he could borrow Kate for the dance, then turned to her. She hesitated.

"I thought we would sit this one out." She looked to Colin for confirmation."

"Oh, go on," he teased. "I know how you love to dance. When the music slows enough for me, I'll squire someone around the floor, if their dates are willing, and then we'll meet up again."

Kate followed her new partner onto the floor. He pumped her hand to the band's beat and spun her out and back again, surprising her. Kate imagined he'd been popular in his heyday. When the music stopped, he thanked her for the dance and returned her to where Colin waited. Kate was flushed and laughing.

"He put me through my paces. Okay, sport. Let's see you get out there while I catch my breath." Soon there was a queue of friendly partners, and they changed often whether the song had finished.

When the set ended a smiling, round, matronly woman towed a florid-faced man to Kate and Colin. Lines engraved in his face reflected his life experiences. Colin greeted them with a wide smile. Intrigued, Kate saw nothing special about the couple.

"Colin, this is my Riley," she said with pride.

Colin shook his hand. "Molly told me about your courtship." He turned to Kate. "This is Molly and Riley."

Molly patted Kate's hand. "Your man is handsome, dear, but not as handsome as my Riley." She beamed at her husband. "You should have seen him in his Army uniform. He was just… dashing."

Riley's bright blue eyes gleamed as he laughed. "Forty pounds and years ago, honey." He patted the paunch that hid his belt.

"We were planning to marry when Uncle Sam drafted him," Molly said to Kate. "I didn't want him to go to war, what with all those terrible things happening in Europe. I waved him off with a smile and cried myself to sleep that night and many others. Like most women my age in our city, the news reports given by Gabriel Heatter on the radio riveted us. We were lucky… still are," and she patted Riley's cheek.

The orchestra shifted to dreamy ballads. "Molly, they're playing our song," Riley said.

Kate and Colin joined them on the dance floor. Colin tucked her hand against his chest.

"I'm glad we came this evening. Are you?" Kate asked.

"I've enjoyed it more than I thought I would. I danced with two or three merry widows and flirtatious females tonight. One of them pinched my ass."

Kate pretended shock before she broke into laughter. "You're a hit. Do you think they recognized you?"

"I don't know." Colin shrugged.

"I didn't get pinched, but two men held me closer than I liked and panted in my ear," she confided.

"Hm. I don't want to share you any more tonight. Are you ready to leave?"

He held her hand as they made their way to the exit. Several couples called goodbye and invited them to come again.

"Hungry?" He smoothed his thumb around her palm as they walked to the car.

"No, too many peanuts. Let's go back to the motel. We can pick up a pizza or a sub if you want something."

"Do you have a Florida driver's license, Kate?" He asked as he held the door for her.

"No, why do you want to know?" She frowned, puzzled at the question.

"While you were snoozing last night, I checked on a few things."

He unlocked the door to their room, closed it, and slipped on the night lock. Kate dropped her evening bag on a chair and stepped out of her shoes while Colin laid keys and his wallet on the dresser top. He turned and took her in his arms.

"Kate, will you marry me?"

She looked at him in surprise. "Are you letting the fortune-teller spook you?"

"No, it's not because of her, although she gave me some uneasy moments. I planned to ask you in a romantic setting with candlelight, flowers, and the works, but I don't want to wait. I don't want to live any more of my life without you." He drew her close and kissed her. "And your answer is?"

"I love you, and it would teach you not to be impetuous if I accepted."

"So, teach me a lesson."

"I enjoy being with you, but marriage… That's a giant step," she hedged.

"I came here to find out how we feel about each other. Didn't you think marriage would be in the picture?"

"No, I didn't expect you to propose." She stepped away to look at him.

"I can feel that damn word coming." He prompted, "But?"

"Your world is so different from what I know, and I'm not sure I'll fit, or if one woman can satisfy you."

"She can if that woman is you," he said.

"I'm afraid you'll grow tired of me, and I won't tolerate infidelity. Don't expect me to look the other way, pretend everything is okay, and make nice until you're ready to come back, if you do. She's right."

"She who?" Colin questioned.

"The fortune-teller. I don't know if I can live your lifestyle. You're surrounded by temptation. I'm afraid my imagination will destroy me when you're in love scenes. It must be so easy to fall in love with your leading lady, to succumb to the setting, and fall in love with love. I think it's why so many show business marriages fail."

"Come on, Kate. I gave up a lucrative job to be with you because I love you. That alone should prove I'm serious."

"Should it? That's just money."

"It's *more* than money. It's what I do, who I am. That show represented the success I've spent my professional life working for." He pulled her back into his arms. "You're the one who turns me on. You're the one I want to make a proper life with, come home to, make love to, wake up beside. Trust me, Kate. I've never felt like this before."

Her eyes shimmered with unshed tears. Did she dare chance it? She had felt so betrayed, so embarrassed, so miserable.

Be honest, Kate, the voice whispered. *You assumed too much too soon, and you're not happy without him. Remember your destiny.*

Kate's thoughts swirled—Zvie in her head and Colin's proposal.

"… no waiting period in Florida if you have an out-of-state driver's license." Colin enthused. "We can get married tomorrow."

"You've given this some thought, haven't you?"

"Did you look at those couples tonight? Really see them? They were young during a time of war and upheaval. They endured separations, hardships, uncertainty, and loss. Still, they found each other." He paced a few steps away to collect his thoughts and turned back.

"Molly was a talker. I learned about her life and about Riley while we danced. Somehow her husband knew when she was talking about him. Their eyes met across the room, and I can only describe it as electric. After all the years together, she saw him as the debonair man who courted her, and she married. I saw them dancing cheek to cheek, and I got goose bumps. They were so in love after sharing forty or fifty years together. I saw several couples like that tonight. I decided then that I want forty years with you, and it still won't be long enough." He tilted her chin and looked into her eyes. "We're one of those couples, Kate. I believe in years to come I'll look at you and see you as you are tonight."

"That's so sweet, Colin. You think so? After all that's happened?"

"Especially after what happened. We're here together, aren't we? You haven't given me an answer. Tell me what you're thinking."

"I told you I love you, but we have things to work out. I need to know what we each expect of the other and agree on some ground rules."

"I expect you to be my wife, my companion, my lover. I expect to be your husband, your lover, your friend, to take care of you. Ground rules? You mean like sex only on Monday and Friday? Eating out on Tuesday and Thursday? Laundry on Saturday?"

"Be serious, Colin," but she smiled. "Not rules, let's call it our foundation for a life together."

"This isn't flattering, Kate. Either you love me and you want to marry me, or you don't."

"I love you. I've never hidden my feelings for you," she soothed. "You've been thinking about this all evening and I had it sprung on me." She eased away from him with troubled eyes. "Marriage between us involves more than loving each other."

"Enlighten me."

"Your career complicates things—the lack of privacy, for example. I wouldn't want to reveal our marriage to the public until we're sure it's working. You told me you don't want another failure announced in the tabloids. I don't want headlines either. No immediate public announcement. Agreed?"

"That's a hell of a condition. I want to shout it to the universe."

"We will—later. Living together and blending our lives will be a major change without doing it in the public eye. No publicity or photo ops right away. And I want our home to be our sanctuary. No guests unless the guest or guests are welcome by both of us. No exceptions, so there won't be any suspicion on either side. I want complete honesty between us. If you ever feel our marriage isn't working or you're attracted to someone else, I want to be the first to know."

"Do you want this in writing, Kate?" Colin's sober expression displayed an underlying mockery.

"Lots of couples write their own vows. We're not having a splashy wedding, but these conditions could be our vows. I'm not asking you for a prenuptial agreement."

"All right. Kate, tell me you believe I love you." He gazed at her, and she felt those beautiful blue eyes reeling her in, making her want to say yes. She shivered and glanced away.

"That sounds a little like a condition. Do you have some of your own?"

"Well, now that yours are out in the open, yes. I want us to agree there'll be no separate bedrooms or separate beds. If I have to go on location to work, you will travel with me. We will not take trouble or anger to bed with us, and by that I don't mean one of us will sleep on the couch until the air clears again. We will not sleep unless we make up."

"Agreed, I want us to frame them so we won't forget."

"Shall I take that as a yes?" He gave her a weak smile. "This has not been the romantic proposal and enthusiastic acceptance I hoped for, but we can make up for it. Are you going to marry me, Kate?" he whispered.

"I love you, Colin. God help us. Yes, I want to marry you."

Chapter -38-

"Ta dum da dum." Colin intoned the familiar opening notes of "Wagner's Bridal Chorus". He lifted the drape away from the window. "It's a beautiful day to get married, Kate."

"Happy is the bride the sun shines on and all that traditional drivel?" She shielded her bleary eyes with her hand. "You're disgustingly chipper for so early in the day. I hadn't noticed that before."

"Today is a special day. I'm getting married, and my bride-to-be is the most beautiful, sexiest woman I know."

Kate eyed the travel alarm. "Colin! Public offices don't open this early. And, flattery won't get you anywhere unless I can snooze longer." She moaned and pulled the covers over her head.

"You could persuade me." He let the drape fall and burrowed under the covers to face her nose to nose.

"That's not fair. I didn't sleep most of the night thinking and worrying and then worrying and thinking more."

"How was I to know you were awake most of the night? I could have helped you relax, and we could have enjoyed the night."

"Really?" Kate thumped her pillow and forced her eyes to focus.

"Kate! Have you forgotten already? You need a refresher course." He pulled her to him so she was resting on his chest. He ran his hand down her back and circled her hip.

"Hmm. Refresher course, huh? It's coming back to me now: crisp hair, thick, a little curl. Is that why you keep it so short?" She tousled it with her fingers. "And oh-so magnetic eyes, the first thing I noticed about you, although right now they're too darn bright and alert for my taste." She smoothed his eyebrow with her thumb. "Your eyes lose their color, become glacial when you're angry. They're clear and blue when you're tender," she said, her voice low and husky. "But I like them best when they darken with passion."

"Your lips tilt like we all amuse you, did you know?" Kate moistened her finger and traced his lower lip. His expressive eyes and inviting mouth had attracted her from the first moment they met. She still felt their magic.

"I like the way you feel." She bent her knee to stroke his calf with her foot and felt him stir.

Colin grasped the hem of her sleep-shirt, drew it over her head and tossed it to the floor. His lips brushed hers. Then, he deepened the kiss, and Kate felt her temperature rise, knew by his reaction he heard her body tell him what he'd wanted to hear last night when he proposed.

"I want you," she whispered.

"You got me," he replied with a teasing smile before lowering his lips to the corner of her mouth, her neck and nibbling his way to her breast. He rolled his tongue around her nipple and felt it pucker. Heat built in her belly, moved lower, and coursed through her. She pulsed as he pressed his arousal against her.

Whispering, she ran her fingertips around his navel, drifting down his pelvis to his inner thighs. She wrapped her fingers around his erection and stroked. "And I like…"

"No more talk," he rasped and rolled her on top. Kate rocked against him. His hands caressed her bottom, then clasped her hips. He thrust until she accepted him deep inside and set their rhythm. He fondled her breasts, and she moaned, tightening around him. With a groan, he gave one last thrust, and she collapsed on him.

*****

Bright sun invaded the motel room when Kate stretched and agreed to coffee and breakfast.

"That's my definition of better sex," she said.

Colin reached for her hand, and pressed a kiss to her wrist, another in her palm. "If best is that much better, I may never get out of bed again."

"Then you'd miss naked dancing, sex with whipped cream, and other pleasures we have yet to try." She gazed at him from under her lashes. "And did I mention you would have to give up your career?"

"Something to look forward to, my dear." He twirled an imaginary mustache with flair. "I hope you don't intend yoga postures or I might make the cover of a tabloid—Unusual Sex Requires Hospitalization."

"We'll try to avoid soiling your new image. I like you borderline scruffy. It's very sexy and gives you a dangerous air, although it's scratchy."

"Sorry, Kate. Does my bride have whisker rash? Lucky you don't want formal photos." He ran his hand down her cheek and sobered. "I scribbled a rough draft of our conditional vows. You can add, subtract, edit, or whatever. We'll recite, print, frame, engrave, even tattoo them."

"That last is too extreme. Editing would have to airbrush your nude scenes."

"Ha! I checked for directions to the nearest courthouse while you recovered from having your way with me."

"You're full of yourself this morning." She pulled a face and made for the shower.

*****

An hour later Kate Dunning entered the county government building and Kate O'Brien exited with a complacent Colin O'Brien. She stared at the marriage certificate clutched in her hand.

"We did it." She looked thunderstruck.

"You are now Mrs. O'Brien. You made a married man out of me… for the last time. We'll frame the official certificate with our vows and hang them in our home. We got the order of things backassward, so let's go buy you a wedding ring."

"And one for you, Mr. O'Brien. Don't think I'll be the only one wearing the traditional symbol of bondage in this union."

"Kate!" He grabbed at his chest and staggered. "You might have wounded my psyche if I didn't know you love me and crave my body."

"I wouldn't want that." She kissed his cheek before she got into the car to revisit yesterday's shopping mall.

"I've been expecting you." The suave clerk in the jewelry store glided forward to greet them. "I saw you looking at our display in the window. I knew you would be back. What may I show you? Engagement rings?"

"Kate? Would you like an engagement ring and a wedding ring?"

"Let's look at wedding rings."

The salesman motioned them to chairs and brought several trays to the counter. He took his stance opposite them with avaricious eyes. He recognized Colin.

"I like this one. What do you think?" Colin asked.

"No, it doesn't look good on my finger." They perused the wares, choosing a full circle of baguette-cut diamonds set in platinum. Colin's ring was similar; small stones edged a wider platinum band. Kate tilted her hand, admiring the flash of the gems. Colin suppressed a smile and leaned to brush her lips.

"Pretty isn't it? But not as pretty as you. Happy, Kate?"

"Yes, and it's a beautiful ring. Thank you."

They returned to the motel after their brief, but expensive, shopping expedition.

"I think it's time to go home. Are you ready, Kate?"

"Yes," she drew the word out, agreeing with reluctance. "I suppose we have to return to the real world."

"I want to tell Zvie our news." Colin said. "Maybe he's heard about the audition for me, uh, us. We'll move your things to my place. Did I tell you I love you today?"

"Yes, but you can tell me as often as you like."

"I'll call my travel agent and request the first flight available. We'll return the rental car at the airport to save time."

"Just remember to make the reservation for you and Kate Dunning." She added at the frown on his face, "The airline will require picture ID."

Later that afternoon, Kate shivered in the back seat of the car carrying them to Zvie's apartment. Colin slid his arm around her.

"Cold?" he asked.

"I guess I got used to Florida weather." She leaned into Colin's warmth. "I should have worn something warmer."

When the car stopped at the curb, Harry opened the rear door.

"Miss Kate! Mr. O'Brien! It's great to see you." Harry's genuine welcome warmed his smile. "Let me get that luggage for you. Are you here to stay?"

"And it's good to see you too, Harry." Colin responded, as Kate nodded.

"Is Zvie in?" At Harry's nod, Kate added, "Please don't announce us. We want to surprise him."

They entered the elevator while Harry assured them he would send up the luggage.

Kate retrieved her key from her handbag and unlocked the door.

"Hello," Colin called. "Where are you?"

"In the kitchen," Zvie looked up as they entered.

"Kate!" He jumped to his feet and hugged her. "My dear, I'm happy to see you. Let me look at you. There's something different… you're thinner, and—"

"There's something else different about her too, Zvie." Colin blurted, holding up her left hand.

"What's this? You've been shopping," he said with a grin. "And you have one too, Colin? You found a buy-one-get-one sale."

"Zvie, you tease." Kate smiled. "You knew before we got here, didn't you? I don't suppose that man with the atrocious wardrobe we saw so frequently was a friend of yours?"

"I confess to a nodding acquaintance with Ezra. He was clumsy in front of the jeweler's window, wasn't he? My best wishes to both of you. I have often seen radiant brides, but I don't think I've ever seen a radiant groom before. May I kiss the bride, Colin?"

"A chaste kiss on the cheek," he said.

"Shall we give a party to announce your marriage?" Zvie asked.

"Kate doesn't want an announcement," Colin replied in a neutral voice, his face impassive "I, however, would love a party and want to take an ad in the newspaper or shout our news from the terrace."

"Kate?" Zvie turned to her.

"I want to wait. Not forever. Don't look at me like that the two of you. I want time to adjust before our every word and act gets scrutinized in the press." She still leaned against Colin with his arms around her.

"The press reported your movements before you went away. Surely you didn't forget." Zvie nudged the newspaper toward her. "Read our friend's column from yesterday's paper."

Morning News

Sam Lewin confided that Melody McIntyre is Colin O'Brien's house guest. Ms. McIntyre and CO met and married in college. According to Ms. McIntyre and Lewin, CO's career was the root cause of their divorce. Lewin implied a reconciliation is in the works.

"Colin?" Kate questioned, foreboding stealing through her, diminishing her joy of moments before.

"Sam has a key to my apartment. I didn't think to ask him for it. It seems I should have. Sam and I parted ways before I came to Florida. I don't know what he's trying to prove with this stunt. Melody's been out of my life for years."

"Let's be frank," Zvie said, "He's vindictive. Sam recognized Kate as a serious threat. Now that he no longer represents you what little stature he had is slipping away."

"This puts a damper on moving into your apartment," Kate said. "Talk about three's a crowd!"

"Sam doesn't know you were with Kate," Zvie said. "The best way to handle Sam is to announce your marriage. We'll invite him and your ex-wife to our impromptu celebration. We'll let Bernard know Sam no longer represents you. That, along with your news, should take care of Sam for all time. I doubt anyone will believe anything he has to say again."

"How will you evict your uninvited guest?" Zvie asked Colin. "You're welcome to stay here."

"I don't know. I… we could go over together and ask her to leave. Kate?"

"Are you entertaining tomorrow night as usual, Zvie?" Kate asked. At his nod, she turned to her husband. "We could stay here tonight and make our announcement at the party tomorrow."

"It's not the way I imagined spending our wedding night." Colin sighed.

"The eviction should be easier and cleaner after the announcement. I think she will want to leave. If not, I'll help her pack." Kate smiled without humor. "Zvie told me so often about your favorite restaurant. Let's all three of us go there tonight."

"What a splendid idea," Zvie said.

"I'm always willing to eat at Maria's." Colin resigned himself to the change in his plans.

"We need to shower and change. Reservations in an hour, or so?" Kate winked at Colin. "Follow me."

After they collected the luggage, Kate led the way to her bedroom. She continued through and switched the light on in the bathroom.

"Jacuzzi for two? Or a shower?"

"This may not be a hardship. Do you think Zvie would merge households or trade apartments with us?" Colin assumed innocence at her quirked eyebrow. "Just a thought. I'll look forward to the Jacuzzi tonight. If we use it now, we'll miss our reservation. I haven't taken you there, have I? It's casual, Kate. Jeans are acceptable."

*****

The hostess at Maria's greeted Colin and Zvie by name and gave them menus They were about to order when Sam and a petite dark-haired woman approached. She was a stranger to Kate.

"Colin, I hoped you'd be here. Someone wants to say hello." His eyes slid over Zvie and Kate, taunting them, before turning to Colin.

"Hello, Melody. I read in this morning's paper that you're staying in my apartment." Colin spared a glance to his former wife, then stared at Sam.

"Hello." Melody exchanged a look with Sam, but hers was quizzical.

"You should have asked me, don't you think?" Colin said to his former agent.

"I didn't think you'd mind," Sam blustered, "with your history and all."

"Our history," Colin said. "All the more reason you should have asked. How long did you plan for her to stay?"

"How've you been?" Melody asked before Sam could reply.

"Busy. What brings you here?"

"Sam offered to help me." She looked to Sam, and he nodded. "I have an urge to try show business."

"Given up the country club and the staid, respectable life?" He turned to include his dinner companions. "I'd like you to meet Zvie and Kate—"

Kate nudged him under the table, and Colin faltered.

"Kate Dunning." He looked at her.

Kate acknowledged Melody with narrowed eyes.

"Sam," she inclined her head.

"Sam, we meet again." Zvie extended a hearty greeting. "I'm hosting Saturday evening with friends, and would-be friends," he added with sarcasm. "Would you and uh Marilyn like to join us?"

"Melody." She and Sam chimed together.

"Melanie, excuse me," Zvie corrected, and she glowered at him.

"Are you planning another floor show?" Sam huffed, curling his lip.

"Something more exciting. You shouldn't miss it." Zvie's calm reply belied his plan.

"If you'll excuse us," Colin interrupted. "We'd like to order."

"Why don't we join you?" Sam suggested.

"Another time, perhaps? The table isn't big enough for five." Sam flushed at Zvie's offhand dismissal. The rosy hue on Melody's fair skin deepened to embarrassment.

Zvie shared Colin's enjoyment of the restaurant and they lingered over dinner. The malevolent glares Sam directed at Kate made her nervous. She dribbled red sauce.

"Excuse me. I'd better treat this before I have a permanent stain." She stopped at the bar for a glass of seltzer then made her way to the ladies' room. When she returned, Melody sat in her chair, leaning toward Colin, her hand on his thigh. Colin appeared riveted by her gaping neckline, and Kate's temper flared.

"Am I interrupting?" She inquired in an icy tone and a sweet smile that countered her temper. Her scorching eyes threatened to fry Colin in his chair. "Should I come back later?"

Zvie hazarded a look at Kate and shot to his feet. Kate gathered her purse and jacket.

"We should be going." Zvie said, leaving bills on the table. "Coming, Colin?"

Without a word, Kate walked to the door. Zvie signaled the doorman who hailed a passing cab. Colin joined them as the car pulled to the curb.

"That was unexpected! How did Sam know you'd be at Maria's?" Zvie asked.

"Lucky guess? I haven't spoken to Sam in weeks, and Melody?" Colin frowned, "Not since our divorce."

"Any thoughts, Kate?" Zvie asked.

"No," she hugged the door to create space between her and Colin.

"I didn't realize Sam knew your ex-wife," Zvie said. "Are they friendly?"

"She met him a time or two. As I remember, he ridiculed her plans. You know, a bungalow, kids and Saturday night at the country club. Sam implied she would hinder my career."

"That doesn't sound like an aspiring actress," Zvie said.

"Yeah, amazing," Colin said.

"I assume Sam wants your help with Melody?"

"That's why she came to our table."

Kate rolled her eyes and muttered under her breath.

"What was that, Kate?" Zvie asked.

"Nothing," she said.

"I told her I was busy and she has to rely on Sam," Colin said. He turned to Kate. "Did you like Maria's? While you were out of town, Zvie and I often ate there."

"It's okay," Kate shrugged and continued to observe the city through the cab window.

Kate huddled in the corner, replying in monosyllables to Zvie's attempts to fill the silence. Dissension shared their ride. She ignored Colin's hand getting out of the cab and maintained her silent treatment in the elevator.

Chapter -39-

"Anyone for a nightcap or coffee?" Zvie asked.

A silent Kate stalked toward her bedroom.

"I'll take that as a no," he shrugged. "Good night."

"Good night," Colin replied and followed his wife into the bedroom. "Are you going to talk about what has your back up?"

"You need to ask? I leave the table for one minute, and another woman takes my place. Not only is this a woman from your past, but she has her hand on your thigh, and you're staring down the front of her dress. Go jump off the balcony, Colin." She stalked into the bathroom.

"What happened to those conditional vows you were hell bent on having?" he asked through the door she closed in his face.

"That was before I saw you damn near drool over another woman, and the ink's not even dry on our marriage certificate, you... you jerk." She opened the door wide enough to snarl. "No damn wonder *Lost in Lust* was such a hit. You're a natural in the role."

"You're the one who wanted to keep our marriage a secret. No announcement, you said. If I had introduced you as my wife, this wouldn't have happened."

"Ah! This is my fault? You haven't the fortitude to say no without a shield?" Kate was so livid she hissed. Her eyes glowed.

"Kate, I was not—"

"'Don't you know how to take a woman's hand off your leg or were you hoping she'd move it higher. Maybe give you a little after dinner entertainment? If I hadn't come back when I did, would a lap dance have been next? What is it with you that you're such a pushover? You did the same thing with the girl in the ridiculous dress."

"Calm down. Melody surprised me. That mistake was over years ago, and I don't intend to revive it. She asked for help."

"This is so familiar." Kate rolled her eyes. "Help with what? Sexual frustration? Does she need an escort to a restaurant? Or a date to the party tomorrow night?"

"Kate, be reasonable."

"'Kate, be reasonable'," she mimicked. "A reasonable *man* would have remembered *his wife* and rejected another woman's advances or at least hid it from *his wife*." She came out of the bathroom in workout clothes and stalked out of the bedroom.

Kate slipped a disk into the DVD player, tried to control her breathing and her pounding pulse. Midway through the routine she gave up. She made herself an herbal tea and carried it to the terrace. Draping the afghan around her, Kate curled up in a corner of the rattan sofa. Only then did she let her tears escape. "Welcome to reality, fool."

Zvie opened his bedroom door. "Kate?" He looked down at her, then sat.

"Our marriage will not work. Sam or another Flora, Kitti or Melody will always lurk nearby. I don't want to wait the rest of my life for the next one to appear."

"Don't be melodramatic." Zvie cut to the issue he wanted to discuss. "What's the reason you didn't want to announce your marriage?"

"I don't want to experience humiliation again! Thank my lucky stars we didn't announce our marriage. How sensational would that have been? Colin ogling a previous wife while his current one watches?"

"Your reaction is playing right into Sam's hands. He made you turn tail and run, and Colin only walked in the door with Kitti."

"Let's not forget she was draped all over him," Kate reminded Zvie.

"This is less meaningful, a meeting with a woman he used to know."

"That woman 'he used to know' was his wife!"

"Sam expects you to indulge in a pity party so Colin will give up on you."

"Maybe meeting Melody isn't as meaningful to you, *an observer*, but seeing my husband with another woman's hand on his thigh on our wedding day is sure as hell meaningful to me!"

"I saw what happened."

"I did too, and I'm not blind. When Colin came to Florida, he said he backed off because he didn't want to make another mistake and read about it in the tabloid press. I don't want to be fodder for a gossip column either. A failed marriage is difficult enough without reading about it in a gossip column."

"Have you considered how Colin must have interpreted your reluctance to announce your marriage? You know how skeptical he was and how far he's come to commit to marriage. If you don't trust him, you shouldn't have married him. Or," he studied her, "is it yourself you doubt?" When she didn't answer, Zvie continued. "Trust me and the celestial powers that granted Betty a second chance. I want only the best for you."

"I know," she whispered.

"To meet Colin and discover love is your destiny, just as you asked, just as he asked."

"It's his career, the temptations and the women he's around. He's so good at portraying a womanizer."

"He may have played the part, but he's had only two brief involvements. The other women were casual or publicity schemes. His audition should come through soon. If he gets the part, his career path will change. His career as a sex magnet, so to speak, will end. There should be less temptation."

"I'm out of my depth, Zvie."

"Stop feeling sorry for yourself. Go look in the mirror."

"We were good while we were away, before we came back. Events moved so fast yesterday and today. Running into Sam and an ex-wife our first night back is too much drama too soon."

"Melody isn't a threat. You showed insight when you recognized Colin as the one, and you perceived the consequences if my mission fails. I know you've questioned why Betty's sacrifices were so much greater than Colin's. This, Kate, is where you did not see the big picture. Yes, Colin received a special blessing. If he had not, he would have become more cynical, but his life would have continued as it was. He is the catalyst in Betty's second chance. This project is about you and Colin. Without him, you would have experienced an interesting life, but it would not have lasted."

"I'm tired; my emotions are on overload. I can't handle the Melody-Sam-Colin triangle tonight." Kate gathered her thoughts. "I love Colin, but I don't want to live with the drama he attracts."

"Go to bed, Kate. You'll think more clearly in the morning." Zvie helped her to her feet and put his arms around her. She drew comfort from him. Then, he urged her toward the door.

*****

"Feeling better?" Colin asked when she entered her room.

She shrugged and turned her back. Peeling off her workout clothes, she pulled on a nightshirt. She crossed to the bed and turned back the covers.

Colin gestured to the Jacuzzi. "I've been thinking about this all evening," and he dropped his toweling robe.

"It didn't look to me like *this* was on your mind. Enjoy." Her voice dripped sarcasm.

"Oh no, you're not sleeping until we settle this. Those vows aren't hung on the wall, but they're real. I gave you time to cool off. Now we'll talk."

"You don't want to hear what I have to say. Let's leave it."

"Are you having doubts about us, Kate?"

"Yes, I am."

"At least you're being honest. That's a good first step. I messed up tonight, but I won't let you give up on me, on us.

Sam has you nailed. Are you going to roll over for him…
again?"

"You must consider me naïve or a fool if you think I'll
accept any lame excuse, any justification you offer just
because you do it with such charm, *darling*," Kate drawled.
"I'm tired, Colin. I didn't think I'd have to climb into the
arena so soon."

"There isn't any competition, Kate. You're all strung out.
The Jacuzzi will help you relax."

"I'll relax when you get dressed or leave. Didn't you tell
me you were nervous about taking your clothes off in front of
me?" she asked, as he stood there naked and self-assured.

"That was before you married me, Kate. Now you have to
take me like I am, warts, flab, wrinkles, and all."

"As if—"

He placed his finger against her lips. She pushed at his
hand, but he drew her nightshirt over her head and tossed it
onto the floor.

"Is this one pleasure we haven't tried yet?" Colin's eyes
gleamed.

"This comes under the heading of trying to avoid saying
or doing something *we* will regret," she said as she tried to
retrieve her nightshirt.

"*We* will continue our discussion in there." He carried her
into the bathroom, lowered her to her feet, and blocked the
door. "Will you get in by yourself or do you need help?"

She glared at him with murder in her eyes, clenched her
teeth, and stepped into the water.

Chapter -40-

"Angel Second Chance, I did not expect you."

"We have a… development." Zvie smoothed his disheveled hair and straightened his robe. "Sam Lewin intervened once more. Kate and Colin returned and informed me of their marriage. They were both happy. Then I showed them Bernard's report in the newspaper. Colin's ex-wife is lodging in his apartment. Sam implied a reconciliation in the offing. To make matters worse, Kate asked Colin not to publicize their marriage."

"Why on earth would she do that?" the Archangel asked.

"Insecurity and caution for two reasons." Zvie waved his hand to excuse her. "We agreed the best way to expose Sam would be an announcement at the Saturday night reception. We went out to dinner, and who should show up but Sam, with Melody, the ex-wife."

"Speak of the devil, and you will see his tail? The man is devious and persistent. Was the happy couple amused?"

"No. Melody acted familiar with Colin. Kate's temper flared, and I escorted them away before there was a flaming scene! Kate later confided that marrying Colin was a mistake and…" Too late, Zvie realized his blunder.

"A mistake? Surely not the same day!" The Archangel made plain his shock and displeasure.

"Remember, her sensory abilities have strengthened. The time limitations of the mission may have influenced her." This thought was a new one to Zvie. Had he been too ambitious? Too complacent? He had questioned the Appeals Committee's judgment. Did he know what was best for Kate? He would have to give that further thought.

"Kate wanted a man she could lean on and Colin coped well." Zvie hastened to assuage the Archangel's disapproval. "He gave Kate some space before confronting her. She attempted to withdraw, but he would not let her. I *had* to exert a bit of discreet influence. *We* had a stormy evening."

"You say they will make an announcement soon? Kate agreed?"

"Yes. I'll make sure our columnist friend, also a Second Chance Academy graduate, knows Sam is no longer Colin's agent and could not have had inside knowledge of his plans. Bernard will witness the announcement and the wedding cake ceremony. I plan to have a private talk with Sam Lewin. I have adhered to our code, never displayed powers to anyone but my charges, and only when necessary. But we must discourage Sam from any further interference in Kate and Colin's lives. With your permission," Zvie hastened to add at the Archangel's frown.

"A *small* demonstration, Angel Second Chance, and no one but Sam Lewin must witness it. *We* are firm that our agents remain anonymous. I agree; however, we must curb this odious person. How dare he impede a celestial project!

We do not tolerate interference!" The Archangel only used the collective *we* when he was provoked.

"I will use caution. Also, completely withdrawing our presence would be a mistake. I must remain on call should a major problem reoccur and Kate or Colin needs me."

The Archangel locked eyes with Zvie and drummed his fingertips on his desk in rhythm with the ticking of the Great Clock.

Zvie drew a deep breath. "Kate confided, and I agree, Colin's career is a factor. He seems to be a drama magnet. I believe she'll come to terms with it, but not overnight. Sam Lewin has eroded her confidence in Colin once again."

"I will present your suggestion to the Appeals Committee." The Archangel blew out a breath and exchanged a grave look with Angel Second Chance. "If only Colin were a plumber."

Chapter -41-

Kate slipped into her robe the following morning, made coffee, and took her cup to the terrace. She watched the steam from her cup rise in the frosty air. *If only my doubts would dissipate like that.* She had to give Colin marks for the way he had handled himself after the scene at the restaurant. He'd persisted until they resolved the Melody and Sam issue. Colin had pacified her, but she hadn't forgotten the drama.

"Good morning, Kate. Just like old times: you, me, and coffee with the morning newspapers." Zvie noted the shadow beneath her eyes.

"Zvie, what will happen to you and me after we reach the deadline?" She nibbled her lip, frowning. "Will I be able to talk to you or will you disappear?"

"Our relationship will change. You and Colin will rely on each other. I have asked the Archangel for flexibility, but the Appeals Committee has to approve my request. An annual session at the Academy would also benefit you."

She nodded as Colin sauntered out on bare feet.

"Good morning," he yawned.

"Good morning, sleepyhead. What happened to the chipper early riser of yesterday? Recovering from having your way with me?"

She turned her head, and his kiss landed on her cheek.

"Let's try that again," and he steadied her chin. "My aim must be a little off after the rough night I had sparring with a tough opponent."

"We'd better go inside." She looked down, ignoring his reference to the night before. "It's cold out here for bare feet."

"Yes ma'am." His meek reply contradicted the twinkle in his eyes. "I would have worn slippers, but they're at my place."

Kate handed a coffee to him. "I like you in jeans," she whispered and patted his butt. "Sexy."

Zvie offered a relieved smile to heaven at the interchange showing they had mended yesterday's breach. Colin wasn't the only one who thought Kate was a tough opponent.

"I think I should buy something special for the party tonight," Kate said.

"Do you always shop before a party?" Colin asked.

"Is that a problem?" She challenged.

"Just asking," Colin smiled.

"Good." She turned to a now smiling Zvie. "Do you need help with the party?"

"I've made the arrangements, as I didn't know you would be here. Enjoy..." With a look of dismay, he stopped mid-sentence. He had to convince the Archangel that his mission was still in jeopardy.

"Zvie? What is it?" Kate shivered. Her chill had nothing to do with the temperature.

"It seems an enterprising rag reporter was at *Maria's*." Zvie's focus shifted to Colin with an inscrutable expression.

He extended the newspaper. The front page of the Entertainment section featured a smiling Melody and Colin.

Et Cetera

You sly dog, Colin O'Brien. Kate Dunning left the room and Melody McIntyre took her place. This writer witnessed the poignant reunion between Ms. McIntyre and her former husband. An intimate caress and soulful eyes lend weight to Sam Lewin's disclosure of a reconciliation. Still, CO left with Kate and Zvie. Any red-blooded man would welcome his dilemma.

"Welcome to reality, Kate, my girl." She blanched; her compressed lips lost their color as she turned away from Zvie and Colin. "This makes a mockery of our planned announcement tonight, don't you think?"

"Kate, I'm sorry. I—"

"It seems I was not unreasonable or the only one who thought you and Melody were up close and personal. You shouldn't have married me if you want to comfort every woman who approaches you with a sob story and an *alleged* problem."

"Kate," Colin tried again, but her lifeless voice continued as though he had laryngitis.

"I think this says it all. Apparently, a damsel in distress takes precedence over a *wife*. Excuse me." A tear escaped, and she swiped at it.

"Where are you going?" Zvie asked, his face a model of concern.

"To my room and I *do not* want company." She hurried out of the kitchen.

"Let's talk about this." Colin said and followed her.

She whirled to face him, hands on her hips. "Is there something wrong with your hearing? *I do not* want company." Kate ran to the bedroom and pulled on the sweatpants and shirt she'd draped over a chair the night before. She slid into terry scuffs and snagged her purse.

"You can't leave. We have to solve this." Colin reached out as she tried to pass him.

"Don't touch me," she demanded with ice in her voice. "We've said all there is to say. Haven't you done enough?" He froze, relaxing his hold. Kate pulled free and sprinted through the door. Colin recovered in time to watch Kate disappear behind the elevator doors. He raced down the stairs.

"Good morning, Mr. O'Brien," Harry said. "I didn't see you come in this morning."

"I arrived very early." Harry's cheery greeting annoyed him. "Did you see Kate?"

"Yes, I called her a cab." He smirked at his little joke.

"And?" Colin prodded.

"One was cruising the area," and Harry related the excellent service he had provided, oblivious to Colin's groan.

*****

Colin took the elevator and with hesitant steps returned to the apartment.

"I see you didn't catch up with her." Zvie stated the obvious.

"Of all the lousy luck, Harry snagged a cab nearby. The car was pulling away when I got down there." Colin looked out at the gray day. "It's cold, and she didn't wear a jacket."

Zvie recognized Colin's concern as a deeper fear he did not voice. Zvie, too, worried about his protégé and not only for the success of his mission. *How fortunate Sam Lewin isn't here.*

"Kate is right." Zvie waved the newspaper. "This makes a mockery of any announcement. If we go ahead with our former plan, we will subject Kate to pity or ridicule. Everyone knows you were unmarried when you left the show. Your absence from the entertainment scene has not gone unnoticed. Gossips will conclude you couldn't be faithful even a day back in the city. Coupled with the scene at the restaurant, they'll label you an adulterer."

"I'm not a violent man, but I could beat the shit out of Sam if he were here. Zvie, how can I fix this?"

"At this moment, I'm at a loss. I'm not even sure Kate will come back." He sipped his cold coffee. "I assume this Scoop person wasn't at the restaurant by accident. Sam's writing is all over this script. I'd wager he's the reason your ex-wife is here. Probably spun her a fictitious tale. Wants to go into show business," Zvie huffed. "Does she have any talent?"

"Not when I knew her."

"If the reporter would confess Sam and Melody staged the scene, we could prove Sam's villainy and preserve your marriage." Zvie checked the newspaper banner. "Come. Let's have a talk with Scoop. He's our best recourse."

Archangel, I hope you approve of what I'm about to do.

Chapter -42-

Seeking anonymity in the teeming sidewalks and skyscrapers of the city, Kate stared out the window without seeing. When the cabbie stopped for a traffic light, she paid with a random bill in her purse and joined the throng. She was unaware of the curious glances her knit shirt and scuffs drew while around her pedestrians huddled in coats. Without a destination, she stopped in front of store windows until jostled into motion. Shivering with cold, she entered a coffee shop and sat by the window. She sipped hot coffee, crumbled a bagel, and watched passersby until she stopped shivering. Then she made her way to the City Museum. From a secluded bench, she stared at the exhibit in front of her until a kindly guard approached.

"Are you okay, Miss? You've been sitting here for some time."

"I'm all right." She attempted a smile.

"You shouldn't be out without a coat. Shall I call a taxi for you?"

"Thank you, no."

She rose and made her way to the exit, stooped and stumbling. At the nearest department store, Kate bought a sweatshirt and sneakers before continuing to roam. When she saw the marquee, she crossed the street, bought a ticket for the matinee, and huddled in the back row of the dim theater.

This morning's gossip column and the oh-so-familiar photo of Colin and a woman had fueled Kate's anger. Same scene, an unfamiliar face, she thought during her cab ride. Is this what life with Colin will be? Her impulsiveness of the morning morphed to despair, and pain pierced her breast. Tears coursed down her cheeks. Would she ever know happiness? Kate wrapped her arms around her waist and rocked.

Poor Kate. The butt of whispers and ridicule once again. I imagine Sam is crowing over the success of his latest scheme to ruin your life. He knew you'd act just like you are, the insidious voice whispered.

"Zvie, why won't you leave me alone?"

The couple in front of her turned to look, and Kate slid down in the theater seat.

Do you enjoy wallowing in misery? After weeks of soul searching, you buried Betty, or did you? Are you going to fume in silence and wish someone would rescue you, like Betty would do?

"I'm not Betty. *I'm not,*" she whispered.

A bump in the road, well maybe a pothole, Zvie conceded, *and boo-hoo, poor Kate's on the run. Betty's sacrifice for nothing. Nothing... nothing... nothing...* echoed until she cupped her ears.

Kate dug in her purse for a tissue, wiped her face. *I'm not Betty! I will not be Sam's victim! I've sacrificed enough!* Kate straightened; rage incinerated her indecision, her helplessness. She bid goodbye to the young girl who had left the dinner table in tears.

Kate vowed to make Sam Lewin, that ugly toad, suffer. *This time I will be in control.* He was about to get his comeuppance; she would see to it.

Zvie's friends knew the best places for whatever their need, and they shared the information. Outside the theater, Kate called a pricey day spa with a reputation for excellence. The salon's services would reinforce her confidence. She mentioned Zvie and dropped the names of several of his friends.

"Yes, we had a cancellation," a cultured voice answered.

Cynically, Kate knew the profit motive had more influence than her connections, but a facial would erase the evidence of her troubled day. A hair appointment always picked up her spirits. She would find a dress to complete her makeover in the adjoining boutique.

"Hello, I'm Kate Dunning," she said and approached the receptionist.

After several keystrokes on her iPad and a glance at the calendar, the receptionist found her name and spoke into her headset. A balding man in a smock and jeans ambled toward her.

"I'm Andre," he offered with a lazy smile. "You want something special for tonight?" Andre eyed her sweatpants and jacket with a raised eyebrow.

"Yes, and I don't want to look like the proverbial girl next door, unless she's having an affair with her neighbor's husband."

He tilted her chin, turned her face from side to side.

"We can manage that. Is there a reason you're hiding underneath these rags?"

"I left my house in a hurry. Don't let these clothes fool you. You understand what I want?"

"Trust me. It will be my pleasure."

"I wish you hadn't said that. I'm not high on trust."

Hours later, Kate surveyed herself in the salon mirrors, a complacent Andre at her side. Highlights streaked Kate's bobbed, chin-length hair. The makeup artist enhanced her eyes with smoky shadow, taupe eyeliner, and charcoal brown mascara. Blush emphasized the hollows in her cheeks, and her lips gleamed with scarlet lip gloss.

Together, Andre and Kate shopped the boutique and selected a black dress with a vee neckline. Its hem above her knees revealed slim legs. Silver sandals with three-inch heels completed her ensemble.

When they returned to the salon, Andre wielded blow dryer and brushes with such fervor her scalp tingled, and her eyes watered. When he finished her styled hair swung free and curved to embrace her chin.

Kate tugged at the dress's neckline, and Andre suggested and produced double-faced tape to secure it.

"And the bride wears black," Kate mocked. Had it not been for Sam and Melody, she would not have chosen black.

"Ordinarily, you would relax an entire day with us, love. You received an abbreviated version, but we worked our magic." Andre kissed her cheek. "Everyone will notice you. I would wish you luck, but I don't think you'll need it."

Kate left with a selection of products and all the bits and pieces that contributed to her image. She looked at her watch. When she arrived, the party should be underway. Her cell phone had rung several times, but she had ignored the calls. By now, she expected Colin and Zvie were in crisis mode. Her clothes of the morning hid in the salon's distinctive bag.

She slid into the cab waiting for her. Taking a deep breath, she muttered, "Game on."

Chapter -43-

Harry opened the door of the cab and gawked. "Miss Kate, is that you?" he asked as she stepped out.

"Yes, Harry." Kate shrugged out of her jacket and stuffed it in the shopping bag. "How do I look?"

"Great… different, but great! Uh, Mr. Zvie and Mr. O'Brien asked me to call if I saw you."

"No need, Harry. I'm going to the apartment. Will you send this up? I don't want to look like a bag lady when I enter," she winked.

He nodded. "Have fun at the party."

"That's the plan," she said. "I'll send someone down with a plate of goodies for you."

Kate drew a steadying breath as the elevator rose. She located her key and opened the door to a buzz of voices, the party in progress. She had hoped to slip in and check her appearance before greeting Zvie's guests, but it wasn't to be. She heard several calls of "Hi Kate," "Nice tan," and an occasional air kiss accompanied by a version of "Welcome back." Before she reached the hallway to her bedroom, Kate pictured a scene from *Hello Dolly* with guests breaking into song.

She closed the bedroom door, leaned against it, and exhaled. Colin lay stretched out on the bed in jeans.

"Hello, Kate."

"Colin! Why aren't you at the party?"

"I wasn't going unless I could go with my wife. Have you seen her?"

"Are you trying to be funny?"

"No." Colin swung his legs over the side of the bed and sat up. "I see Kate Dunning's going to the party."

Kate had primed herself to face a disgruntled or angry Colin. His calm and dispassionate demeanor, his quiet statement puzzled her.

"I missed Kate O'Brien today. Strange, isn't it? I've been married such a short time," he said, followed by a guttural sound of derision. "How was your day?"

"All right. I kept busy. And yours?"

"I've had better. I worried about you, Kate. Why didn't you answer your phone?"

"I needed time alone to think."

"What did you do? Where did you go?" he asked.

"I went shopping, to the museum, a matinee, consulted a plastic surgeon about breast implants, and ended at The Magic Mirror."

"Breast implants! What the hell for?" He demanded, goaded from his calm.

"I thought if I got bigger tits my husband wouldn't be tempted to look down other women's necklines." Temper flashed in his eyes. Wary, she hastened to add. "I'm teasing."

"Ha! Your hair is different. Shopped for a dress?"

"I needed a boost to my confidence before I faced the inquisition."

"I heard a warm reception." Colin said. "I'm surprised to see you. I didn't expect you to come back."

"Don't I *always* do what's required?" Her lip curled.

He shrugged. "I thought avoidance more your style."

"Don't go there, Colin. I took most of the day to decide not to run, and it's still a possibility. I dislike confrontation."

"Sometimes it's the only way. During your thinking time, did you have an epiphany? Maybe reach a decision about me? About us?" Colin shoved his hands in his pockets. "Where do we go from here?"

Kate shivered with a frisson of fear. This Colin didn't push to talk or negotiate. This Colin was indifferent.

"What do you want to happen?" she asked.

"Ah, Kate, must you always answer me with a question? All right, I'll commit first if it will help. Nothing has changed for me. I'm the same guy who asked you to marry me, who loves you, but damned if I know where I stand. You spent the day deciding issues, not joint decisions, as I didn't give an opinion. I suspect you're having a second or even third doubts. Nothing has gone right since we came back."

"Reality's not like a TV script, is it? I can't decide if you create drama or you attract it. Whatever, I'm not handling it well. Maybe I never will. Last night is why I didn't want an announcement. Again, I'm the object of ridicule. Let's get on with this."

"Is that what this new look is about? Defiance?"

"Got it in one." Kate's chin jutted daring him to criticize her.

"Dammit, Kate." He grabbed her upper arms. "I've never been violent with a woman, but I sure as hell would like to shake sense into you. This morning my wife flirted with me, grabbed my ass, and my world was as good as it gets. Then you read a distorted account by a second-rate reporter in a disreputable rag, and you run out of here like the hounds of hell are after you. You won't answer my calls and come back looking like a call girl. I want my wife if she still exists."

"Oh! A call girl!" Kate bristled. "Let's discuss appearances."

"I preferred the woman I married, and we have more important issues to settle. You're blaming me for something I didn't cause and couldn't control. You're quick to heap blame on me, Kate. That's not playing fair."

Zvie stood in the doorway observing the pair. Although they stood face-to-face, eddies of conflict and dissension swirled around them. Colin acknowledged him with a nod and left them. Kate heard the shower.

"You need an update," Zvie warned in a low voice as he came to her.

"Is Melody here?"

"Yes, she's with Sam. The reporter from *Maria's* is also here…at my invitation."

"You asked him here? I wouldn't have believed it," she whispered, crushed at his betrayal.

"Before you judge me, Colin and I met with him today. He confessed to receiving a phoned-in tip. Sam hired the photographer. He masterminded the scene."

"That's no surprise, is it? Still, Colin isn't innocent."

"He feels terrible. The poor guy worried about you…and so did I."

"Colin always feels terrible afterward," Kate huffed. "That's not news."

"You're very callous, Kate. Do you want to drive him away? A man's pride will allow him to bend only so far. When he reaches his limit, he either breaks or flees. Be sure you know what you're doing. Remember what I told you about do-overs? You could cause an irreversible event. Allow Colin and me to neutralize Sam."

"Zvie, I don't know your plans, but I do *not* want our marriage announced tonight."

"Kate—"

"Promise," she pleaded.

Zvie considered her for a heartbeat before reaching a decision.

"I want what's best for you, Kate, even if you question our beginnings, and I hoped that you had relegated it to the past. I've been your mentor, your champion, and your friend, but I *cannot* and *will not* promise that. This morning I could have understood tears or even a tantrum, but you were impulsive, thoughtless, and childish. I gave you credit for more strength, more maturity than that. The Academy should have instilled courage, self-esteem, and empathy."

He held up a hand to silence her when she would have spoken. "That newspaper report wasn't only about you; it smeared Colin's character too."

"Zvie—"

"Stop this foolish, asinine practice of avoidance. It's unworthy of who you are and the gift you received. Face your problems; fight for what you want; and forgive!" Zvie paused, made sure she met his eyes. "This may be the most important talk you and I will ever have. If you do not love Colin, tell him so; let him move on. Don't play games with him."

Kate froze. Zvie's stern voice and expression, his eyes like laser beams made him a stranger.

"Colin was resistant. He seemed determined to throw away the greatest opportunity of his life, but you had the benefit of the Second Chance Academy and my mentoring," Zvie scolded. "I can't pretend to know what your fate will be or the discipline the Celestial Appeals Committee will exact if you defiantly renounce your second chance. I've never failed before. Archangel Rafael has stressed the Committee's certain displeasure if the mission fails." Zvie looked to the ceiling for inspiration and blew out his breath. "You need to see this."

Zvie swept his hand through the air, and a scene wavered like ripples on a stream before it sharpened. In a commonplace setting, children moved in slow motion, followed by grim, silent nannies. A solitary dog lumbered after a ball; other canines dragged along on leashes. As though a master painter had run out of color, everything was gray—trees, flowers, people, animals. Kate saw people she knew and walked among them. She tried to attract their attention, speak with them, but no one acknowledged or appeared to see her. She was a shadowy outline with no substance—unseen, unheard, alone.

"Some souls that mortals know as ghosts or spirits cannot leave Earth until there is no one left alive who knew them or remembers them. Is that the future you want, Kate? To wander the Earth, alone and friendless? The Great Clock is ticking."

Kate dropped into a chair, shocked by the vision and Zvie's austere countenance.

Again, Zvie motioned. Kate saw Colin approach a house set in a manicured lawn. Vivid flowers and blooming trees swayed, and a blue sky colored the scene. "Honey, I'm home," he called at the open door. His teasing smile acknowledged the trite phrase as he opened his arms to embrace her.

"You must make an ultimate choice, because I and I alone will judge the mood of our guests. I will decide when and if the time is right to announce your marriage." Zvie's eyes flashed, lighting the corner of the bedroom.

Kate bowed her head, then nodded agreement.

"Splendid," he said and rejoined his guests.

Colin came out of the bathroom and removed a garment bag from the closet. He dressed in trim dark trousers and a pale blue shirt that showed off his suntan. He shrugged into a tailored dark jacket.

"I expected you would wear the clothes you had with you in Florida," Kate said.

"Don't let your imagination run away with you, Kate. I didn't sneak over to my apartment behind your back today. You're not the only one who went shopping." His blatant cynicism pierced her.

"I didn't mean… I wasn't suggesting anything," Kate defended, still shaken by what she'd seen.

Colin's mouth set in a grim line; his eyes were gray and cold.

Remorse at his unhappiness vied with Kate's own distress. She smoothed the collar of his shirt; her fingers crept of their own volition to brush his cheek.

"I'm sorry," she whispered.

Colin caught her hand. "At least you're still wearing your wedding ring. That's in my favor." His arms closed around her, and they stood close together for a few moments before they joined the party. The buzz of conversation diminished a beat. Questioning faces turned toward them, but the room soon resumed its rhythm.

"Zvie told me that reporter is here tonight. Why, Colin?"

"It's part of Zvie's plan."

"I have to eat something before we make nice," Kate murmured.

They passed through the buffet, and Colin guided her to a vacant chair by a small table. Kate watched the guests form groups, break apart, and form new ones. Early in her role as Zvie's hostess, she had described it to him as the conversational dance between the informed and the curious. She spied Sam and Colin's ex-wife through a gap created when one guest shifted position.

"Kate, how lovely to see you again."

She stood as Bernard ambled over. A fixture at Zvie's parties—reporter, admirer and friend—she air kissed his cheek while Colin beckoned to a waiter with a tray of drinks.

"So, you're back at last. I missed you. Florida, wasn't it, and a fresh look?"

"Yes, after several weeks in the sun, I needed The Magic Mirror—" Melody and Sam sidled up before she completed her reply.

"Colin," Sam acknowledged. "Kate, you look…different." He gave her a once-over.

"And you're wearing a suit. You look almost presentable," Kate purred, unsheathing her claws.

Melody glided to Colin's side. Bernard watched Colin shrug off her attempt to link her arm through his, saw her surprise. She clasped her hands in front of her. Their quintet drew the interest of guests standing near, and the hum in the room lowered a decibel. Zvie strode over to take part in the unfolding drama.

"Care to comment on the alleged reconciliation Sam shared with me?" Bernard asked Colin, waving a casual hand in his ex-wife's direction. The seasoned reporter sensed a story in the love triangle before him.

"What I know about it I read in your column. I've been out of town with Kate these past few weeks."

"You've been with *her*?" Melody's mouth dropped open and her brown eyes widened. "That's not what Sam—"

"I don't know what fairy tale Sam spun for you, but it's time you face reality." Colin interrupted. "It's been a real hassle for me with you in my apartment. I want you to find other accommodations so I can come home."

Melody flushed and then paled. "But...but where will I go?"

"Move in with Sam or check into a hotel like other out-of-town visitors."

Bernard's mouth twitched, and he pulled a notepad from an inside pocket.

"Sam," Colin continued, "I didn't think to ask you for the key to my apartment when I dismissed you as my agent. It was a mistake on my part. You had no right to put *your* guest up there."

"You don't represent Colin anymore, Sam?" Bernard questioned with keen interest.

"It's a misunderstanding." Sam slid a glance at Colin. "We're negotiating."

"I am representing Colin," Zvie said. "There's no misunderstanding. A studio on the West Coast is casting. I advanced Colin's name through a friend of mine. He's scheduled to read for a part."

Kate turned to Colin with an unspoken question.

"Later," he murmured.

Zvie held up his hand to forestall further questions. "You know I can't give you any details, Bernard, but in a week or two I'll fill you in." He turned to Sam with a disarming smile. "You and I need to have a few words in private."

"You told me you could bring Colin around," Melody's accusation rang out. "Why did you bring me to New York?"

"Melody, keep your voice down," Sam said. "We'll talk later."

"I want to talk now." The room grew quiet.

"You lied." Her trembling lips and shrill voice drew curious eyes.

"It's what he does best," Kate said.

Melody's eyes filled with tears. Aware of the room's attention on them, she tried to hide behind Sam's bulk.

Kate took Melody's arm and led her to the foyer. "Colin, please ask Harry to get a cab," Kate said with a look back over her shoulder. "You should go, Melody. You must have a lot of packing to do before tomorrow."

"You just want me out of the way." Melody accused jerking her arm away.

"I do, but not for the reason you might imagine." Kate studied Melody's pale face, her trembling lips and swallowed the insulting words she'd wanted to say last night. "Colin wants to get back into his apartment, and there isn't room for all three of us."

"He asked you to move in with him?"

"He's my husband, Melody. Where else would I live?" Melody wilted, and Kate pitied her for another of Sam's victims.

"The cab is waiting," Colin said as he joined them.

"I'm sorry Sam misled you," Kate said. "I don't want to add more drama to the scene we've played tonight, but when you pack your bags, don't forget to include your dreams concerning my husband. Good night, Melody."

"Goodbye, Melody," Colin said as he held the elevator door until she was inside. Together they watched the door close on Colin's past.

"Whew!" Kate turned.

"Feeling better?"

She nodded. Her hair swung forward to conceal her face. "Getting there." She'd wanted to be vicious, but Sam had used Melody just as he'd used Kitti and countless others. Melody, too, was a victim of Sam's unscrupulous nature. He had a lot to answer for.

"When did you find out about the audition?" Kate asked.

"Zvie got the call this afternoon. We haven't discussed details because of the party preparations and your absence. We'll talk after the guests leave." His expression softened. "Was it so hard to tell Melody I'm your husband, Kate?"

"Actually, it wasn't," she admitted. "We'd better go back so everyone can see we're not bruised and bloodied—at least not on the outside."

When they returned, Kate thought the buzz of voices was louder than usual, and all but a couple of guests looked their way. Soon the tinkle of ice and the background music signaled the party had resumed. Zvie's friends would discuss Melody's departure, but their interest in her was superficial, not lasting. Kate greeted a couple she knew as Zvie motioned Colin over where he stood with Bernard and Scoop.

Sam edged over. "Abandoned, Kate? Even with that dress, new hairdo? Didn't do the job. Tsk, tsk," he shook his head. "What's it gonna take for you to get you don't have what it takes to keep Colin interested?"

"Still here, Sam? That's right. I would have seen the slime trail if you left."

"You think you're clever, don't you?" His smile was nasty.

"Clever? No, but I'm thoughtful. The Academy taught me to treat guests with consideration but not what to do with a rude and obnoxious jerk. I planned to ignore you, but I can't."

From Sam's smug look and slight smile, he misinterpreted her words.

"I wasted time feeling sorry for myself and being angry at Colin when you were to blame. I'd like to reveal you for a lying piece of foul-smelling scum, humiliate you, but you have to possess decency to feel embarrassment." Kate's eyes glowed with righteous anger.

Sam took a step back, but she followed, jabbing her index finger in his chest. Eyes that had covertly watched, riveted on them. Still, Kate kept her voice low.

"I would have tried to get along with you for Colin's sake. I didn't understand why he allowed you to manipulate him or how you deceived him into thinking he owed you. You've developed treachery to a fine art."

"Thank you, Kate." His complacency needled her.

"You are a pathetic excuse for a man who lives vicariously through someone else, and until now it's been Colin."

"Who the hell do you think you're talking to?" Sam sputtered as his face flushed.

"You must live in some kind of hell," she continued, oblivious to the ears straining to hear, "never experiencing a woman's caress because she feels something for you, knowing you're only the gateway to her career, that you repulse her."

"Why you—"

"Is a woman's kiss partial payment of the price you exact to represent her? You must have envied and hated Colin all the while you professed to be his friend."

"I made him." Sam hissed.

"No, he made you. Without him, you will be nothing."

"Colin won't leave me."

"He already has. He sees you for what you are." Kate spared him a pitying look.

"I'll make you break again," Sam said with an evil smile. "He only had to walk in with Kitti, and you took off. You haven't got the guts to go up against me."

"Fight you? I'll scrape you off the bottom of my shoe like garbage. I told Melody to forget Colin. Now I'm telling you."

"Or you'll what?" he demanded.

"Zvie and I have friends. A word or two dropped in a receptive ear, allusions, innuendos—you know how it works. You've done it often enough. A word or two at the proper time, and the environment becomes unfriendly to you and your clients. Your reputation will suffer."

"I've got friends too, more than you and Zvie," he blustered.

"Maybe so, but do they have any influence? The reconciliation you leaked branded you as a liar. Did you think you could manipulate Colin's affections?"

Her focus on Sam, Kate didn't see Colin approach.

"You interfering bitch! That publicity hound will do whatever I tell him to get a line or two out of it. He'll come around and beg me to take him back. You'll be out on your ass." Sam clenched his fists and moved closer.

Colin stepped between them, backing Sam against the wall.

"Don't talk to my wife like that," he said with an eerie calm. "I heard you, Sam. If I hadn't fired you before, I would now. You can't think we could work together after Melody."

"You don't mean that. You can't choose her over me." His eyes opened wide; wider than Kate had ever seen them. "After your last mistake, you said only fools get married."

"I was wrong." Colin was sheepish for only a moment. "We got married only yesterday. Thanks to you it seems longer. With Melody in my apartment, my wife and I couldn't go home."

Sam narrowed his eyes at Kate. His mouth worked, but no words came.

"You look like you need a drink," Zvie said to Sam as he joined them. Touching his shoulder, he guided him to the kitchen.

"I thought I heard congratulations are in order." Bernard said.

Kate gave him a wry grin. "Yes, Bernard, we… I," she corrected when Colin squeezed her fingers, "didn't want to live our first weeks together in the glare of flashbulbs and newsprint. I know publicity is unavoidable because of who Colin is, but I wanted him to myself. You can understand that, can't you?" She gave him a wistful smile, met his understanding eyes.

"My editor wouldn't forgive me if I didn't report it. It's all news: your marriage, Sam's dismissal as Colin's agent, and that Scoop fella was most forthcoming about Sam's part in the false reconciliation."

"You must have heard the rumors of why you left *Lost in Lust*," he addressed Colin. "The audition is newsworthy."

"Trust me, Kate," Bernard smiled.

"Those two words give me chills, but I know you have a job to do. You're a dear friend," and she leaned to kiss his cheek.

Bernard stood a little straighter.

Colin rolled his eyes and moved closer. "Flirt," he whispered in her ear.

The caterers wheeled a cart to the serving table, cleared it, then returned with fresh plates, flatware, and a lavish cake.

Zvie returned from the kitchen alone as waiters carrying trays of champagne circulated. He strolled up to Kate and Colin, stopped a passing waiter, and lifted flutes of amber liquid for each of them.

"It's time, Kate, Colin. You gave an admirable performance tonight, my dear. I believe everyone here will wish you happy, and I, for one, always enjoy a glass of champagne." He tapped his glass and raised his voice.

"I propose a toast to Kate and Colin," and looked at his watch. "They were married the day before yesterday. I'm sure all of you wish them a long and happy life together and join me in the hope Colin's apartment will soon be available to them."

Kate, Colin, and Zvie touched glasses and sipped.

"Hear, hear!" "Salud!" Their guests drank to the couple's future.

Kate lifted her face for Colin's kiss.

Betty's plea for true love had led to this moment. Kate fast-forwarded memories. Heartbreak and disappointment had dogged her every step. She had found love, but the journey had been an emotional and difficult one, even with the help of a project angel.

Kate and Zvie exchanged a long, loving gaze acknowledging their special bond. They had shared so much.

Why did she feel so melancholy? *Why couldn't it have been you?*

Zvie's slight nod acknowledged her silent question. With a cheerful expression that denied his sad eyes, he turned away.

"Happy, Kate?" Colin whispered.

She nodded and reached for his hand.

"Now, my friends, if Kate and Colin will do the honors," Zvie said, "this cake is a favorite of mine. I persuaded an elite chef, a culinary instructor, to prepare it from his secret recipe."

"All You Need Is Love" - Words and music by John Lennon and Paul McCartney.

"You Don't Bring Me Flowers" - Words and music by Neil Diamond, Alan Bergman, and Marilyn Bergman. Duet by Neil Diamond and Barbra Streisand.

"Some Enchanted Evening" - Music by Richard Rodgers; lyrics by Oscar Hammerstein II.

"You Were Meant for Me" - Music by Nacio Herb Brown; lyrics by Arthur Freed.

"Cry Me a River" - Words and music by Arthur Hamilton.

Armaros - From Jewish legend. One of the legions of angels cast out of heaven for fornicating with mortal women and passing on to mankind the forbidden knowledge of casting spells.

Maggie - The last in a parade of unwanted and neglected animals that Betty Parker adopted and loved.

Mara Light, artist extraordinaire, whose painting, *Guidance,* is *Becoming Kate's* cover.